THE

SAVIOR

a Paul Dodge Novel

THE

SAVIOR

a Paul Dodge Novel

CHRISTOPHER FLORY

 Torchflame Books

Durham, NC

Published 2022, by Torchflame Books
an Imprint of Light Messages
www.lightmessages.com
Durham, NC 27713 USA
SAN: 920-9298

Paperback ISBN: 978-1-61153-497-9
E-book ISBN: 978-1-61153-498-6
Library of Congress Control Number: 2022919122

CHAPTER 1

THE STREETS OF THE SMALL EAST COAST CITY were oddly clean. A week of summer rain had forced the dirt and grime into the gutters and eventually to the sewers, out of sight. Unfortunately for Sarah, it hadn't taken the meanness with it. In her world, the streets belonged to the night dwellers. She was a guest here, making a living walking the same streets as murderers and common street trash, selling her body, her pride, one trick at a time.

The rain and lower-than-normal temperatures made it hard for Sarah to earn a living, and the growling in her stomach bared witness to the lack of money she had earned over the past week. Her rent was due at the motel. The manager would trade sex for rent if the girls couldn't pay for their roach-infested rooms, but Sarah swore she would never stoop to that level. Sure, she sold her body to pay the rent, but her body—her choice. Having a man that smelled of old fish and curry force her to pay off a debt by spreading her legs, or worse, her lips, made her physically ill. Acid shot from the pit of her stomach into the back of her throat, causing a gag reflex. It was all she could do to keep from vomiting at the very idea of his hair-covered, sweat-drenched body pinning her to the bed for even one second.

She washed her mouth out with the small flask she topped off with vodka every morning and kept stashed in her purse for such emergencies. The burn from the alcohol helped kill the taste of vomit in her mouth. The clear liquid also rinsed away the thoughts of the men she would have to be with tonight. It was only a job; she kept telling herself. No different from that of a secretary or a waitress. Her whole life, she had heard stories of powerful men using secretaries to fulfil their deviant desires and then discarding them like an empty beer can tossed to the side of the road. The thought spurred a memory of the time even she had to drop to her knees, to avoid from getting fired from a greasy spoon where she worked as a waitress for about two months. The smell of grease clinging to the owner's clothes resurfaced every time she was with a customer. That was the moment she decided if she had to endure disgusting men invading her personal space to keep a shitty job, it might as well be on her terms. Sarah took another swig of vodka. It did little to drown out the horrible memories racing through her head.

It had been a slow night. Higher than normal temperatures paired with oppressive humidity were keeping people indoors, in the cool grips of air conditioning. Her first actual customer approached at half-past eleven. He stopped his decades old BMW ten feet short of where she stood. It was part of the game for many of the men that frequented prostitutes. They felt as long as the woman had to approach them, it wasn't their fault they were cheating on their wives and girlfriends. His eyes scanned every inch of her thin figure, like he was assessing if she was good enough for him. Did she meet his stringent requirements for anonymous sex in the front seat of a car in an alley? She already hated him and wanted another swig from her flask as she approached the passenger's door.

"What'll it be, sweetie?"

The man was nervous. His eyes darted left and right, as if he expected someone to jump out from behind a building, or parked car, gun drawn, screaming he was under arrest.

"Come on, baby. I don't have all night," she said.

"How much?" he asked.

"That depends on what you want."

"I'll give you fifty to watch me."

Sarah thought about the offer. She had heard about men like this. The ones that would get off making women watch while they took care of business. It made her nervous. It didn't seem right. But fifty bucks was fifty bucks, and she needed to make some money if she wanted to avoid the nightmare scenario with the hotel manager for one more night. That was all she would allow herself to think about.

"Whatever floats your boat."

The thin, attractive prostitute opened the passenger door, climbed into the front seat, and the man drove two blocks before turning into an unlit alley, stopping the car between two dumpsters. The performance was over in ten seconds after the man unzipped his pants. Once finished, he tucked in the front of his shirt, tossed the wad of napkins onto the back seat, and screamed at Sarah to get out. Then he threw a wad of money through the open door, forcing it to slam shut as he sped away.

Sarah bent down to pick up the money which had landed at her feet in the street. The bills were wet, dirt and pieces of leaves stuck to their face. She counted the money. Thirty dollars. He had shorted her twenty.

"What an asshole," she said to no one, before stuffing the bills in her bra and returning the two blocks to her corner to wait for the next customer.

It turned out she didn't have to wait long as a white van eased up to the curb and stopped. The van had a metal ladder strapped to the roof and no windows. The owner secured the side doors with padlocks, the kind you see attached to the outside of a shed, or basement door, to keep people from getting in. This trick was over before it started. She had a rule about vans. There were too many shows on television about hapless women who willingly got into white windowless vans and were never heard from again. She swore that would not happen to her, so she waved the driver away.

"Whore," he yelled, as he sped off. Sarah couldn't help but think the driver would easily find a girl willing to get into his mobile crime scene. Money was more important to some street girls than safety. She shuddered at the thought of the next person he solicited.

She watched as the van slowed, coming to a stop a few blocks from where she stood. A young girl worked that corner. New to the game. Like many of the girls on the street, she was a runaway, abused by her father and ignored by her mother. Sarah spoke to her occasionally, even offering to buy the inexperienced girl breakfast after one particularly slow night. More streetwise, Sarah gave her tips on surviving a rough trade — the first being: Don't go with customers in windowless vans. But who could blame her? In this line of work, you never knew when your next hot meal might come, and rarely did anyone do you a favor without wanting something in return. Apparently, the girl hadn't listened, too busy gobbling up the free meal plopped in front of her.

Concerned, Sarah rose to her tiptoes and waved her arms frantically. The young prostitute never turned her head. Her focus stayed on the customer. The light from the brake lights faded, and the van pulled away from the curb with its new passenger, turning right on the first street and out of Sarah's sight. She went back to her curb, leaned against the brick wall of the storefront, and waited for her next customer to arrive.

An hour later, the same white van rounded the corner and crept past her. The driver's icy stare as he passed sent chills up her spine. Once the van reached the corner where he had picked up the young girl, the driver hit the brakes. Only he didn't stop to let her friend out. Sarah watched nervously as the van's taillights faded into the distance and out of sight. She didn't see the young girl for the rest of the night.

By morning, exhausted and hungry, Sarah had enough money for breakfast and two more nights at the motel. She walked to a diner popular with women of the night and ordered a large breakfast of eggs, toast, pancakes, and bacon. She turned down the free coffee, as she didn't want the caffeine to keep her from falling asleep.

After filling her need for food, Sarah took a short walk to the corner where the young girl usually stood. The spot was empty. Full of breakfast and tired, she made the walk back to the motel. Pulling wadded bills from her bra, she paid the manager, who still offered himself as payment, which she declined. Again. She was asleep as soon as her head hit the pillow. Not a thought of the young girl or the white van until later that night.

The images on the computer screen put his mind into a

relaxed state. It was the same routine every day. A quick glance at the police blotter to check for offenders on his caseload arrested the night before. Next, he would type the violation reports and request arrest warrants from the parole board if any names matched the ones in his file cabinet. Parole violators were not eligible for bail, but it was often a race to get the warrant signed by the parole board and served at the jail before some low-level magistrate who didn't know the law cut the offender loose.

On this day, he didn't see a single name he recognized.

Two hours passed and Parole Agent Paul Dodge had suffered through an appointment with a parolee who refused to admit his child pornography addiction was a problem for his recovery efforts. Another appointment with a convicted rapist was scheduled in thirty minutes. It was looking to be a busy day, and busy days were bad in the law enforcement business. Slow days were good. *People don't get shot on slow days*, he thought. Dodge had a few minutes before the next appointment and opted for a cup of coffee from the mobile coffee truck parked in the street in front of the building. He stood and made his way through the bullpen area toward the elevator, but before he got there, the booming voice of his chief echoed through the maze of desks and cubicles.

"Dodge, get in my office."

The tone in the chief's voice was familiar, but he couldn't think of anything he had done recently to warrant a scolding by his boss. Turning back toward the door, he walked past the other agents working in their makeshift cubicles, all eyes upon him as he stepped into the chief's office.

"What can I do for you, Chief?" Dodge asked.

"You can start by closing the door," Chief Johnson said, as he eased into the seat behind his desk.

The door creaked as it swung closed, catching the attention of another agent sitting close by. Dodge winked at him through the glass as the door latched shut.

"This seems ominous," he said.

Chief Johnson was scanning a file on his desk. He was one of the few people Dodge had difficulty getting a read on. There was rarely a hint of emotion, other than anger. Formerly a parole agent for over two decades, the chief had seen just about everything. When you are shocked by very little, emotional responses are few and far between.

"How's your caseload look?"

Dodge leaned forward. "It's fine. I have a few guys I am paying a little more attention to than normal, but overall, most of them are squared away. Why do you ask?"

"I'm the chief. It's my job to ask."

"True story, but normally you yell at me from across the bullpen. You don't have me come to your office and shut the door." Dodge used his thumb in hitchhiker fashion to point at the door behind him. "So, why don't you tell me what's on your mind, so you can scold me? I can apologize, and then get back to work."

Chief Johnson was an old head of the department. He didn't tolerate sass from his subordinates, even if it was coming from a highly respected and decorated agent. Dodge knew something was wrong when Chief Johnson glazed over the comment.

"The locals found another body this morning," Chief Johnson said.

"Another prostitute?"

"They didn't say, but based on where they found her, I would guess she was a working girl."

The idea of another dead anyone bothered Dodge. He shifted in his seat and ran his hand through his slightly graying hair. "How many does that make?"

"Three."

"Who has the case?"

"That's why the door is closed," Chief Johnson said. "The task force caught the case."

"Are the suits downtown at police headquarters requesting me? I'm not sure a dead prostitute, or even three, is something I can help much with. I mean, the other bodies didn't show any signs of sexual assault. Is this one different?"

"They haven't done the preliminary autopsy yet, but I was told there are no apparent signs of sexual assault. The first officers on the scene said the girl's body was fully clothed. Not even a tear in her underwear."

"So, why call me? They have plenty of detectives in homicide capable of handling a murder."

"Your buddy Renquest drew the short straw on this one. He's the one asking for you."

Dodge couldn't think of a reason Renquest would want him involved in a straight murder case. The task force normally called him in when there was a sexual component to the crime, opting to leave the spouse killings, murder for hire, and myriad of other killings to the six detectives not assigned to the task force. Maybe it was because there were multiple victims now, but he had never worked a serial killer case before. Why would they ask now?

"Why don't I call him and try and figure out what is going on?"

"That's a negative. They want you at the crime scene now," the chief said. His eyes met Dodge's in a Mexican standoff. "Personally, I would rather have you doing the work the state pays you for."

"You should try telling them that," Dodge said.

"That is exactly what I told the sons-a-bitches."

"I feel a *but* coming on," Dodge replied.

The chief leaned back and glanced at the phone on his desk and then back at Dodge. "The Secretary of the Department of Corrections called me shortly after my conversation with Renquest. He said you were to report to the crime scene and to do whatever the locals ask of you. And it wasn't a suggestion, Dodge. It was an order."

"The Secretary asked, ordered, me to interject into a local murder investigation? What, was this girl a daughter of a senator or something?"

"I don't know what is going on, but I plan to call in some of my markers and try to find out," the chief said. "As for now, you better get to the crime scene. Detective Renquest should have sent you a text with the address."

An unopened text icon flashed on Dodge's phone. He realized he had muted his phone during his last appointment and turned the phone back to ring mode. "Anything else?"

"Yeah, one more thing. The secretary said you were to be attached to the task force full time on this. You don't come back to the office until the locals say you are no longer needed." Chief Johnson stood. "Give me your gun and badge. You won't be needing it for the foreseeable future."

The chief's request for his firearm alarmed Dodge. An agent working a series of homicides without a weapon seemed ludicrous. "What the hell is going on? Turn in my weapon? What am 1 supposed to carry, pepper spray?"

"There will be a State Police Captain at the scene, and he will provide you with more details." Chief Johnson held out his hand, signaling for his most trusted agent's ID and weapon.

Dodge pressed the magazine release button, dislodging the magazine. He then slid the weapon from its holster, and ejected the round from the chamber, leaving the slide locked to the rear. The weapon clanked on the hard surface of the desk's wooden top as he slid it over to Chief Johnson.

"Dodge, one last thing. Be careful with the state police. They tend not to play well with others."

Feeling naked without the weight of his duty weapon strapped to his side, he nodded and headed for the elevator. Once on the street, he stopped at the coffee truck parked outside and ordered two black coffees, one with sugar for himself and one without for his partner Detective Renquest. It was a ritual he had become accustomed to when the task force caught a new case and requested his assistance. Then he walked into the parking garage, climbed into his truck, and headed in the direction of the address Renquest had texted him.

CHAPTER 2

ORGANIZED CHAOS SEEMED TO RULE the crime scene. Patrol officers directed traffic away from the alley and tried to keep the growing crowd of gawkers from pushing forward to catch a glimpse of whatever was happening behind the yellow caution tape. Crime scene techs placed numbered yellow placards by everything in the alley that might be evidence, then took photographs. They then placed every piece of scrap paper and empty beer bottle into clear plastic bags. Detective Renquest stood right in the middle of it all, like a general commanding his troops, using his hands to guide each soldier exactly where he wanted them. Dodge loved watching his partner work. *He was good*, Dodge thought. Though he would never say it out loud.

Dodge carefully walked the perimeter, noticing a woman standing on the sidewalk about a hundred yards south, and a rusty white van parked up against the curb. Dodge guessed the van belonged to a construction worker working in one of the many buildings on either side of the street. He couldn't read the license plate from such a distance, so he focused his attention back toward the crime scene.

Dodge approached his partner, offering out the cup of coffee in his left hand.

"Two sugars?" Renquest asked.

"Yeah, but it might be cold by now. What have you got?"

The detective took a sip from his cup and used his thumb to point over his shoulder. "We have one dead girl and very little to go on. The heavy rains for the past week have kept everything drenched. The print boys don't think they can pull a single latent from anything other than the body."

"What do you have on the victim?"

The two men walked toward the white sheet spread out over a mound of cardboard left for the recycling truck to pick up. Renquest asked the medical examiner to pull the sheet back—the body of a young woman lay beneath. Marks on the neck and the purple specks in her eyes, also known as petechial hemorrhaging, showed signs of strangulation.

"May I?" Dodge asked the medical examiner, as he reached to move the sheet so he could see more of the body.

The coroner nodded.

After carefully pinching the sheet between his fingers, making sure not to touch the body, he slid the white covering all the way to the victim's waist. "All of the clothes appear to be intact," he said.

"Same as the other two vics," Renquest said.

Dodge reached backward, over his head and snapped his fingers.

Renquest pulled a pair of black surgical gloves from his jacket pocket and placed them into the outstretched hand. "I hate when you do that."

Dodge smiled, though his partner couldn't see his face, and stretched the gloves over his hands. He then slid his index finger across a small section of her stomach exposed from when the medical examiner lifted her shirt to insert the thermometer to gage liver temperature and estimate time of death. The body was pale and cold. Her skin flexed under the slightest pressure and returned to its original shape after a few seconds had passed. It reminded Dodge of how a stress ball reacted after being squeezed. The whole thing seemed unnatural for such a natural process. Death, not how she died. That was humans at their worst.

When he pulled his hand away, Dodge noticed a shine on the glove of his index finger. He brought his finger up to his nose and sniffed. Nothing. "What the hell is this smeared all over her body?"

"You saw that too?"

"It's hard to miss. When the light hits her the right way her entire mid-section shines like a new penny."

"The medical examiner thinks whoever killed her, wiped the

body down with some sort of oil. Maybe mineral oil or another odorless product."

"Why? And was it applied pre or postmortem?"

"Your guess is as good as ours. Once she is on the slab, we should know more. But I got to say. I hope it was after, because I can't imagine anyone letting someone smear oil, or whatever the hell that stuff is, all over their body for any amount of money. Especially a working girl. They work on quantity, not quality. She would be in the shower for a week trying to get that off. Her night would have been over after this trick."

Knees popping from kneeling on the hard ground, Dodge grunted as he stood. "It's called sploshing, and there are plenty of people that enjoy it as part of their bedroom ritual. Just be glad it's oil."

The detective stared at his partner. "What else could it be?"

"Some people use water. Others are darker and use animal blood."

"Jesus Christ, Dodge. You need to stay off the internet. No one should know that."

"Believe me, I don't want to know half the stuff I do. But I had a guy on my caseload once who was into that sort of thing. And he didn't use oil, water, or blood."

"Do I want to know what he used?"

"Probably not, but you asked," Dodge said as the medical examiner pulled the sheet back over the girl's head. "The guy kept all his semen in mason jars for a month. He would then pay a hooker to come to his house for a splosh party."

"That is the sickest thing I have ever heard. I don't know how you do it. I would want to shoot every one of them in the head at the first meeting."

Dodge shook his head. "Someone must do it. If not me, who?"

Renquest nodded. "I'm glad it's you and not me. I just arrest them, and I'm done. I don't have to get too deep into their sick little minds. I need just enough to justify a charge and a cell."

"Sometimes I envy you."

Dodge carefully slipped off the gloves and placed them in a brown paper evidence bag. He then passed the bag to an evidence technician that had been watching him examine the body. It was important to keep everything from the crime scene, even the little blue booties you had to put on before going into an indoor crime scene. The items the police and crime scene people wore could be tested if there was DNA contamination of the site.

He looked around at all the people bustling about. He noticed one man leaning against the front fender of a late model sedan. The man wore a black suit with a red tie over a white button-up shirt. But it was the shoes that caught Dodge's attention. On his feet were white sneakers with the letter "N" on the side. It wasn't odd for people to have sneakers on with dress clothes anymore. People did it all the time at the courthouse. Staff would go for walks on their lunch breaks, and it was more comfortable than dress shoes. A lot of the secretaries Dodge knew kept a pair of running shoes under their desks and would put them on while doing filing and other tasks that required them to get up and down repeatedly. Dodge also imagined the sneakers had to be warmer than open-toed heels. As common as the practice was at the courthouse, Dodge had encountered no one in the field wearing athletic shoes with a suit. Then he remembered Chief Johnson told him there would be state police at the scene. It would be just like a state trooper to pair a suit with white sneakers in the field.

"Is that the Statie?" Dodge asked, tilting his head in the man's direction.

"Yep. That's Captain Blanchard. He's just been waiting over there, leaning against the hood of his car. Typical trooper behavior. Park his ass on a cruiser while we do all the heavy lifting."

"I was told a State Police guy wanted to see me."

"I'd bet he is the one that asked for you. I believe he's the point person from the state police working the other two murders."

Dodge shifted his gaze from the trooper back to the white sheet on the ground. "Why do the state boys care about a couple of dead prostitutes?"

"Normally, they wouldn't. But they found the second body outside city limits, in the Sheriff's territory. Only the good sheriff didn't want to deal with a murder, as it's an election year and unsolved murders, even those of prostitutes, don't play well in the press. So, he put in a call to the state police, and we get Captain Comfy Shoes over there."

Renquest had clearly noticed the shoes. *Nothing gets past him,* Dodge thought.

Dodge approached the person responsible for his being at *this* crime scene and stuck out his hand. Captain Blanchard took his hand and squeezed tight. The man's grip was powerful. It was like having your hand inserted into a vise. Unable to pull free, Dodge winced, and the state police captain let go.

"Agent Dodge, I assume."

"Nice to meet you. And you can just call me Dodge."

The state police captain pushed away from the front of his cruiser, leaving only a foot of distance between the two men. Dodge stood close to six foot two, and the man towered over him by a good three inches.

"So, you are probably wondering why I asked the Department of Corrections for your help."

Dodge, a little humiliated by the handshake earlier, tried to regain his alpha status by taking over the conversation. It was a kind of job interview, only he didn't want it to seem like he was the applicant.

"I more wondered why the state police would want in on a prostitute? Not a case an outsider usually likes to get involved in. Unless there is a sexual component to the murder you aren't telling me about? Other than the vics occupation, that is."

If the comment had gotten under the captain's skin, he did nothing to show it riled him. He was quiet for a moment. Dodge assumed he was sizing up his new partner. After a moment the tall, well-built man in sneakers spoke.

"Honestly, I thought the same thing. But the brass didn't want to be left out of a serial killer case. Told me to work with the task force on the other murders and keep them apprised of the investigation. Which reminds me..." Blanchard turned and reached in through the passenger side window and grabbed a black leather bi-fold wallet and handed it to Dodge. "Inside you will find credentials, a badge, and an access card to the state police post off Highway 22. I have a small cubical set aside for you with a laptop and phone. The IT team is getting you hooked up with accesses to all our systems so you can get working on this as quickly as possible."

"Accesses to your systems? When I'm called in on a case, I usually work out of city police task force office."

"Didn't your chief or Detective Renquest tell you?"

"Tell me what?"

"The head of DOC assigned you to me on this one. You will report directly to me and will work out of the state police post."

The idea of being a statie, even for a few weeks, annoyed Dodge. By statute they were the ones tasked with maintaining the Sexual and Violent Felon Registry. The registry was a list of people who were convicted of a sexual or violent crime and therefore had to register their addresses and employment with the state. Any member of the public could then look up an address and see if any sex offenders or murders lived in their neighborhood. The whole thing was a feel-good publicity law meant to make the state appear tough on crime, while doing nothing to prevent future transgressions. A dirty secret known to those in the field was that for every person on the registry, there were ten that had not been caught. The point being that even if the search results said no predators lived in the area, chances were there were going to be a few peepers, pervs, and wife beaters living next door. Besides, people should be looking from within the family and household. That's where most of the sexual assaults came from. Crazy Uncle Chet or Cousin Bobby. Those are the real threats.

Running the registry fell under the prevue of the state police by statute. It was one of the worst jobs in the state police and assigning troopers to oversee the massive list of sex offenders was usually a punishment rather than a promotion. While it was the responsibility of the convicted offender to provide certain information by law, the troopers overseeing the registry had to ensure the home addresses and employment status supplied were kept up to date. The troopers were also tasked with making sure the addresses reported by the sex offenders met the mandatory distance requirements from schools and parks, using mapping software, and many times, they had to drive to the locations in question for a more accurate measurement. Due to those facts, most troopers once in charge of the program in their area of responsibility did just enough work to not get into trouble and get reassigned as soon as possible. Always someone *new and learning the system*. It was a colossal bureaucratic mess.

On top of issues with the way the state police handled their duties concerning the administration of the registry, Dodge also didn't like being treated like a commodity—his services sold to the highest bidder. He was comfortable with the people on the task force and trusted the officers he worked regularly with. He didn't trust anyone with the state police because he didn't know them well enough. So, when in doubt, follow the rules. Trust no one and play it close to the vest.

"When do l start?"

"You already have. Which reminds me, do you need a weapon?" Blanchard asked. His eyes glanced at the empty spot on the right side of Dodge's waistline.

"I have my own. l didn't have time to go home and get it." Dodge said, his hand reaching over the spot where his weapon usually rested.

"That's fine. You will need to come down to the post and qualify with your own. State police rules."

Weapons qualification was never an issue for the veteran parole agent and at this point in his career, he felt it was more of an annoyance. A slap in the face, really. He taught firearms at the corrections academy, and he never understood why state agencies wouldn't have a reciprocity agreement in place. It all seemed like a huge waste of resources and money. It was difficult but the veteran agent choked back his indignation before answering.

"I'm free tomorrow morning."

"Good. Be there at seven and we will take a cruiser over to the range," Blanchard said. "What caliber? So, l know which ammo to bring."

"Forty."

"Good. That's what we carry as well. I've got plenty of that caliber lying around. The whole thing shouldn't take more than half-an-hour. Depending on how much warm up you need."

"l prefer to shoot cold," Dodge said.

Blanchard shook his head and patted Dodge on the back before circling the car to reach the driver's side. "Alright then. I'm going to go back to the post to see how the IT department is coming with your accesses. You can hang out here and help with the crime scene. Call me later today and let me know how things are progressing." He stopped and glanced back at his new employee. "Don't forget, you work for the state police now. You take the orders we give until we decide you are no longer needed. Understand?"

Dodge said nothing. He didn't like being given commands. And being reminded how to do his job plain pissed him off. He took a deep breath in. The stench of rotting trash was beginning to fill the air. The crime scene team had cordoned off the alley early that morning before the trash collectors could empty the dumpsters. Trash continued to pile up as businesses opened for the morning rush of customers, adding to the already growing odor. He blew out his breath, regaining his composure before returning to where Renquest was still barking orders to the crime scene techs.

"How'd it go?"

"About as good as can be expected."

"He'd heard of you, huh?"

"Funny. What do you know about Blanchard?"

Renquest was still sipping his coffee. "Not much. He has only been with the state police for about a year. He came here from out west somewhere. California or Arizona, I think. You want me to ask around?"

The two men watched as Blanchard's car turned right, disappearing into the mesh of buildings and traffic.

His eyes were still fixed on the spot where the state police captain's car sat a minute ago. "l suppose I'm being paranoid is all. No need to make any more enemies than necessary. Catching this perp is going to be hard enough without starting a ruckus over my feelings being hurt."

Renquest let out a howling laugh.

"What's so damn funny?"

Renquest washed down his laughter with the last swig of coffee. "Nothing really. Just the thought of the great Paul Dodge having feelings is funny to me. More like ego, I'd say."

What his friend said wasn't all a lie. It *was* more likely his ego was hurting than his personal feelings. Unfortunately, with his success in clearing cases over the last few years, his sense of self-worth had only grown larger, and he was keenly aware of that fact. It was only a matter of time before something, or someone, took his legs out from under him, putting him back in his place. Rolling with it this time seemed like the prudent course of action.

"Where you headed after this?" Dodge asked.

"Back to the office to oversee the techs while they log evidence. Then I'll a head over to the medical examiners to watch the initial autopsy. You?"

"I'm going to head to the house to grab my back-up weapon and vest. I'll meet you at the ME's office around noon. We can get some lunch after the cut."

"Sounds good," Renquest said.

Dodge walked to his truck for the quick trip back home, but as he sat in the driver's seat staring at his phone, he scrolled through names in his contact list until coming to the S section. He looked at the third name on the list, Beth Samuels. She was a state investigator in Arizona he had worked a case with when he was in the Air Force. She had extensive contacts all over the west coast and could easily check on Captain Blanchard's past. His thumb hovered over the call button as he wondered if she would have any memory of him. It had been over ten years since they last spoke, and he didn't leave the situation with her on the best of terms. After several minutes of back and forth in his mind, he decided not to make the call. Yet.

Flipping the phone shut, he turned the key in the ignition and the engine came to life. Then, at a break in the traffic, he pulled into the street. The trip home took less than ten minutes, but his mind was working overtime. He needed to concentrate on the death of the young girl, and the autopsy room was a good place to start.

CHAPTER 3

THE MAN IN THE WHITE PANEL VAN sat parked two blocks down from the alley where hours earlier he had placed the young girl's body. A makeshift curtain made from a surplus green wool army blanket, purchased at a surplus store two towns over, stretched from the driver's side to the passengers behind the front seats to block any curious eyes from peeking into the back where he did his work. The blanket darkened the interior more than he liked. He enjoyed gazing into their eyes while he worked, but what he was doing demanded privacy and compromises had to be made when using a mobile workspace. It really wasn't any different from that of a dog washers or companies that drive to your home and fix damaged windshields. Although, his van was different in one aspect. Once a customer was inside, they never left alive.

He never thought of himself as a psychopath. The killing brought him no joy. Nor did he have any empathy for his projects. Simply put, the expiration of life was an unintended consequence of his work. He had to test the ones lucky enough to be chosen. To make sure they were worthy of his services.

He was a free-er of tortured souls. The girl last night, Monica, appeared more lost than the rest. Such a young girl, doing such horrible work. The pain she endured before he set her free must have been an unbearable burden. He didn't believe in heaven or hell, though he did believe in God. To him, life was about peace and suffering, and his girls were at peace when he finished.

He liked to return to the drop site, once someone found the body and police arrived to admire what he had done. At first, he thought the daring move a risk, staying far away from the scenes. But as time passed, his confidence grew and so did his curiosity.

After all, doesn't an artist enjoy seeing their creations hanging in a gallery? He was an artist of sorts. A Michelangelo of corrupt souls. Besides, if he were to continue cleansing the souls of troubled girls and not have his work interrupted by being arrested and jailed, he needed a better understanding of how the police examined and processed the crime scenes. He had watched every show imaginable on television but knew none of that replaced actual life experience. Over the years, he had found much of what he saw on television crime shows was exaggerated for effect. Capabilities police didn't actually have. Why spend time planning for an eventuality that would never come?

He always left the newly saved in a place to be found easily by a passerby or early morning delivery driver making his rounds at the local businesses. He didn't pose the body. Only those who enjoy the act of killing complete such an act. Egomaniacs who want the attention cast upon themselves. His was an act of compassion. He was helping the people he chose, not trying to feed the monster inside himself. People consumed with themselves infuriated him, driving him into an almost rage-like state. He took a deep breath and continued watching the scene unfold a few blocks away.

The hardest part of his work involved figuring out how to work out of a vehicle in plain sight that most people associated with child molesters. A white, windowless panel van was necessary, but it drew attention everywhere he went. Television shows and movies always showed the abductor pulling up in a big, white windowless van and snatching children off the street. In reality, it wasn't something that happened often. But when people are continually shown the same information, real or not real, they begin to believe it, leading to personal bias. He noticed it soon after purchasing the van that police would take notice and follow him for several blocks before ultimately losing interest. He always obeyed traffic laws, used his turn signal well in advance, and drove just under the speed limit. But he couldn't control everything. And being followed by police was an unacceptable consequence. He needed anonymity.

Then one day, a flash of genius struck, and a solution was born. It was simple and cheap, and he could perform the work himself.

He bought some tubular aluminum pipes at the hardware store, paying in cash to leave no paper trail. Fashioning the metal into two long runners, connected in three spots with cross members, he installed the contraption as a ladder carrier on the roof of the van. He found a couple of old metal ladders at a garage sale and bolted them down. He never needed to use the ladders, so permanently fastening them to the rack was not an issue. And it kept them from sliding off if he had to slow or speed up quickly. Now he could park in front of any rundown, dilapidated building. No one would give him a second look, thinking he was simply another painter or carpenter trying to squeak out a living in the city.

"Sheep, only concerned with themselves," he mumbled.

This day, he parked further away. The streets were empty, leaving his view of the scene unobstructed. But there was something different about today. A new face caught his eye. He knew the other cops at the scene, but the one who brought coffee to the fat one, he had never seen before. Oh, how he hated the fat cop. He was a walking cliché, exuding all the characteristics of a television detective. Overweight. A cheap suit haphazardly put together from mismatched pieces, and most of all, he appeared to be lazy. Unwilling to do any of the work himself. A person who rode the coattails of others to success.

But the new guy seemed different somehow. There was an air of confidence about him. Others watched with intent when he examined the body. Even the state cop, Blanchard, seemed to give up some of his usual dominance to him. That surprised the man. He had never seen the state police captain act this way before. Finding out who this new player was would be a necessity. Someone new in the game could alter everything. He didn't fear change. In fact, change was a necessity. He just hadn't planned on doing it so soon. Had he been too good? Did the local police need to bring in an outside expert?

"Who is he?" he murmured under his breath, mesmerized by the others' reactions to the newcomer.

He watched the man work for a little while longer, then decided, in the end, it didn't matter. His work would continue.

Souls needed to be cleansed.

Then a young woman approaching his van caught his eye. At first, he didn't recognize the face, but as she drew closer, he knew the face. It was the slut that waved him away last night, denying him his first choice. His face flushed with anger. He wondered if he could grab her right there. Would anyone even notice? Certainly not the cops down the street. Not the fat one. He forced his urges back down. It was a bad idea to break away from the plan. He needed to make sure she was worthy of his service before releasing her tormented soul.

He had thought it out so meticulously and it worked. It was important to never allow his emotions to take over. It was not personal. Making it personal will get you caught. But he couldn't forget about her either

—∿∿—

Fear for the girl she watched get into the van the night before had kept Sarah from sleeping more than a few hours after returning to the motel. Awake and anxious, she threw on a pair of shorts and a t-shirt, then made her way back to where she spent her nights to see if young Monica had returned.

As the corner the young girl worked came into view, Sarah saw the police and fire trucks. She didn't need to see a body to know why they were there. Sarah stopped and watched the scene from a distance. Years of working the streets had provided her with a sixth sense of sorts. A gut feeling, really. She remembered the man who tried to pick her up last night. The man in the van that picked up Monica. And she always listened to her gut. It was kind of a rule.

She watched as officers pulled more yellow crime scene tape across the mouth of the alley, tying it to the mirrors of the patrol cars parked on both sidewalks. Then the cops, one man and one woman, stood guard. She imagined there were two officers recreating the identical scene at the opposite end of the alley. The ambulance drivers stood by their rigs. She knew that meant the person the ambulance came for was likely dead. Her fears were confirmed when one of the EMTs pulled a white sheet out from the back of the ambulance and disappeared into the alley, only to reemerge a few moments later, his hands empty.

She couldn't see the body in the alley, but she knew the body now covered in a sheet was Monica. She could feel it in the pit of her stomach. A street girl's intuition. The reason she had never been found face down on the cold ground and covered with a white sheet.

"That poor girl," she whispered.

Two unmarked police cars approached the yellow caution tape and parked. She recognized a cop car when she saw one, lights or no lights. Two men climbed out, one from each. The first man was heavyset and looked a little disheveled. His shirt was wrinkly and the tie he wore didn't match the rest of his suit. If she had gone out each night looking that way, she would have to pay her rent the same way the other girls did. The second man was tall and lean. He reminded Sarah of a cowboy in one of those black and white westerns shown on TV every Sunday morning, right after the preacher's shows ended. Instead of going into the alley, the second man leaned up against the front of his car. Not a single person approached him, and he spoke to no one. He just stood there, watching everyone else work.

She was turning to leave and head back to the dirty carpets and the chemical smell of her motel sheets when a third man arrived. He stepped out of his big black truck, his eyes scanning the streets and sidewalks, appearing to look for nothing, but at the same time looking at everything. He locked eyes with her for a second before turning and disappearing into the alley. She waited a moment, but when the man didn't come back out, she walked away. About halfway back she passed a van that looked like it belonged to a house painter or handyman, parked on her side of the street.

She continued to the end of the block and turned left toward the motel.

CHAPTER 4

IT WAS ONE IN THE AFTERNOON when Dodge pulled into the medical examiner's office parking lot. A stop at the parole office to fill in Chief Johnson on the situation at the crime scene turned into an hour-long debriefing session with the parole agent that would work his caseload while he was temporarily reassigned to the state police. The department had recently hired a new sex offender specialist for the office, Laurel Wiggins. Dodge had trained her for six months, showing her the ropes and introducing her to city police officers and community partners, like social services and child protective services.

She was good. But what worried the veteran agent most was Laurel's safety when conducting home visits. While he often conducted field visits solo, he preferred less experienced agents to work in pairs. The idea being that one agent would stand watch, maintaining control over the main entry and exit point while watching for anyone else who might show up unexpectedly. This allowed the lead agent to concentrate on interacting with the parolee. Laurel was smart and had a good eye for trouble. He had confidence in her abilities but emphasized the importance of working in pairs in the field. She told him she understood and would use a partner when conducting home visits. Before heading to the autopsy at the medical examiner's office, he stopped at the coffee truck on the street outside the office, and ordered two blacks, one with sugar and one without.

Detective Renquest was waiting in the lobby of the medical examiner's office. Dodge handed his partner the coffee with sugar.

"Thanks. This is going to be a friggin long day."

"Where's the coroner?" Dodge asked as he sucked the coffee

that had pooled on the lid of his cup on the drive over.

Renquest took a sip of his coffee, burning his lip. "Damn, that Benito makes a hot cup of joe." He blew on the liquid before taking another sip. "The ME is out to lunch. The secretary said he should be back in about fifteen minutes."

The sound of the bell ringing above the door made both men turn. Captain Blanchard, no longer wearing a suit, but still adorning those white sneakers, stepped through the door and into the lobby.

Dodge nodded in his direction.

"Well boys, we gonna see a cut today?" the captain asked.

"As soon as the Doc gets back from lunch," Renquest said.

"What do we know so far?"

"From what we could get from vice, her name was Monica. Last name unknown. She was a runaway and came into town about six months ago."

"A runaway? If she was a minor, why didn't vice roll her up and send her back to her parents?" Blanchard asked.

"She was seventeen when she left home, and by the time..."

Captain Blanchard cut Renquest off before he could finish. "She was eighteen and no longer a minor."

"That's right. There was nothing they could do except bust her for soliciting."

Blanchard shook his head in disgust. "If someone would have done something earlier, she might still be alive."

Dodge spoke up. "There are hundreds, same as her, all over the city. My guess is she looked healthy and if her face didn't show signs of scars or bruises, they likely had more serious cases to deal with."

As part of the sex crimes task force, Dodge had dealt with abuse victims working the streets. Some were old hands, and some were young, like Monica. It always upset him when anyone died but he tried not to take their deaths personally. He had allowed himself to fall into the trap not too long ago and it almost cost him his life.

Dodge noticed a hint of personal conflict in Captain Blanchard's voice when he spoke about the victim. Maybe he had a daughter? Maybe she was the same age as the victim? There were a million reasons a case could affect a cop, but there was only one way to deal with it: working the case and following the facts to a resolution. That is the only peace you could find in a homicide as a cop.

The medical examiner stepped into the room as the men finished talking. He waved at the receptionist to buzz the door that led to the autopsy area, and the four men filed through, down a long hall and into a locker room where they put on blue gowns and slid paper booties over their shoes. Blanchard put on a facemask to cover his thin cop-like mustache. It was important no foreign hairs found their way onto the body before an examination, corrupting the integrity of the evidence. Most detectives had a DNA profile on file at headquarters to be ruled out if they contaminated a scene, but the state police captain hadn't submitted one since taking the job.

A microphone hung by a long cord centered over the autopsy table. The doc called out the date and time, along with the names of everyone present in the room before beginning his examination. First was the victim's sex and approximate age, followed by the condition of the body, the liver temperature, and an approximate time of death.

"I'll be able to narrow the time down more, once I get the organs out, recorded, and weighed."

When the medical examiner grabbed the bone saw and started removing the top of the skull to reveal the brain, Captain Blanchard had seen enough.

"Well, if you two have this under control, I will head back to post," he said before taking one last glance at the bone saw ripping through the thin walls of Monica's skull. "Dodge, don't forget to come by in the morning with your weapon for qualification." That said, Blanchard turned and exited the room.

Renquest said, "A little weak in the knees."

"Too much time behind a desk," Dodge said.

"Why aren't you leaving then?" Renquest burst out laughing as the words passed over his lips.

"I would, but some asshole keeps calling me because his

detectives can't solve a simple murder."

"Can you two either shut up or leave?" the medical examiner said while holding his hand over the dangling microphone.

The two men looked at each other, embarrassed at being chastised by the doc.

"You'll call us with the early results, doc?" Renquest asked.

"I'll call as soon as I have the initial findings. But I'll tell you now, it's going to be asphyxiation," he said, pointing to the bruise marks on the neckline. "My guess is, I'll find the hyoid bone fractured when I open up the neck cavity."

"Alright, Doc, please keep us in the loop," Dodge said.

They hadn't gleaned much information from the initial examination, but both men felt seeing the cut was important. The autopsy was a crucial part of the investigation and a body on a cold slab, being dissected, was a great reminder that all victims count.

Dodge held the door for Renquest and followed him into the prep room, where they removed all the protective gear and placed the gowns and footies in brown paper bags to be kept until the DNA evidence from the body finished processing. Once in the parking lot, the two men decided on a local diner to grab a late lunch and review what they knew about the case, which was next to nothing at this point. For the average citizen, eating right after viewing an autopsy seemed callous and revolting. For cops who dealt with murder every day, there was nothing odd about it. You eat when you can.

After filling up on greasy diner cheeseburgers and fries, Dodge decided he wanted to get a second look at the alley where they found Monica's body. He drove the twenty minutes through the heart of town, past his office, and by Café le Chez, stopping for a group of pedestrians crossing to get their afternoon caffeine fix. He couldn't help but look for her. It had been her favorite place to sit and watch people coming and going from work and shopping. It had been a while since he had thought about Anna. They hadn't spoken since she left that day in Puerto Rico, and he had hoped she would be waiting when he returned, but she wasn't. He even drove by her apartment once—the window coverings were open, and the place was empty. It appeared she had picked up and left. Not sure where she could have gone, but sure she didn't want to see him again, he moved on. He was good at moving on. Tuck your emotions deep inside the box and smash the lid shut. He always found room in the box for one more memory.

Arriving at the alley, Dodge drove the few blocks surrounding the area to get a feel for who might be watching. He looked for ATMs and liquor stores, anyplace that might have video cameras that could have caught a vehicle or the victim in the moments before and after her death. He saw none. People in this neighborhood didn't have bank accounts. Transactions were cash-based and paid in full at time of purchase. There was no way an ATM would last more than a few hours before someone hooked one end of a chain to it and the other to a vehicle, yanking it from its base. In fact, there wasn't even a bank in sight. Only liquor stores, pawn shops, and check cashing stores advertising ten percent payday loans, and none of them appeared to have outside surveillance cameras.

Satisfied there was no camera footage that would make this an open and shut case, he retraced his steps back to the crime scene. The alley was clean. As usual, the evidence techs had bagged every sliver of paper, soda pop can, cigarette butt, and anything else within ten feet of the body. The alleys surface was in good shape. No chance for tire prints. But finding a smoking gun wasn't the point of this exercise. He was interested in why the perp picked this place to dump the victim. Why had there been no attempt to hide the body? Leaving the body in the open was a bold move. Which meant the killer wanted the victim found. Or did he panic?

Dodge hoped for the latter and not the former. Panic was good. Mistakes happen when a killer panics. A hair gets left behind. A footprint is left in the mud. That's how most crimes get solved. But bold. That was something very different. Bold meant calculated. Planned. Meticulous. Less mistakes made. It's harder to find evidence and pin down a suspect or timeline when a killer is making bold moves.

Dodge thought about the body at the morgue. He closed his eyes and pictured Monica on the ground. He played the scene backwards in his head. It was fuzzy because he didn't have all the details. The picture usually cleared as he put pieces and faces together. Monica flew up into a vehicle, a car maybe. The door closed. No, *that wasn't right*, he thought. She had no scratches or scrapes on her body. Her clothes were clean. If the killer pushed her out of a vehicle, her clothes would have had dirt and gravel from the alley stuck to them. He or she must have carefully removed the body and placed it carefully on the pile of cardboard next to the dumpster. That took time. A couple of minutes at least.

Then a blank scene. He didn't know what happened before the dumping, other than she was strangled and the killer rubbed her body down with oil. A job like that takes time. Dodge noticed, at the medical examiner's office, the oil covered all the victim's body. Meaning removing her clothes, lathering the entire body, and redressing her postmortem. That kind of routine takes time, a work area where he wouldn't be disturbed, and patience. It was doubtful he panicked, dumping her body in the first place he found. A patient, motivated and confident killer. Every city's nightmare.

Serial killers drove fear into the heart of a city. People stayed inside, restaurants closed early, and police phones rang non-stop with calls from concerned citizens who think the killer is their next-door neighbor. And the prank calls, oh, the prank calls never stop. Dodge needed to see the files on the other victims. But first, he needed to come back downtown later that night to talk to the other working girls. He hoped one of them knew Monica or could at least tell him if his victim had a pimp. H also knew that prostitutes kept a sort of mental list of all the Johns who like the weird stuff or are violent. That could give him a few leads to run down. Right now, that was all he had.

As the sun dropped out of sight behind the city's facade, shadows crept in. The same streets that were full of people running errands and buying goods in the daytime were transformed. People sat on their balconies, drinking and conversing. The working girls were claiming their territory. He watched them in amazement as they made their way to their little piece of the city. It was like workers filing into a factory waiting to punch a timecard. Occasionally, fights broke out when one prostitute tried to set up her wares on a corner claimed by another, but the alpha eventually ran off her challenger.

Dodge couldn't help but think, as he observed the area where they found the last victim, it looked like the spot where a newcomer to the streets might work from. The corner was at the end of the run. The sole source of light came from a floodlight attached to the wall of a business on the opposite side of the street, but construction prevented anyone from using the sidewalk on that side. As if selling your body to survive wasn't enough, having to do it from that spot could make a person appear almost non-human.

After a few minutes, he turned his attention toward the busier stretch of the street, searching for the right girl to talk to, then someone caught his eye. She looked familiar. Brown hair. Thin build. Even the way she stood reminded him of someone. Then he realized it was the same girl he saw watching the crime scene earlier that morning. Seeing her twice was not a coincidence.

Dodge hopped out of his black truck. He crossed the street and walked down the block to where the woman stood. "Excuse me, ma'am."

The girl watched him as he approached. An untrusting gaze. Her eyes darted from his head to his feet and then back again, but she made no move to approach.

"I was wondering if I could ask you a few questions?"

She turned and walked in the opposite direction.

Dodge sped up casually, so as not to seem more threatening than he did. "It's ok. I'm not with vice."

The girl stopped, turned to face her pursuer. "But you are a cop. I saw you this morning."

"Actually, I am not a cop. I work for the Department of Corrections. I am a parole agent."

"So, why is a parole agent hanging around where they found that dead girl?"

Dodge eased his stance and relaxed his shoulders to make

her more comfortable. He noticed a change in her posture and her hands dropped to her sides. "Well, sometimes the local police call me to help if they think the crime in question could involve a sexual component."

The girl stood silent.

"What's your name?"

"Sarah."

"Hi, Sarah. I'm Dodge."

"Dodge? No first name?"

"My full name is Paul Dodge, but you can call me Dodge, he said, trying to reassure her he was a friend. At least not a foe. "Are you on this corner every night?"

"Most nights. But if it is raining, I might stay home or find a place with some cover."

"Where's home?"

"The Sunnyside Motel. For now," Sarah said.

Dodge nodded. "I know the place. One of those pay as you go motels. Did you know the manager is a registered sex offender? Convicted of rape fifteen years ago. You need to be careful around him."

Sarah laughed. "He makes some girls pay rent by getting on their backs. But not me. He is disgusting and smells horribly."

"I can talk to him if you would like? It might help."

The laughing smile turned to grimace. "Or he gets pissed off and throws me out on the street."

Dodge stood silent for a moment. He knew she was probably right. Then he looked back up the street, where they found the last victim. "Did you know the girl murdered last night?"

"Yes. But we weren't friends or anything."

"When was the last time you talked to her?"

Sarah rolled her eyes upward, trying to recall an event she hadn't thought of in a while. "I took her to breakfast a week or so ago. The night was rainy, and we were all miserable and I felt sorry for her. I'm not sure she had a customer all night. She is so far off the main stretch and only the desperate guys wander up that far for action."

"Did she say where she lived or where she came from?" Dodge asked.

"No. She was pretty quiet. Ate like a horse, though! It cost me ten dollars when she finally finished."

A feeling poked at his gut as if Sarah were holding something back. "Is there anything you can tell me about her that might help me find out what happened up there last night?"

"Do you think it's the same person who hurt the other girls?"

"We're not sure yet. But, if 1 were you, 1 would be careful out here at night. We believe women are getting into his vehicle willingly and they wind up dead not long after."

Dodge reached into his pocket and pulled out a business card. "My personal number is on the back. You can call me anytime, day, or night, for any reason. Even if it's only to have a cup of coffee or a bite to eat. Tell me where you are, and 1 will come get you."

Sarah smiled as she took the card from his hand.

Dodge said, "Thank you," waited for a break in traffic, and crossed the street back to his truck. It had been a long day and he could feel it in his bones and joints. He needed rest. Besides, the next morning he had to qualify for Captain Blanchard. Being an excellent marksman, not qualifying was the least of his worries. He hit what he aimed at. But he wanted to be ready mentally. A curiosity to know more about him still tugged at him. And to learn about something, you first must prepare. Prepare open-ended question and have responses ready for any answer. All while maintaining the tact to do it with someone who understands the interview process without tipping your hand.

Fifteen minutes later, the exhausted parole agent stepped into his living room, poured a glass of Blantons, and lay back on the couch. His mind raced. He could barely form a coherent thought. A sip of bourbon seemed to calm it. He took another swig and closed his eyes.

CHAPTER 5

MORNING SUNLIGHT DANCED across the sleeping agent's face, warming his skin, and forcing him to turn away from the window. Dodge stretched and groaned all the kinks away in his aging body before wiping the crusty sleep from his eyes and pulling himself up. The previous day had been long and tenuous. The plan to drag himself off the couch and into the bedroom before dozing off never materialized. He didn't remember when he finally fell asleep, but the empty glass on the coffee table signaled the event took place after the last swig of Blantons crossed his lips. A cautionary tale, as the brown liquid had been scarce in recent months. A fire at the distillery's warehouse limited supply, and he didn't want to waste what little remained in his stash by falling asleep and spilling a valued commodity. He attempted to switch to another label to ride out the crisis. But in the end, he always enjoyed, or needed, a glass of Blantons with one ice ball, a little more after watching an autopsy.

After a quick shower and what must have been a time record drive across town, Dodge arrived at the state police post right at seven. Captain Blanchard watched as he drove in, leaning up against the hood of his cruiser, making a glance at his watch as Dodge climbed out of his truck. He grabbed the drink caddy holding the two cups of coffee he had bought at the convenience store about a mile before the police post. In his other hand, he held two creamer cups and several sugar packets.

"I wasn't sure how you took your coffee," Dodge said, pulling one of the foam cups from its resting place in the caddy and sliding it onto the hood of the cruiser.

"I take my coffee in a teacup," Blanchard said.

Strike one. Something about a cop that doesn't drink coffee never sat right with the veteran agent and coffee enthusiast. "More for me," he said, reaching for the cup, which had slid a few inches down the car's hood.

Blanchard pushed himself away from the cruiser and moved to the driver's side door. Opening it, he said, "Hop in. The range is only a few miles from here. Unfortunately, only official state vehicles can enter, so your truck will have to stay parked here."

Dodge placed one cup of coffee on the roof of the car. Opened the door with his free hand and climbed inside. Blanchard pressed on the gas and the car lurched forward before Dodge could shut the door, his arm stretching out the window, bending up, snagging the extra cup of coffee right before it tipped over and spilled down the side of the cruiser. He shot a glance at Blanchard, who was smiling.

"Nice reflexes. It's good to know your partner is quick on the draw."

Dodge stared back blankly. "So, we are partners?"

"Sure. As much as you do what I say and stay out of trouble," Blanchard said.

"Have you been checking up on me?"

"I would be a fool not to. Wouldn't you say? I am sure you did the same thing for me."

He thought back to the phone call he never made to his friend in Arizona. "I don't know enough about you to know where to begin."

The two men rode in silence the rest of the way to the range. Blanchard finally broke the tension as they turned to enter the front gate of the range.

"Sit tight. I have to unlock the gate."

Once out of the car, Blanchard removed a key from his pocket and slid it into the lock which held two ends of a chain that had been wrapped around the gate and a wooden post. The padlock fell to the ground. The chain free from the gate, he then swung the gate open. Blanchard climbed back in the car, slowly pulled through the opening. Dodge thought it strange the captain didn't close the gate behind them. The two men rode in silence as the gravel crunched beneath the tires.

The firing range was spread out over an area about the size of a football field. There was one building, probably used to store targets and extra shooting glasses and ear protection. The range was long and narrow, with the first twenty-five yards covered in gravel with two-foot strips of concrete spanning from side to side every five yards to mark distances to the target. Beyond the collapsible target holders at twenty-five yards was another seventy-five yards of open ground. At the end were three permanent metal "T's" in front of a fifteen foot high sand berm lined with old automotive tires meant to stop any stray rounds from traveling past the end of the range. It was not the worst range he had been to.

Once inside the building, Blanchard instructed Dodge to grab two silhouette targets with clips and hang them up at the end of the first two lanes. Qualifying would comprise of two targets, with the shooter firing fifty-four rounds. Any round in the black area of the silhouette scored a point, and he needed a final score of eighty percent to qualify.

"Load your primary mag and then your spares," the police captain said, donning his red firearm instructor hat and handing his charge two boxes of forty caliber ammunition.

Dodge followed the orders. The range was a serious place. No matter how experienced a shooter you were, on the range, you did as the person in the red hat told you. No questions. Dodge waited for the next instruction. After Captain Blanchard positioned himself behind the control panel, ten yards to the rear of the firing line, he shouted the next command.

"Shooters to the line."

A bright yellow line ran the length of the range at the near end.

"Eyes and ears."

Dodge donned his ear protection and shooting glasses. Then a slight pause and the next command.

"Shooter. You have one minute and forty-five seconds to complete the course. The clock will stop between sequences and when you need to replenish your magazines. Acknowledge."

The shooter waved his hand above his head. The universal sign on a range you understood the command.

Blanchard paused for a moment as he set the controls to work the target. "Shooter. Fire six rounds at the first target that turns. Next fire six rounds at the second target that turns. You will not know which target turns first. You can move and shoot, but if you cross the firing line, I will disqualify you. Acknowledge."

Again, he waved his hand, took in a deep breath, and exhaled. Inhale then Exhale.

"Shooter ready," the man in the red hat yelled.

The first target to turn was the one to Dodge's left. He was right-handed, so he slid one step to the left. Anticipation for the recoil from the weapon caused the first round to hit low and to the left. A simple correction to make, and the next five rounds landed center mass. He kept his spot on the line. Expecting the turning of the second target to his right, he adjusted his stance. Waited. When he heard the air release from the lines, he squeezed off two quick rounds, both kill shots to the chest. Then he fired four more once the target completed its swing. Three landed center mass, but the fourth was high and to the right. Still within the target's black silhouette. The half-empty magazine clanked as it hit the ground and he slammed a fully loaded one into the receiver.

"Shooter at the ready position."

Dodge lowered his weapon, pointing the muzzle downrange, but well below the target.

"Shooter. The next round is alternating targets. Their order will be random. You will fire all rounds in the fresh magazine and perform an exchange. Then place one round in the head of the next target that turns. Acknowledge."

Again, Dodge raised his hand.

The targets turned. First one, then the other. Sometimes in order and other times back-to-back. Dodge placed all fifteen rounds at center mass, which began to look like Swiss cheese. The last round after the magazine exchange was right at the spot on the target signifying the bridge of a person's nose. Twenty-eight rounds fired so far. All on target.

Dodge took five minutes to reload the three mags, then returned to the firing line. Sweat began to form on his brow. An expelled casing had ejected over his head during the last firing sequence and landed on the collar of his shirt. The hot metal burned his skin, and he rubbed it with his left hand.

"Shooter. This is the last sequence. You will fire the remaining twenty-six rounds at the targets as they turn. If a target advances on you, you may cross the firing line and close the gap to engage. Once in the kill zone, you must remain in front of the firing line. I encourage freedom of movement. Acknowledge."

Dodge raised his hand for the last time.

"Shooter to the ready," Blanchard said.

Targets flipped at random for the first ten shots. There was no pattern to the turning targets, and adrenaline pumped through his veins. Dodge could no longer hear the air releasing from the lines. His ears rung from the crack of the exploding shells, even with double ear protection. The purpose of this drill was to work on reactionary shooting. Anticipation became his enemy. On the twelfth round, the first target advanced on him. Dodge fell to one knee and fired before the silhouette moved three feet. He then stood and entered the kill zone. Some targets flipped and others came at him. He continued to walk toward the targets, closing the gap while administering lethal justice on the paper foe. The last round struck the silhouette on the right in the gut area. Dodge holstered his weapon and turned to walk back to the firing line.

Captain Blanchard ran the targets up the line and retrieved the battered pieces of paper. He tried to add up the scores, but the center of the target was one giant hole. It looked like a rat had chewed it.

"I guess I'll have to pass you," he said.

Reassuringly, Dodge said, "They are all there."

"What happened to this one?" Blanchard asked while pointing to the single hole in the stomach area of the silhouette.

"I shot his buddy in the chest three times and he still advanced on me. That rates you a gut shot in my book. He can lie there in pain until the ambulance arrives to take his dumb ass to the hospital."

Captain Blanchard nodded and let out a grunt. "Let's clean up and head back to the post. Load your mags with state-bought ammunition before leaving. Consider it your duty ammo."

Blanchard returned the unused ammunition to the shed and locked the door. Dodge policed his brass on the range, dumping it in a fifty-gallon barrel, and slid a box of ammo into his back pocket before meeting Blanchard back at the cruiser.

"That was some impressive shooting, Agent Dodge," Blanchard said. "We could use an instructor at the academy if you are interested. The pay sucks and we usually do re-qualifications on the weekends."

"That's quite a selling pitch. But 1 like my weekends."

The two men chatted about old cases on the way back to the post. Each one trumping the other's tales. The contest ended in a stalemate.

Once back at the station, Captain Blanchard showed Dodge to the cubical containing a desk, laptop, printer, and a solitary monitor. He was used to his setup at DOC, where multiple monitors enabled him to transition across several platforms, completing multiple projects at once. The chair looked comfortable at least, but he didn't plan on spending much time here.

"Any chance 1 can see the files on the other three victims?"

Captain Blanchard led him to another room. A long conference table sat in the center, covered with file boxes. Dodge counted five in total. All labeled with the moniker Jane Doe. Two boxes had the number one and three after the name and three boxes with the number two.

"We don't have IDs on any of the three vics?" Dodge asked.

Blanchard looked at the boxes lined up on the desk. "We know two of their names. They originally classified the third as a drug overdose, but 1 added her to the mix because she was a prostitute and 1 figured better to be safe than sorry. Then, 1 used the moniker Jane Doe, because 1 didn't want to give too much to the media too early. Reporters are sniffing around and will figure it out soon enough, but 1 figured why not make them work for it."

"Good idea."

Blanchard paused for a moment, then reached across the table and pulled one box toward them. The box labeled Jane Doe #1. Reaching inside, he pulled out a manilla file, tossing it on the table. "Open that, but what's in there stays here. Understand?"

The cover of the file folder made a swishing noise against the wooden tabletop as Dodge pulled it closer, allowing him to sit before examining its contents. After spreading out several of the photos in front of him, the first thing he noticed was the fully dressed body. Same as the victim from yesterday. Then the shine on her skin caught his eye.

"This victim's body looks to have had the same oily substance rubbed on it. I assume this matches the latest victim. Meaning the killer redressed her post-mortem?"

"That matches what we found." The police captain paused, taking a deep breath before continuing. "Her name is Jessica."

Dodge studied the photographs, going over each one from top to bottom, then left to right. Next in reverse order. Even turning some upside down to provide an abstract view, anything he could do to spot something he might have missed at first glance. If he was present during the initial investigation, he would have viewed the body from every angle. Standing. Kneeling. Since he wasn't there, manipulating the pictures was the next best thing.

As he shuffled the photos around, he built a timeline. Once he had the photos arranged in a way he felt most likely resembled the facts of the scene, he stood back. Captain Blanchard had been hovering so close over his shoulder, that the two men collided when Dodge stepped back.

"Sorry," Blanchard said, moving off to the side to give Dodge room.

Staring at the collage of photos, he noticed that in each shot, the victim's shirt was scrunched up at the bottom, revealing a small portion of her stomach. He leaned in closer and could see a small mark above the navel. It appeared to be the bottom of a birthmark or possibly a tattoo.

"What's this?" Dodge said, pointing at the mark on one of the pictures.

"I was wondering if you would see that," Captain Blanchard

said. Then he removed a picture from another file inside the carton, pulled out a photograph, and handed it to Dodge. "That's why I labeled the cartons as Jane Doe."

Dodge took the photo and his eyes widened at what he saw. The killer had written the words *The Savior* in red across the victim's stomach.

"What does *The Savior* mean?"

"Couldn't tell ya."

"You know what this means, right?"

"I just said I have no idea what it is."

Dodge looked over at Blanchard, who had slid a few feet away after handing Dodge the picture. "I get why you labeled the boxes Jane Doe now. If the press caught wind of this, they would give this guy exactly what he wants, fame. I assume no one knows about this except us and the coroner?"

"One reporter found out, but I got her to back off by appealing to her sense of civic duty. I told her there was no need to panic the entire city with rumors of a serial killer until we know for sure that's what we have here. But she will only hold off for a week. Maybe two. And if the bodies keep piling up, she will write the story and I can't stop her."

"Who was the reporter?" Dodge asked.

"Her name is Angela Cortez. She works for Channel Six," Blanchard said.

Dodge shook his head.

"You know her?"

"Yeah. Not sure if she will take my call, but I can reach out to her."

"You two got a history or something?"

"You could say that," Dodge said, rubbing his hand though his short, sandy brown hair. He decided to change the subject. "Did the boys at the lab find anything out about this writing on her stomach?"

"They said the substance used was probably lipstick. Not sure if it belonged to her or not. They found no cosmetic products at the scene. A chemical analysis is being done to determine the exact manufacturer. Once we have the maker, we can canvass the local stores to see who sells that brand."

"It would be a huge waste of time."

"Why do you say that?" Blanchard asked. A look of annoyance on his face.

"This isn't some high-end call girl we are looking at. She is a street walker. Local too." Dodge picked up one of the photos from the autopsy. "Look right here," pointing out the small bruises on her arms. "Those are track marks. She's a 'hype', an IV drug user. The only place she spends her money is the shooting gallery with the rest of the junkies."

Blanchard stepped closer. Dodge could smell the gun powder from the range on his clothes.

He continued, "Girls like her get their makeup at the cheapest place possible or steal it. Either way, when you get the results of the analysis, you'll find that that brand is sold in every drug store in town. Hell, even some convenience stores I would bet. You'll be chasing your own tails all over town."

"You seem pretty sure of yourself."

"Look. You called me in for my opinion. Now you have it. You can do with that information what you want."

Now Dodge was annoyed and began to shuffle through the pictures. Rearranging them again in front of him. Studying each one, as if it was the first time he ever laid eyes on them. Being able to empty his mind when taking a second look at evidence was one skill that made him a brilliant investigator.

"Are there photos of the other two victims?" Dodge asked.

Captain Blanchard removed the lid from the box marked *Jane Doe #2*. Pulling out a file, he said, "Her name was Patti."

"Still is," Dodge said, as he spread the pictures across the table above the photos of the first victim. "Give me the shots from the third victim, Monica."

The captain removed the file from the box labeled *Jane Doe #3* and spread them out across the table.

He placed the pictures above the photos of the second victim. Concentrating, he scanned every picture, looking for the slightest detail that might jump out at him. "Did the second girl have the writing on her as well?"

The captain moved in behind Dodge and leaned in over his shoulder. "No. The first one only. What are you looking for?"

Dodge was silent. Studying. Then he saw it. "Give me the autopsy reports from both."

Captain Blanchard dug back into each of the boxes, rustling through mounds of paper until he came out with two reports from the medical examiner. He handed them to Dodge. "What do you see?"

After examining each report, he slapped each one down on top of the pictures of the victims they referred to, then turned to Captain Blanchard. "Your timeline is off."

"What do you mean, my timeline is off?" The state police captain scoffed. "We found Jessica seven days ago on a road leading out of town toward the dump. Patti, two days later, inside a vacant house on the south side. The coroner pinned the time of death on both. Jessica died before Patti."

Dodge slid all but two of the photos off the table, one each of the first and second victims. their bodies splayed out with a little yellow evidence card marked with the number one positioned off their right shoulders. He waited. Blanchard stared at the photos. He wasn't seeing it. After a few moments of silence, Dodge tapped his fingers on the picture of Patti. Right on her face.

At that moment, Dodge saw Blanchard's eyes open wide, then close as he shook his head. He recognized what they had missed. He stared at the red lipstick on Patti's lips. The shade appeared to match the color used to write on Jessica's stomach.

"Son of a bitch," he yelled.

"The autopsy results show Jessica died before Patti, so the killer had to have both girls together for a short period. Have the lab sample the lipstick from both bodies. It will be an exact match."

"Ok. But if Jessica died before Patti, why does it matter?"

"Maybe it doesn't. But it would be easy enough to alter the time of death for each victim. He locks one girl in a very cool room and stashes the other in a hot room. The bodies cool at different rates, altering the liver temperature. 1 mean, the times listed on the coroner's report even overlap by a few hours. But if both girls were still alive, in the same place, that could help us narrow down where he might maintain his little shop of horrors."

Captain Blanchard pulled out a chair and fell into the black leather cushion.

Dodge gathered up the pictures he had swiped off the table. It was a bit dramatic, but it worked. He then sorted and placed them back in the folders, replacing each in their respective boxes.

"We need to rework the timeline and dig more into Patti. Grabbing one hooker off the street is easy. But taking two and having them both alive in the same place, or at least the same time, takes planning and a place to work where the killer feels safe."

The captain nodded. "I guess I was right to bring you on. That's good work, Dodge."

"Sometimes a fresh set of eyes is good. You would have gotten there eventually."

"Is that how you would feel?"

Dodge laughed. "God no. I'd be mad as hell, but it doesn't make it wrong."

The two men spent the rest of the morning reworking the theory of the crime. They switched the two victims on the timeline and began forming a plan. Starting with victim two, Patti. Dodge took the lead and pieced together a new timeline and using a map on the wall, marked the locations of where they found the three bodies. The captain had some addresses where the second victim had lived and hung. He placed a pin on each of them on the map. Dodge told him about his meeting with Sarah the night before and he also marked the corner where victim three, Monica, worked. It was the beginning of a murderer's comfort zone. Once they nailed down Patti's locations, they should be able to shrink the search radius by half. The more points on the map they could get, the more accurate the comfort zone would be. Dodge liked how things were progressing, but he knew something would go wrong. Another murder more than likely. He saw nothing that made him think *The Savior* would be stopping anytime soon. His feeding grounds were ripe with potential victims. The thought gave Dodge a sour stomach. He swallowed deep and continued working. It was all he could do. For now.

CHAPTER 6

A MYRIAD OF QUESTIONS SWIRLED in Dodge's head as he left
the meeting at the state police post. He wasn't sure what to make
of all the new information he was hit with, and his new partner,
or boss as Blanchard kept reminding him, was even more of an
enigma. Missing the lipstick on the second victim was a rookie
mistake. One Dodge thought a cop with the time in service
Blanchard had shouldn't have made. It's not as if he hadn't made
his share of mistakes. Hell, he had made plenty. Some even cost
lives. But not putting the lipstick clues together was different. It
was careless. A lack of attention to detail, which was something
Dodge had little tolerance for. The whole thing made him feel
as though he couldn't trust anything the state police had done
on the cases up to this point. He would need to go over all the
evidence again. Piece by piece. Photo by photo. Had the detectives
interviewed anyone on the streets who may have known the
victims? He saw nothing in the files suggesting Blanchard even
made any attempts to canvas the streets for witnesses, or anyone
who may have known the victims. Mistakes were one thing, but
laziness was something he had trouble seeing past. But first, he
needed to know more about his new boss. Where did he work
before coming to the state police in Virginia? Why did he leave?
They were all questions he needed answers to before he could
fully trust the man.

He pushed the button on his steering wheel and a dial tone
replaced Steely Dan's "Peg" on the truck's speakers.

"Call Beth."

The screen on the LCD display read "dialing..." After a few
moments, the phone rang. A familiar voice from his past picked
up on the other end.

"This is Detective Samuels."

He tried to speak, but the words clogged in his throat. His stomach knotted. The two had left it open and amicable, but something had always tugged at him when it came to her. Late at night, when he was alone with a drink, he often wondered if *the one* slipped through his fingers. While their time together was brief, a couple of weeks, it felt like they had known each other for years. They had clicked on every level.

"Hello?"

"Beth, I don't know if you remember, but this..."

She interrupted, "Paul Dodge!"

"The one and only," he said, wishing he could take it back almost immediately.

"How long has it been?"

"Ten years, at least."

"Seems like yesterday to me." Her raspy voice spewed confidence.

"Me too."

"So, what've you been up to, Pauly? I saw you on the news a few years back. I even thought about catching a plane to come out east and see you."

She was the only person he ever let use that name. He hated it, but coming from her lips, it sounded endearing.

"Why didn't you?" Dodge asked.

"You know? Things got busy. I had too much work. I needed to wash my hair."

"Wash your hair?" Dodge said. "You're giving me the "I had to wash my hair" bit?"

"It's better than the shitty goodbye I got, or more like didn't get."

He wondered if this call had been a good idea. He had been so nervous about talking to her, that he never considered how she might feel about hearing from him after so many years.

"Yeah, I'm sorry..." he hesitated. Partly, because he didn't want to say the wrong thing. But also, he wasn't sure *what* to say. "I mean, I was an asshole. There's no excuse for how I left back then. I really am sorry."

Dead silence.

"It's ok," she finally said. "I wasn't ready for anything serious back then, anyway. Newly divorced, I was looking for a hookup. You were available and had a great ass."

The conversation had veered off course and was in danger of smashing into a tree. He decided to try and rein it back in.

"The reason I'm calling is that there have been a series of murders out here involving prostitutes."

"Changing the subject, huh?"

"It wasn't going well for me," Dodge said.

"Well, it had some time to fester."

"If you want to finish making me feel like a total wanker, I got some time."

Beth said, "Nope. I think I got it all out. So, somebody is axing hookers, huh? What do you think I can help with?"

Over the next five minutes, he filled her in on what he had learned so far about the murders. Even though he hadn't seen Beth in close to a decade, she was still third on his trust list, behind Renquest and Chief Johnson. It was one of his rules. Once someone earned your trust, hold it tight until they give you a reason not to. So, he included the part about writing on the second victim's stomach in red lipstick. Dodge wasn't trying to get her advice on the case, anyway. The call was to gain insight into his new boss, Blanchard.

"Are you wanting to know if we might have similar cases here in Phoenix? Cause I can tell you now, we find at least one dead prostitute a week in the city. I would need a little more detail about the murders. Time, place, condition of the body and, of course, physical descriptions of the victims."

Beth was a capable investigator and for a moment, he considered running down the cases from beginning to end to see what new insights his friend could provide. *An outside perspective hurt nothing*, he thought. That's the reason he was on the case. Or so he was told. Besides, she had a knack for details, and she might even find something he had missed. The thought fleeted, and he stuck with his original plan.

"Actually, I'm not looking for help with the case, per se."

"If you don't need help with the case, why did you call me?"

"The State Police are running point on this one and the lead detective is a Captain Blanchard. I think he is out of your part of the country, originally. Maybe Arizona or California, or even Nevada," Dodge said. "Ever heard of him?"

The phone went silent.

"Beth?"

"Don Blanchard?"

Her voice was low, and the tone gave him chills. Dodge jerked the wheel of his truck, not even checking the mirrors for other cars, and turned into a McDonald's, pulling into the first open spot he saw. He grabbed his phone from the cup holder, swiped the screen, turned off the Bluetooth function, and placed the device to his ear.

"You've heard of him?"

"Yes."

Dodge waited for what seemed like a minute. "Jesus Christ, Beth. You gonna tell me what the hell is going on, or you going to make me play twenty-one questions?"

"It's twenty questions and I don't want to talk on the government phone." More silence. "What are you doing tonight?"

"I planned on working. I need to go back and visit the first crime scene to get some perspective. I found some things and the timeline changed. I need to put fresh eyes on everything. Why, you want to call me later? I can make time to take a call." Dodge asked.

"No," she said. "I can be there in five hours. There is a flight out of Sky Harbor that leaves in two hours, and I'll call you when I land. Text me your address."

"Now you're freaking me out a little. If there is something I need to know, for God's sake tell me now."

"We can talk more tonight. And Dodge, be careful. I have got to go if I am going to make that flight." The line went dead.

Dodge sat in the cab of his truck, not sure what to make of the call. Be careful, she had said. He had his doubts about Captain Blanchard after they first met, but he based that feeling on the quality of work he had seen, along with his natural reaction to trust nobody after first meeting them. Nothing gave him a reason to worry about his personal safety with a cop. Reaching into the console between the front seats, he pulled open the lid and dug down until he found the pack of cigarettes he kept for emergencies. Then he rolled down the driver's window and stuck the filter end between his lips and lit it. He hadn't smoked in nearly three months, but the urge was always there. Besides, he did his best thinking when he was sucking the wonderful hot smoke into his lungs. He knew it was the addiction talking, but he didn't care.

As the rush of smoke entered his lungs, his mind cleared. It was the addiction, he told himself again. Another drag, then an exhale. He felt his muscles relax and leaned his head back. Closing his eyes, he ran the conversation with Beth through his head. Did she know Blanchard personally? Were they partners and something had gone wrong? Was he on the take and she crossed the Blue Line and turned on him? Or were they once lovers? He wasn't sure what happened but knew if it was enough to make her fly across the country to explain in person, he needed to watch his six around Captain Blanchard until he got the full story. The Beth he remembered wasn't reactionary or paranoid. Which was why her behavior was so worrisome.

After taking the last drag and flicking the butt out the window, he checked for traffic and pulled back onto the street. He headed to the location where the first victim was found. Dodge pressed his finger to the LCD screen, which controlled the radio and navigation in his truck, and typed in the nearest address to the crime scene, on Old Town Road, which ran east out of the city toward the dump.

After typing the directions into the onboard computer, Dodge turned the Bluetooth function on his phone back on and said, "Call DT." Renquest answered on the second ring.

"Dodge, I was wondering when you were going to call."

"Sorry, I was at the state police range this morning, qualifying. I was feeling naked without my piece."

"I assume they passed you out of pity," Renquest said, an attempt at humor.

Dodge glanced at his watch. A quarter after four, getting Renquest to go out this late in the afternoon would be a challenge. "I need you to meet me out on Old Town Road. I think another pair of eyes would be good at the dump site."

"It's been over a week since they found her, and rain would've washed away anything missed days ago. Besides, the techs went over the scene with a fine-tooth comb. Hell, they even crawled into the drainage culvert and took sediment samples. What is it you think you'll find?"

"Maybe nothing," Dodge said. "But I have some updates on the murders and I can fill you in while I'm walking the scene."

Dodge could hear Renquest sigh, but he encouraged his partner to join him "Don't make me drive all the way back to the task force office. It'll take you half an hour to get to me, tops."

"Alright. Where you at now?"

"I'm on my way there."

"I got to wrap up some things here, and I'll head over as soon as I am done. Should be there within the hour."

"Ok, thanks. I'll see you in a bit," Dodge said and rung off.

Dodge glanced at his watch when Renquest parked his blue four-door cruiser on the shoulder. The drive had taken him forty-five minutes.

"Glad you could make it," Dodge said.

"I told you I needed to finish some things before I left. Damn Dodge, take it down a notch."

"We are losing daylight fast and once the sun goes down; you couldn't see a semi-trailer parked ten feet in front of you out here."

"Relax. I'm here now. So, what is so important you had me drive out here to redneck... God damn. It smells like shit out here."

"Future hamburgers," Dodge said, pointing at a herd of cows in a pasture on the other side of the road.

"I wish they'd hurry it up. I didn't get lunch today."

The job always came first for Dodge, and his partner's comments annoyed him. But he put his annoyance aside and started walking the crime scene. Renquest followed close behind.

Dodge climbed into the drainage ditch. The ground was wet, but not muddy. "Where exactly did they find the first victim?" Dodge asked.

Stepping alongside his partner, Renquest pointed to a spot in the ditch about ten feet from where they stood. "Right there."

Dodge paced out the distance to the edge of the road. He took five wide steps. "About fifteen feet."

"Eighteen and a half, to be exact."

"That's what I wanted to talk to you about." Dodge knelt on one knee to get a better angle. "Captain Blanchard had the timeline all wrong."

Renquest was now standing directly over Dodge's right shoulder. "His timeline was off?"

"It's true this is where they found a victim. Her name is Jessica, and she was the first one abducted, but she was killed after he snatched his second victim, Patti."

"Wait, you're telling me, the guy who did this grabbed our vic... what did you say her name was?"

"Jessica."

"Jessica. He then kept her locked up somewhere until he could lure another girl... Patti?"

"Yes, Patti."

"So, this psycho snatches two girls. Holds the first one hostage somewhere until he can get his hands on another girl. Then he keeps both before killing them, and dumps the bodies at different locations on different days around town?"

"That's how I see it."

"Why? Wouldn't it be easier to just kill the vics right after taking them? I mean, keeping two hostages requires planning and a place to stash them. Somewhere he feels comfortable and away from prying eyes."

"You're pretty good at this."

"Piss off."

Dodge smiled, then told Renquest about the pictures Blanchard had shown him earlier at the state police post. He told him about the lipstick and the writing on Jessica's body and how the staties missed the fact that Patti was wearing the same red lipstick.

"Jesus, Dodge. If this guy is signing his work, we are dealing with one crazy son of a bitch. That's bold. This is not the work of a first-timer. I'd bet dollars to donuts he has done this before."

"Me too. Keeping a victim alive longer than you have to? That either makes him the dumbest possible serial killer or the most confident one I have heard of. Outside Bundy and maybe Dahmer," Dodge said, peering over his shoulder at Renquest.

"The question now is, if he has killed before, where?"

Dodge said nothing.

Renquest nodded. "What else have you found, given you've been on the case for a day and a half?"

Dodge hesitated before answering. Renquest was his oldest friend, whom he trusted with his life. But he wasn't sure if he wanted to bring him in on his fishing expedition concerning Captain Blanchard yet. Depending on what he found out from Beth, he could stir up a hornet's nest and the last thing he wanted was to put his partner in a bad spot. Caution being the better part of valor, he decided to wait until after speaking with Beth.

"That's about it. I thought you might help to locate information about Patti. Everyone was concentrating on Jessica, using her as a jumping-off point because she was the first victim found. I think we should start with Patti. If we find out what corner she worked, where she lived, and who she hung out with, we may be able to place those two together at some point. I'll look into Monica, the third vic. Maybe together we can piece some of this new timeline together."

"Ok. Ill' get an analyst to start working on arrests, addresses, and hospital records. Maybe one of them had a history of running into doors."

Dodge knew what Renquest meant about running into doors. He was referring to domestic abuse victims and the excuses told to hospital workers when they showed up in the ER with black eyes and broken noses. In this case, his partner was talking about the girls possibly having a pimp who might have been beating on them. It was a good idea. One that he also had pondered.

Dodge stood. "We need to work fast. Blanchard has a leak at the state police post."

"Someone talked to the press. That's just great. Any idea who it was?"

Dodge nodded.

"Who was the reporter?"

Dodge said, "Cortez at channel six."

Renquest smiled. "You going to talk to her?"

"I said I would."

"When was the last time you two spoke?"

"After we took down that child porn distributor. Haven't talked since."

"You banged her and then burned her on the story!"

A little embarrassed that his partner would bring up his indiscretions, Dodge looked to the ground. "It wasn't like that. It just happened."

"It happens a lot."

"Shut up."

"Look, I'm not saying I blame you. Hell, I would if I ever got the chance. But try to see it from her point of view. You meet up about this case. She gives you information that eventually leads to you putting cuffs on a real bad hombre, and somewhere in between all this madness, you have a tussle between the sheets. The optics are bad, man."

Again, Dodge said nothing. Mainly, because he had no defense for the allegations his partner had thrown at him. Secretly, he had always felt bad about the way things went down. Deep down, he even wondered if it was all true. Had he used her? After the story broke, he justified his actions by telling himself she was using him as well. She was a reporter, after all. She used people all the time to get stories and even had some sources inside police headquarters feeding her tips. He didn't fault her for it. Hell, it made him respect her more. But he still felt bad and never shook the feeling.

Dodge nodded. "I'm not sure if she will even talk to me, but unless you want to try talking to her, we don't have another option. It is way too early in this investigation to have the press trailing our every move and trying to interview the people we talk to."

Renquest agreed. He took one more look around and headed for his cruiser. "You coming?"

"In a minute. I need to think for a bit."

"Got any smokes?" Renquest asked. A jab at his partner who he knew had been trying to quit the habit, unsuccessfully.

Dodge said nothing as his thumb pointed behind him toward the truck.

Renquest got into his vehicle and pulled out onto the road. Honking the horn twice as he sped away.

Dodge looked at his watch again. It was a quarter after six. Beth would land in less than an hour. He needed to go home, pick up the place, and change clothes. There wasn't much food in the house. He had planned a trip to the market tomorrow night after work, so takeout would be on the menu for tonight. There was a nice little Thai place on the way home. He also needed to get a bottle of wine. Beth preferred white if he remembered correctly. He would choose something a little stronger. He was nervous about a woman for the first time in a while and he reveled in it.

The sun approached the spot in the sky where shadows were long, stretching for what seemed like miles as the sun dropped to just above the horizon. He decided on a whim to visit the resurrection site, not giving much thought to the idea the police might watch, giving a quick check for anyone that lingers too long or pays too much attention while driving past. He knew the police in this town. They were lazy, incompetent hicks. The only one he had seen with an ounce of investigative integrity was the fat one, and his gluttonous lifestyle would take care of him. Fried pig fat for breakfast and cheap beer and pizza for dinner. He had watched him for weeks, taking notes on his routines before taking Jessica. He was confident in his ability to outwit the detective.

The new arrival, though, was a twist he hadn't expected. Local departments never called for help. Sharing the limelight with others would make them look incompetent. At least it appeared that way to him. It was a matter of ego. He guessed that not one cop wanted to be the one to tell their superiors the officers couldn't deal with a few dead prostitutes. But the new one seemed different. He had an air of confidence, the way he walked, his stature. The Savior needed to know more about him.

As he approached the spot where he had released Jessica's tortured soul, the faint glow of taillights caught his eye. He eased off the accelerator slightly, slowing a few miles per hour. An instinctual reaction. Years of avoiding being caught in speed traps, with a bound and gagged girl in the back of his van, had taught him that.

The lights became brighter as he drew closer to the hallowed ground. He could make out the vehicle as a pickup truck. Black, he thought. Then he realized he had seen the vehicle before. It was at the alley where he freed Monica. It belonged to the new arrival. What was he doing here? The Savior had put days and weeks, even months, into planning, to assure the outcome would be the one he desired. The one he needed. He could feel his skin warming. He was jealous. This was his place, and he didn't want to share it with anyone.

"Get out of here," he mumbled.

As the van got closer, he slowed even more. At that moment, the realization of how much he had decelerated hit him. He eased his foot back into the gas pedal, moving it a fraction of an inch at a time. The van hesitated at first—the lack of horsepower from the old V-8 engine rearing its head at the worst possible time. But after a few moments, the transmission caught, and the van lurched forward. The new arrival was standing, staring into the field that bordered the ditch. The concentration on his face drew admiration from the van's driver. He wondered what the man was thinking. What was he searching for?

The man turned towards the road as the van passed, nearly catching him off guard. He swiveled his head to the left to avoid a full glimpse of his face. Using the passenger's side mirror, he watched as the new arrival's silhouette faded into the distance until he could no longer make out him or the truck. He knew he had more work to do. Starting with finding out all he could about this new player before he could risk taking another soul. He relished the challenge.

CHAPTER 7

SARAH TURNED THE FAUCET to the left. Water spurted out, splashing onto the edge of the tub, spilling over the side, and pooling on the rubber mat she had purchased as a way to keep her newly cleaned feet from touching the faded and cracking tile floor. She jerked her hand back as the ice-cold water ran across her fingers. No hot water again. Living in the motel had turned into one bad dream. Life on the streets wasn't a nine-to-five job and rarely provided the income stability needed to qualify for an apartment. Not that anyone would rent to a prostitute, anyway.

She dreamed of one day getting off the streets, no longer selling her body and her dignity to the lowest bidder. She would be a call girl. The kind that sits in the swanky hotel bar and seduces rich business executives wearing five-thousand-dollar suits, or dinner parties at swanky restaurants. Those suit types were going to pay a high price for her to drop her skirt. It was going to be a better life than the one she had. *One day*, she thought.

The manager of the motel she called home was becoming more aggressive in his rent collection. Three weeks ago, an older thin woman sported a black eye the morning after paying her rent on her back. Sarah tried to talk to her, but the battered woman moved out shortly after. While working her corner, Sarah kept an eye out for the woman, hoping to catch a glimpse of her one night, but she never returned. Then the cops found a body in a field on the outskirts of town, on the road that led to the dump. What a metaphor. The news said her name was Patti. Nobody seemed to care enough to find out what her last name was. That's how it was on the streets. Anonymity.

Street savvy and always up on the local news, Sarah noticed a frightening trend. Girls disappeared more frequently lately. There were always new girls coming and old ones leaving. It was the nature of her profession, but usually, they became pregnant or moved to another city to get away from an abusive pimp. Never had working girls turned up dead in an alley before now. Not in this town, anyway.

Sarah jumped into the shower, lathering, and rinsing her body so fast, she accidentally poked herself in the eye while washing her face.

"That's just great!" she yelled. Another blemish on her prematurely aging body. No one wants damaged goods.

The water was freezing. Goosebumps formed on her arms and legs as the soapy water ran down her body. She decided against washing her hair. It was too cold. Her hair dryer had stopped working last week anyway, and she couldn't afford to buy a new one. Once out of the shower, she patted herself dry. Starting with her face, working her way down. Arms, then legs, finishing sitting down on the edge of the tub with her feet. Next, she rolled her hair into a bun on the top of her head and applied some makeup. She was careful not to overuse any one product, but she liked the way she looked with a little too much eyeliner and mascara. Her eyes were her best feature and the best damn closer a woman could have.

Next, she planned her outfit for the coming night. She settled on skintight shorts showing enough to get the men's attention, but she was careful not to give away too much for free, forcing them pay to see what was hidden from view. Everyone loves unwrapping presents. Build the anticipation but leave something for the imagination. Her outfits were built on the same ideal. Instead of a bowling ball or bottle of cologne, they got supple breasts and more. She slid on a pair of sneakers. A girl never knew when she was going to have to run, and she had seen enough horror movies growing up to know that women in heels die first. A splash of perfume, a refill of her flask, and she was out the door, ready for another night of self-deprecation.

Within ten minutes, Sarah was standing at her corner and

greeting her first trick of the night. The encounter was a quick one, placing her back on the corner in fifteen minutes. As she waited for her next John, she rinsed out her mouth with a sip from her flask and sideways glanced toward the corner where the girl they found two days ago used to stand. Another woman was using the spot now, not much older than the previous. She shuttered at the thought. The whole thing felt like walking across someone's grave. As her eyes turned back to the street in front of her, she was happy to see the creepy white van was no longer parked directly across from her corner. Nothing drives away customers more than a windowless van. To most people, it was either a cop or a child molester. Neither was good for business. She leaned back against the wall, half looking for new customers and half staring at the new girl up the street.

—⁓—

The kitchen smelled of searing meat and steamed vegetables. Dodge had planned on picking up Thai carry-out, but instead, he decided to stop at the market on his way back from the crime scene and bought a couple of beef filets and fresh vegetables. He browned the steaks on both sides in a cast-iron skillet and slid the pan into the oven, setting the timer for fifteen minutes at three hundred and eighty degrees. As he placed the green beans into the boiling water for a quick blanch, the front doorbell rang. Dodge grabbed a couple of wine glasses, setting them on the table as he walked to the door.

As the door swung open, his stomach knotted. He hadn't thought about what to say when she had finally arrived. Thoughts about the case occupied his mind for most of the day, keeping his mind from wandering.

She stood on the stoop, dressed in a t-shirt and shorts, cloth sneakers, the kind in style when he was a kid, no socks. The sight of Beth standing at his front door took his breath away. He hadn't imagined she could look better than he'd remembered. But there she was, all five-foot-seven inches. Her weight spread out evenly across her frame. He instantly remembered what first attracted him to her. It was her presence. The way she filled a room. The brains and sassy attitude were icing on the cake. She was stunning.

"You going to invite me in, or stand there with your tongue hanging out?"

Dodge realized he had been staring. He wasn't sure for how long. Embarrassed by his lack of couth, he stepped to the side. As Beth passed him, he felt her arm brush his chest so slightly. The smell of her perfume wafted by him, triggering a primal urge in his inner brain as a tidal wave of memories rushed in. He placed a hand on the small of her back as he closed the door and gestured toward the dining room. She hesitated, using her body weight to lean into his hand, before entering the dining area.

"I hope you like filets," Dodge said. "I picked a couple up at the market today. Thought you might be hungry after a long flight."

"I'm famished," Beth said.

Dodge stepped into the kitchen. "Excuse me for a moment. I don't want to overcook and ruin your dinner."

"You didn't have to go through all this trouble for me."

"It's nothing, really. I was going to have a filet tonight, anyway. No extra work in preparing one more." He poked his head around the corner of the wall. "You can have a seat anywhere. Make yourself comfortable. Dinner should be ready in about five minutes."

Beth had moved to the wall displaying the various awards they had given Dodge over his career, both in the Air Force and in his role at the Department of Corrections.

"Got anything to drink?" Beth asked, her eyes bounced from one commendation to another.

"There's two glasses on the table and a bottle of wine in the globe bar." Dodge had purchased the bar after seeing it in the home of a federal judge while working a case. Someone killed the judge a few days after Dodge met him. He was shot in the head and his daughter was taken hostage. Dodge visited the daughter during the sale of the property and purchased the earth shaped bar from the estate after she caught him admiring it. Some would have thought it macabre, but he saw it as practical. It was a beautiful bar and was being used for what it was intended.

Beth lifted the top and the globe split at the equator and

opened to reveal three bottles of wine and a battery-operated corkscrew. She held the electric wine bottle opener over the cork until it popped out of the bottle, then poured two glasses, and returned to the makeshift wall of honor.

"You sure seem to have been busy the last ten years."

"What?" Dodge said, popping his head around the corner again. "Oh, those. They give those away anymore."

Beth turned. "No. No, they don't."

Dodge ducked back behind the kitchen wall, embarrassed by the compliment. His face turned red, though she couldn't see it. Moments later, he reappeared with two plates, one in each hand. Placing the first plate on the table and nodding to Beth to sit. He placed the other plate in front of the only other chair at the table and slid her chair back from the table.

"Thank you," Beth said. "It all looks so appetizing."

"It's nothing, really."

She smiled. "You still can't take a compliment, can you?"

He blushed again. Sitting down, he picked up his wineglass and extended it in a toast. "To good food."

"And good company."

Beth smiled and their glasses clinked together, each taking a drink and placing the glasses back on the table. Dodge ate the steak first while Beth ate all her vegetables and some from his plate.

Once done eating, she helped clear the table and dry the dishes after he washed and rinsed them. Dodge refilled Beth's wine glass and poured a double shot of bourbon for himself, then he led her into the living room where they sat on the sofa.

"So, why don't you tell me why you had to drop everything and fly halfway across the country at the very mention of Blanchard's name?"

Beth took a sip of wine. "How much do you know about him?"

"Not very much. I really don't have that much contact with the State Police. They run the sex offender registry, but they assign those duties to troopers low on the seniority pole or to guys who can't stop stepping on their own toes. We don't even have a statie on the task force."

"Sounds about right." His guest turned her attention to the coffee table positioned in front of the couch. "Do you still smoke?"

"I kind of quit. In theory."

"In theory?"

"I always keep a pack around. Helps me think sometimes," Dodge said, rising and walking to the bedroom. When he returned, he held a fresh pack of Marlboros. He tapped the pack against the palm of his hand until one butt poked out above the others. He handed her the cigarette, then pulled the Zippo lighter out of his pocket, flipping the lid and lighting the flame in one motion.

Beth leaned in and took a drag. She exhaled the smoke, waving her hand to break up the white cloud.

"Don Blanchard." She paused and took another drag and a sip from her wineglass. "I should start at the beginning. I first met him at a sexual assault conference our department sponsored about three—maybe four—years ago in Phoenix. Blanchard was a detective from Las Vegas assigned to a special homicide unit dealing in cold cases with a sexual component. You know what I am talking about?"

"Yeah, I've assisted in a few of those cases in the past. Not a lot of fun. Most of the time you can't find witnesses and you're at the mercy of the original investigating officers' reports," Dodge said.

"Exactly," Beth said. "Anyway, Blanchard was a good cop, as far as I could tell. At the conference, we took part in a discussion panel concerning trace DNA evidence and proper collection techniques. I got to tell you, he really seemed to know his stuff. When we broke down into groups, I got paired with him. He had some great insights and led the discussion most of the time."

Dodge nodded and swallowed a shot of bourbon.

Beth continued, "After the conference, about ten of us went out for drinks and Blanchard said he wanted to tag along. We ended up at the bar Alice Cooper owns downtown. Everyone was laughing and getting piss drunk. Everyone except for Don Blanchard."

"He didn't drink at all?"

"Not one drink. I mean, it's not like we expect everyone to drink, but most of the guys were buying rounds and having a good time. I called it a night around eleven. Blanchard said he was staying at the hotel the conference was being held at and asked if I cared to share a cab. I needed to go back to get my car and figured, what the hell. On the cab ride, he just started talking."

Dodge leaned forward, closer to Beth as she spoke.

"He had been working a couple of unsolved murder rapes for about six months. They had little to go on at first, only a few bodies of hookers masquerading as exotic dancers during the day. But Blanchard saw similarities in the victims and the method in which they died. Tortured horribly and all of them were sexually assaulted post-mortem. He ran down leads on the victim's families and employers, including what blocks they frequented." Beth pressed the cigarette into the ashtray, extinguishing its glowing ember. "It wasn't long until some of the other working girls began telling him about a pervert that cruised the streets looking for women. He targeted a particular type of girl. The loners. The ones none of the other girls would talk to. Once in the car, he would demand they give him a blowjob while he preached about Jesus and saving their everlasting soul."

"That's not how I remember church," Dodge said.

"That's funny, because that is exactly how I remember it," Beth said, emotionless. "Where was I? Oh, yeah, Blanchard had been putting some of the bigger puzzle pieces together when another woman turned up dead. Same victim type and same cause of death, asphyxiation. Only this time, there was no sexual assault."

"And Blanchard thought there was a connection."

"That's where things got weird. The killer left a note for the police. Or, I should say, for Don Blanchard."

Dodge was silent for a moment. "What do you mean, a note? Like a letter pinned to the vic's shirt?"

"Not exactly. The suspect wrote on the victim's chest and stomach with a permanent marker. He was taunting him."

The veteran investigator's mind processed what Beth told him. The cases in Las Vegas and his town were eerily similar. Throw Blanchard into the mix and the coincidences started piling up. And Dodge didn't believe in coincidences. He asked, "How does this story wind up with Blanchard in my city?"

"That's why 1 flew out here. There were rumors. Rumors about his involvement in the murders after three more bodies were found spread across the city. Last thing 1 heard, he quit the department and disappeared into civilian life. 1 hadn't thought about him in years, until you called me out of the blue the other day."

"How long ago did he leave the LVPD?"

"1 really don't know. Like 1 said, 1 hadn't thought about him in years," Beth said.

Dodge stood and made his way to the bar, where he poured another glass of bourbon. A triple. This time, he swallowed it in one gulp. He could see Beth staring at him out of his peripheral. "What?"

She stood. "What are you not telling me?"

"Nothing."

He wanted to tell her, but the alcohol was kicking in. First, he needed to get something off his chest. Sitting the glass down on the table, Dodge walked back to Beth. He reached for her hand and pulled her close. The scent of her perfume was strong.

"1 owe you an apology," he said.

"She looked up at him. "1 was only giving you a hard time. It was probably for the best. You being in the military and me living in the desert. 1 can't seem to make a relationship work with someone in my own building; no way 1 get one to work with a ladies' man in uniform halfway around the world."

"Ladies man?"

"Oh, please. 1 was thinking about getting you into bed five minutes after we met. It was all 1 could do to keep my hands off you during the stakeout in the car the third night. Are you telling me you didn't feel the same way?"

"Well, maybe 1 have a little more control than you," he said, smiling down at her.

"Please!" She punched him in the shoulder. Hard. "You are a liar."

"1'm kidding," he said as he reached up and rubbed his shoulder. "You were probably right. Besides, you were way too good for me."

"Were?"

She grew closer to him. Until her chest touched his. Placing his right hand behind her head, he gently pulled her toward him and kissed her. It was as if they had never been apart.

The two lay in bed, sharing a cigarette, both wet with sweat and breathing heavily. Dodge looked at Beth and she smiled.

"That was fun," he said.

"Fun! It should have been mind-blowing. Some things I did, I will spend an hour in the confession box."

"You're right," Dodge said. "It was good."

Beth laughed and smacked him on the shoulder. Again. She rolled over, laying her head on his chest. He flexed his arm to pull her closer.

"Don't think for a second sex is going to get you out of telling me about your case."

Dodge took the last drag from a cigarette the two had shared and doused it in the ashtray. "One of our vics had writing on her. The suspect used another victim's lipstick to write the words, *The Savior* on her stomach. Blanchard reacted more like a father than a cop. It caught me off guard is all."

"What color was the writing?"

"He used red lipstick."

"I would have to do some checking, but I think that is the same shade of red the perp in Vegas used to taunt Blanchard."

"Too many damn similarities. Him being here and the dead prostitutes are not coincidences." Dodge sat up, leaning his back against the headboard. "You wanna go out for a bit?"

"What, now? I was hoping I could keep you in this bed a while longer." Beth sat up and slid one leg over his waist. "When we get back," he said.

They both put on the clothes they had discarded an hour before. Dodge grabbed his badge and weapon. He looked back at Beth, who was teasing her hair into place.

"You bring your piece?"

"Didn't think I was going to need it. I accomplished the two things I wanted to do in coming here." She said, smiling.

"I got an extra in the safe in the closet. It's a snub-nosed revolver, but it should do fine."

"Where the hell are we going, Dodge?"

"Downtown to talk to some girls," he said as he handed her the tiny revolver, which she placed in her purse. "You sure you can get to that in there if you need it?"

"I'm with the great Paul Dodge. Why would I ever need a to?" Sarcasm dripped from her tone.

Dodge smiled. The pair finished getting dressed and began the short ride to the corner where Sarah worked.

CHAPTER 8

IT'S BEEN SAID THAT THE TEMPERATURE has a direct effect on traffic volume. Both pedestrian and vehicle. It was a warm night and people were out in droves. Dodge couldn't think of a recent night where he had seen the number of people just mingling on the sidewalks and sometimes in the street as he did that night. It was wall-to-wall people. He wondered if there was some kind of local street festival happening that he was unaware of. Then he remembered that there are no festivals in this part of town at night. Families and the other law-abiding citizens, the ones who want to have community events like fairs and block parties, usually stay inside after dark in this neighborhood. Tucked away, safely behind locked doors. Even the food trucks packed up for the day just before the sunset.

An increase in activity appeared to be good for the girls working the downtown streets. Within five minutes of parking the truck, Dodge and Beth saw three solicitations go down. A third driver spotted the pair and sped away before stopping. He threw up his left hand to shield his face as he passed the pair crossing the street.

"That was strange. I mean we don't look like regulars, but... Damn it Dodge!"

Dodge looked at his friend. Her eyes were fixed on his waistline. He looked down and realized his weapon was showing. Before he could move his hand to cover it with his shirt, which had ridden up when he climbed out of his truck, Beth reached over and tugged on the bottom, and the shirt fell over the butt of the Glock.

Beth laughed. "That will not endear you to anyone down here."

"Yeah, we should move a few blocks that way," he said pointing to his right. "The girl I spoke to the other day mans a corner a few blocks down."

The couple cut at an angle across the street, dodging traffic by walking between cars whose drivers had stopped, waiting for the light to turn green.

"So why do you want to talk to this girl? I could throw a rock and hit fifty girls from here."

Dodge's eyes remained focused. If he saw her before she noticed them, the pair could split up to prevent her from darting into an alley and out of sight. "She is the only person I know who had direct contact with the last victim before the murder."

"Do you think she knows something she isn't telling you?"

"I think she saw something. She may not think it was important or is too scared to say anything. Either way, we need to find out what she knows," Dodge said, tipping his head toward a young woman leaning up against the side of a building thirty feet in front of them.

Sarah's outfit was more conservative than her co-workers. She wore short jean shorts, but not so short her ass hung out, and a t-shirt cut off at the waist, high enough to show some navel but it covered her breasts completely. She was an attractive girl. If he had met her in a bar, under different circumstances, he may have shown an interest in her. She was younger than him, but who wasn't these days? Beth tugged on his arm.

"I think you should take the lead. She knows you," Beth said. "If she isn't receptive to your charms, as hard as that is to believe, I can step in and play the trusting and helpful female companion."

Dodge nodded, and they approached Sarah slowly, as unthreatening as two people wanting to talk to someone committing a crime could be.

Sarah saw Beth instantly. "Agent Dodge. I see you got a partner now."

Dodge smiled. She was smart and appeared to have a keen eye for trouble which would serve her well in this profession. The pair stopped about five feet from her and glanced around.

"I don't have a pimp. You can relax."

He moved closer. "Nice to see you again, Sarah. How are things at the motel?"

She shrugged. "The same. Nothing much changes for us working girls."

"I don't want to take up a lot of your time, but I have a few questions. I think you can help me with a problem I have."

Sarah glanced in each direction, then waved at the two to follow her into an alley. They went with her, but Dodge noticed Beth hesitate.

"You can stay out here if you like. Keep an eye out and make new friends."

Beth shot a glare in his direction. "I'm fine. Just not a fan of dark alleys."

Sarah led the way, Dodge was next, followed by Beth. The veteran agent found a spot with his back against a wall and a clear view of both entry points into the alley. Beth took his cue and followed suit on the wall opposite him. Four eyes, two directions.

"Ok. No one should see us now. Is there something you want to tell us?"

Sarah kept glancing back toward the street. It was clear she felt nervous about talking to them.

"How many girls are dead now?"

"Three," Dodge said.

"Were the others like my friend?"

Dodge nodded. "Mostly. I mean, they were all working girls, and young."

"What was your friend's name?" Beth asked.

"Her name was Monica."

The light in the alley was dim, but Dodge could see tears forming in the young girl's eyes. He reached into his pocket and realized he didn't have any tissues. It was a habit he learned early in his career. Always keep a small package of tissues in your pocket when you know you are going to interview people. People under stress tend to get emotional and the act of handing them a tissue shows empathy and can build trust.

Beth dug into her purse, pulling out a few wadded-up sheets, and handed them to Sarah. "Never underestimate what a woman keeps in her purse," she quipped.

The comment seemed to break the tension, forcing a smile from Sarah. Dodge had forgotten how good Beth was in the field. She had a commanding presence, but her demeanor made people comfortable, and she always knew what to say. Or what not to say. It was a talent few investigators possessed. He knew of only two others as good as her, Renquest and himself.

"Did Monica have any enemies or someone that paid a little too much attention to her? Maybe an angry pimp or a repeat customer she had recently had a problem with?" Dodge asked.

"Not that I know of. She was new to the life. No one had gotten their hands on her yet. Pimps want to make money, so the low earners and new girls get little attention."

"Ok," Beth said. "Did you see anyone paying close attention to Monica the night she died? Did anyone approach her and she rebuffed his advances? Maybe a car that came around more than once?"

"Like I said, she was young and naive and didn't have the sense yet to say no. I tried to give her some pointers a couple of times, but obviously it didn't help."

Then Sarah paused, looking up like she was trying to find a thought lost somewhere in the air around her.

"What is it?" Dodge asked.

"Nothing," she said. Her eyes came back, locking with Dodge's.

"Are you sure? Sometimes the most innocuous of details might be the break we need. What were you thinking about a second ago?"

"It's nothing."

"Why don't you tell us and we will decide if it is important."

A short silence went by. Then she spoke. "I was thinking about a guy I turned down that night. There was something about him that gave me the creeps. Maybe it was because I couldn't make out his face or that he was in a van with no windows."

"What do you remember about this guy? Was he white or black?"

"White, I think. I didn't get a real good look at his face. It was like he was trying to hide it."

"What do you remember about the van he was driving? The color? The make?"

"White. It was white and had ladders strapped to the roof."

"Ladders? Like a painter or handyman might use?"

"I guess. I don't really know anything about that stuff."

"What did he do when you turned him down?" Beth asked.

"He gave me the finger and called me a bitch."

"Then what did he do?"

"He circled the block and then headed for Monica's corner. I tried to get her attention, to get her not to go with him, but she wasn't paying attention to me." She took a deep breath and let it out before continuing. "Do you think he is the one that might have killed her?"

"And after he picked her up, you didn't see him drop her back off?" Dodge asked. A quick glance at Beth.

"Not until the cops showed up. I mean, I didn't see her then either, but I knew it was her lying in that alley."

Beth nodded.

"Do you think you could identify the van?" Dodge asked.

"I doubt it. The van looked like a hundred I see driving around this place every day."

Dodge paused, giving her time to think and maybe keep talking. She said nothing, and he decided she had told them everything she knew or wanted to. He could always make another run at her later. His hand slid into his front jeans pocket and came out with a twenty-dollar bill. He thanked her for her time and handed her the bill. The pair left Sarah in the alley and made for his truck.

Once inside the cab, Dodge pushed the key in the ignition but didn't start the engine. He stared out the windshield, down at the busy street in front of them.

"What is it?" Beth asked.

"I don't know. Something Sarah said is gnawing at me and I can't figure it out."

"About the van, or the driver?"

"I just don't know. But a white panel van with a ladder on the roof? I probably see a hundred of those a day. Without a description of the driver, it would be like looking for a needle in a haystack of needles."

Beth nodded, placing her hand on his leg. "Why don't we head to your place? We can have a drink and a smoke and talk it out."

Dodge smiled at her, took one more glance at the scene in front of him, and started the engine.

―⁓―

The next morning found the couple hurriedly getting dressed, bumping into each other. Beth had overslept and stood a real chance of missing her flight back to Phoenix. Before the two fell asleep, he had mentioned she could take some time and stay a few more days, making it seem as if he needed her help. But the real motive was simpler. He didn't want her to leave. She fawned over the idea for a few minutes, but then decided she needed to get back to her job. Finding the time to get away and wanting to get away were two different things. If there was one thing Dodge understood, it was how important this job can make a person feel. True or not, being a badge had a way of inflating a person's sense of importance.

The two had a long embrace in the entryway before Beth hopped into her rental car and drove away. A sense of loss came over him. He was not good at goodbyes, so he said nothing. Just another memory to stuff in the box and close the lid, he thought. And that is what he did, for a while.

CHAPTER 9

IT WAS EARLY, BUT THE MERCURY ROSE to over three-quarters of the way to one hundred degrees. It would be in the eighties before long, and the streets downtown would bustle with shoppers and pedestrians going about their day. Many just mindlessly walking the streets, sipping coffee and taking in the sunshine. Others, the smarter ones, planning for the day ahead. Planning was good, and it was one of Dodge's steadfast rules. Always have a plan.

First, he needed to check in with Captain Blanchard. Sarah's revelations the night before could be helpful, and needed to be added to the case file while still fresh in his memory. The story Beth told him about his new boss also gnawed at his gut, the one part of his body he trusted above all others. As he mulled over the details of the case in his mind, the voice in his head kept echoing that something was wrong. Murders happening in Blanchard's town and he just up and quits? No reason. Then the murders stop, and only after resuming his police duties in another city, do the killings start again. Everything about this case, and the captain, seemed tainted with the stench of decay.

As he maneuvered the city streets, his mind was working overtime trying to process his case and figure out where it and Las Vegas came together. Outside of Blanchard, of course. On one occasion, he thought he may have run a red light. That's how his mind worked sometimes, but he decided it was better if he paid more attention to his driving for the moment. He could focus on the case once at the State Police Post.

The post was nearly empty. Only the dispatcher and desk officer were in the building. Dodge used the key fob Blanchard had given him to enter through the employee entrance. The lights, operated by motion sensors in the ceiling, turned on one by one as he made his way to the small cubical the IT people had set up for him in a back office. It only took him about twenty minutes to type up the notes on his meeting the night before, including the part about the white panel van Sarah had seen the night Monica died. It wasn't the best lead, but more than the team had so far. The number of white panel vans in the county must reach into the thousands, but he tried to remain positive and looked at the argument from the other side. There were more people that didn't own a white panel van than did own one. Maybe three to four times as many? He had just ruled out seventy percent of the county's residents as suspects. It was an accountant's trick, but it worked.

The first shift of troopers began funneling into the office as Dodge finished updating the case files. Still no Captain Blanchard. Tired of waiting, he decided it might be a good idea to fill in Renquest in the recent developments. Both in the case and Blanchard. Bouncing ideas off his partner helped provide a different perspective. It also helped ward off tunnel vision, focusing on just one theory of the crime, which could grind an investigation to a halt if the leads ran out.

The task force office couldn't have been more different from the state police post in the morning. Phones rang. Copy machines buzzed to life. Officers drank copious amounts of coffee and bustled around the office with purpose. The contrast between rural and city policing was obvious to even the untrained eye. And it wasn't about the number of crimes or officers. There was always a sense of urgency downtown. The urgency lessened as you crossed into the suburbs and all but disappeared as one entered the farm areas outside the city limits. Personally, the hustle and bustle of the city suited Dodge. He felt oddly at peace amid chaos.

His partner sat at his desk, shuffling from one file to another. A television hung on the adjacent wall—the local news playing in the background.

"Anything new to report?" Dodge asked.

The detective peered up from under the frames of his reading glasses. "Have a seat. If you can find one in this disaster."

There were several files on the chair facing Renquest's desk. Dodge placed them on the floor and brushed an old French fry off the seat before sitting.

"Afraid you'll dirty your jeans?"

"Afraid I'll need a tetanus shot."

Renquest turned his attention back to the stacks of paper on his desk. "What have you got for me from your new pal at the state police?"

"Nothing more than I had yesterday. But I found out some interesting facts about our captain."

The detective's brow curled, his face stone cold. "What have you been up to?"

"Nothing to be concerned about. I did a little digging with some people I know."

"If he finds you have been looking into his past, he will kick you off the case and you'll be back scanning pervs' computers for porn," Renquest said. "What made you want to go digging up bones on Blanchard?"

"Call it a gut feeling."

"Great, another Paul Dodge gut feeling. The last time you had one of those, I had to shoot someone. At least tell me you found something worth it."

Dodge hesitated. "Are you sure you want to know? Right now, it is just me, but if Blanchard finds out you're involved, it could put you and the task force's involvement in this case in jeopardy. Is that something you're ready for?"

Dodge knew the question challenged his partner's bravado. He intended just that, and it worked. He felt a little bad about manipulating his friend and partner. But sometimes it was so easy, and he really needed cover on this one.

"Let me tell you something, no one at the state police, or anywhere else, is going to scare me by using the task force as leverage. Especially not some over-paid ticket writer. So, what do you have?"

Dodge filled the detective in on everything he had learned about Blanchard from Beth over the past two days. From the killings in Las Vegas to his sudden disappearance and reemergence in their town a year prior.

The old wooden chair squeaked and moaned under the detective's weight as he leaned back, placing all of his two-hundred and fifty pounds on the old hinges. His eyes stared at a spot on the ceiling, as if an answer would suddenly appear from between the cracks in the tiles.

"Let me get this straight. Our good captain was a cop in Vegas during a murder spree. He up and quits, disappearing for several months, before winding up in my town just as a series of killings, very similar to the ones in Vegas, start?" Renquest said.

"That about sums it up."

"And your friend in Arizona, she is reliable?"

"Trust her with my life."

The chair let out another growl as the detective stood. "I'll see what I can find out about him. I have a friend or two in the Vegas PD. They should be able to tell me something without it getting back to Blanchard."

"Sounds good but be careful who you trust. The thin blue line will come out in force if they think one of their own is in jeopardy."

Renquest nodded. "Where you headed today?"

"I have to talk to Cortez at Channel Six."

Renquest shook his head.

"You think this is a bad idea?" Dodge asked.

"I think *you* talking to her is a bad idea. There's a difference."

"Cortez has some inside information about the murders. I need to find out exactly how much she knows and try to convince her to hold off writing a story for a few days. At least until we can nail down a suspect."

"You know as soon as you show up, it confirms her suspicions? She will smell blood in the water. Reporters are like sharks. Once they get their teeth in something, they won't let go."

"You're thinking of gators."

"Both will eat you."

"True."

"Plus, doesn't she still hate your guts?" Renquest asked.

"Last time I checked."

"Oh, would I love to be a fly on the wall when she sees you."

"You want me to take pictures?"

"Nah. I'll just stick with the scene in my head."

"Try not to hurt yourself."

"Let me know if you find anything out."

The walk to his truck provided time to plan out how he would handle the meeting with Cortez. They had a past, and their fling hadn't ended well. It would never have led to anything more than sex for Dodge. He assumed she felt the same way at the time. He used her for information, and she did the same to him. She was a reporter, and most reporters didn't have large numbers of close friends. They had sources. Sources for stories and information, to be tossed aside when no longer needed. And Cortez was no different. Or so he thought. Turns out she was different in one way. Her feelings for him were genuine. But his preconceived notions about her, and other reporters, ensured the relationship would not blossom, instead wither and die. Doomed to failure.

Earlier in his career, Dodge had used Cortez to plant a story on the local news about an internal investigation. The carefully worded story said the Department of Corrections was looking into a matter concerning a local parole agent suspected of taking bribes and fixing parole hearings. The news desk at Channel Six made an on-air plea asking former and current offenders for any information that might help them unmask the allegedly crooked parole officer. The news channels attorneys would investigate any allegations they considered credible with guaranteed anonymity for those brave enough to step forward.

Dodge placed surveillance teams on Cortez, twenty-four seven. Every meeting with every offender photographed and logged. He hoped the play would force the absconder to come out of hiding. He had complained about his conviction for years. Oddly, the parole agent felt some of the offender's claims had merit. But it was irrelevant. The courts had upheld the conviction. Time had been served, and it was his job to protect the public and ensure compliance with early release supervision conditions. Everything else was background noise. Well above his pay grade.

On the third day of surveillance, Cortez met with an offender who said he was on the run and had information about the agent the news team was looking for. It was the easiest bust the task force ever made. Cortez and the absconder met in a busy public space, which they probably thought provided anonymity and protection. In reality, the location allowed the agents to hide in plain sight. Individual sights and sounds were drowned out by a sea of people and movement. Officers were on top of him before he could take a step. Cuffed and stuffed in less than two minutes. A perfect takedown.

Cortez was a smart woman and an excellent investigative reporter. It took her all of five minutes to put the puzzle pieces together. It was the last time Dodge had spoken to her. Until today.

The elevator doors opened to the fourth floor, and he gazed into the lobby of the Channel Six business suites. His left hand tremored and he stuffed it in his pocket. It was normal to feel nervous at the thought of seeing a past lover when things had ended poorly. Usually, the result of something he said, did, or didn't do. He didn't hold any romantic feelings for Cortez. Any emotional ties were shed years ago. Truth be told, Cortez intimidated Dodge. She was strong, independent, and intellectually superior to him. He was street smart, but she was brilliant. Her moral compass pointed North, but she wasn't afraid to veer off course to get the results she wanted. She was a lot like him. And that's why it would never work.

The receptionist took his name, and he signed in. He barely had sat down when he heard a familiar voice.

"If it isn't Paul Dodge."

He tried not to look surprised. Or scared. "Cortez. It's been a long time."

"Not long enough," she said. "What the hell are you doing here?"

"I was just in the neighborhood and thought I would stop by and see if you wanted to get a cup of coffee." Dodge realized how dumb the statement sounded as soon as the words slipped past his lips. Law enforcement and reporters didn't meet in public. It was always in private. Strike one.

"Bullshit. I saw you on television at the last murder scene. I also saw that state police captain, Blanchard, there as well. Did he send you down here to try and get me to sit on the story longer? The Savior. Kinda has a ring to it, doesn't it? My editor loves it."

Cortez was enjoying this. Dodge scanned the lobby for any busybodies that may be listening to their conversation. No one caught his eye. But it was still a floor full of reporters whose jobs were to listen and notice little details, like a cop and a reporter having an awkward meeting in the lobby of a major news channel. Strike two.

He took a deep breath to regain his composure. "Who said I am working on those murders?"

Cortez laughed. Her eyes never broke contact with his. "A series of murders in this town where the victims are all sex workers and the Great Paul Dodge not involved. Please, don't insult me."

Strike three. She was brilliant, and he needed to come up with a fresh approach. "Is there somewhere we can talk in private? I think I can make it worth your time."

The seasoned reporter stared, sizing him up, studying for any tells or signs of betrayal. After a moment, she said, "You have ten minutes before I must leave for an interview. But I swear to God, if you are jerking me around, I'll crush your nuts and you'll wish you were never born."

Dodge knew Cortez didn't make idle threats. She meant what she said and had the fortitude and connections to make his life a living hell for a few months, minimum. But she also knew sexual crimes and murder drew ratings. The one thing her bosses cherished more than even her.

The two sat at a table in the far corner of the small break room, out of earshot of the people congregating in the lobby. A simple glare from the reporter scared away anyone using the room for a reprieve from the never-ending news cycle. Both sat in awkward silence, neither wanting to be the one to start the conversation. It was a power thing.

Finally, Cortez, gave in. "You have nine minutes," she said.

"First let me start by saying I'm sorry for..."

Cortez cut him off. "Let's not start by dragging up that old shit. Look, we had a fling. You used me and flicked me away like a finished cigarette. What's there to talk about?"

Dodge looked down at his hands on the table and noticed the tremble was back. "I only wanted to say I am sorry about that. If I had to do it over again, I don't know if I would have done things differently, under the circumstances, but I wouldn't have waited so long to say I was sorry. For what it's worth."

She rolled her eyes, and he knew it was time to move on.

"I know you have a source inside the state police post. I also know he gave you the information about the writing on the victim's body."

"So, I have a lot of sources in all the police departments."

"I know better than to ask for your source. But I need a favor from you."

Her eyes narrowed and the lines around her mouth became more pronounced.

"The type of favor that gets repaid in big story currency," Dodge said.

"Go on," she said. Her eyes widened, just slightly.

"I don't know if I can tell it in eight minutes."

"It's six now and don't be a smart-ass. Tell me what you are talking about."

Dodge told her about the murders in Las Vegas several years ago, explaining Captain Blanchard's role in the case, even laying out the timeline concerning the state police captain's abrupt departure from Vegas and his arrival in their town. When finished, he watched as Cortez processed the information. Dodge was a skilled storyteller, and he had lathered the details on thick, hoping something would resonate and stick. He could almost hear the wheels in her head turning. How would she play it? What would the angle be when pitching it to her producers? What would her angle be in trying to get more information out of him?

Still, she said nothing. But the look on her face gave away her answer. He didn't need to put the rest of the puzzle together. She was in.

After another minute of silence, she asked, "What is it you

want from me?"

"I need you to hold back what the killer calls himself. We have no leads and if he is seeking attention, well, he could escalate his attacks."

The secretary from the lobby appeared in the doorway. Cortez waved her hand, motioning the young woman to leave, and she scurried away like a frightened child.

"What do I get?"

"I'll make sure you get the exclusive when the story breaks about *The Savior*." He used the name as a hook. If he was willing to say it, out loud, to a reporter, she had to think he was on the level.

Cortez sipped from her coffee, taking time to think about her answer. "I'll wait two weeks on the name. But only two weeks." Her finger stretched out inches from his nose. "You burn me here and I'll run both stories and make sure I name you as my source. You won't be welcome in a police station for three states."

Dodge nodded. The reporter slid out of the bench seat and leaned over. She then took a napkin and wiped the remnants of red lipstick off Dodge's lips, turned, and walked away. He watched her, remembering how he found himself in bed with her the first time. She was stunning.

CHAPTER 10

THE WHITE VAN SAT PARKED OUTSIDE the motel, its engine running ensuring the air conditioner warded off the heat from the summer sun. The van was an uninsulated hollow metal can that was hot in the summer and cold in the winter. He was getting tired and sweat formed on his brow and slid down his face, soaked up by a yellow stained shirt collar as it rolled down his neck. A handkerchief he kept stuffed in his shirt pocket worked perfectly to wipe the moisture from his forehead. When finished, he carefully placed it into a plastic sandwich baggie, ran his fingers across the zipper action, and sealed it shut. No need to leave any traces of DNA on the side of the road, he thought.

The motel was quiet this time of day. He had been observing the old brick structure for weeks. Watching. Waiting. Making mental notes of who lived alone. When the desperate ones came and went. Most of the tortured girls that called it home only came out at night to go to work. She was different, though. The routine never seemed to change much. Out in the morning for breakfast, then a quick walk around the area surrounding the corner, where she commits her sins. Afterward, she went back home to the motel, only to leave again under the cover of darkness. He wished he knew her name. It was all so impersonal without names. The service he would provide to her was very personal. It was all about her. Not knowing her name made it seem less important. He would find out so everything would be perfect when the time came.

He watched through the grime-covered windshield another few minutes before settling on a plan, deciding to get her name from the manager of the hotel, a disgusting man always trying to scam the girls in his motel out of more money. Or worse, forcing them to perform sexual acts for shelter. Since the first time he came across the despicable human, he dreamed about hurting the motel manager. Teach him a lesson. But he knew he couldn't touch the pig behind the front desk. It wasn't his job. That was for someone else to decide. He would stick to women in need of his services.

A set of windchimes rang as he opened the door. He reached up and grabbed the bell, stopping it from ringing again as the door pushed past it to close. The front desk was clear except for a small metal bell with a sign that read, "Don't Touch." He couldn't contain the urge to break a rule. Not once. Not twice. But three times. Ding, ding, ding. He stepped back and waited. No one came. He looked around for cameras. There were none. No mirrors or windows that someone watching from a secret hallway or room could use. Just a small office and reception desk. And silence.

He concentrated. A low groan. More of a moan, really, coming from behind the desk. He leaned in, stretching across the front desk until he was on his tiptoes. The noise grew louder. He noticed a small crack in the wall behind the desk that ran from floor to ceiling. It appeared out of place. He searched the wall for another and found it about three feet to the right of the first one. He squinted. Wallpaper covered the entire surface of the wall. A simple design with black diamonds every few inches. But the installer had been sloppy. Along the edges of the cracks, the lines creating the diamond shapes didn't line up. They were offset by an eighth of an inch. Looking at the floor, he noticed a semicircle of wear in the carpet directly between the vertical cracks in the wall. There was a door. No visible knob or hinges. It had to be triggered by a button. From under the desk maybe. He slid back and crept around to where he could have a better view of the back side of the reception desk.

The edges of the desk were rough and coated with a heavy brown stain. Except for one area. Just to the right of the center. A spot maybe three or four inches long. He looked at his hand and back at the faded spot. It was about the size of an average man's hand. His hand slid across the underside of the desktop. Slowly.

Cautiously. Then he felt it. A small rise in the surface. Round and hard. He pressed his finger into the surface. A clicking sound came from behind him. The door cracked open. The moaning got louder. Sliding his fingers into the newly discovered crease, he eased the door open enough to peer into the room. What he saw made him sick. It was the manager, his back to the door. He could see a young girl on a filthy, stained couch. She was naked and her mouth taped shut. The manager's shirt was off, and his pants were pushed into a wad below his knees.

He wasn't sure what the disgusting man was doing, but it wasn't right, and he had seen enough. The girl was clearly a tortured soul who needed to be set free. The manager, a casualty of war. Collateral damage. The Savior now had a reason to kill the manager. It was now his problem. The hinges of the well-balanced door were silent as it easily pulled wide enough for his thin body to slide through. It closed behind him as smooth and imperceptible as it had opened. The young girl's eyes opened wide and she stared at him as he sidled up behind the half-naked manager. It was over in an instant, and the room fell silent.

———

The downtown area bustled with shoppers, business owners, and the after-work crowd that mingled around the bars and cafes, complaining about their day and delaying their long commute back to the suburbs. Back home to wives and children, homework help, and reheated microwave leftovers. It all sounded too real to Dodge. It was one reason he never married or had children. The repetitiveness of it all didn't appeal to the bachelor. Even the few times he had been in serious relationships, he was clear from the beginning, no children. It had cost him a few loves, but he tried not to dwell on it. He just didn't get the same warm and fuzzy feeling other people got at the sight of a baby or small child. Babies made people all gushy, changing how they talked, making up words, and acting as they had never seen a small human being before. The whole thing escaped him. All he saw was a screaming poop machine. A perfect glob of Freud's ID.

As he continued watching, gazing at the crowds of people, he realized the scene unfolding in front of him wasn't much different from his routine, except for the wife and kid part. He had a job, albeit much different from what most of his fellow citizens did for a living, but a job he had to report to every day. Today had been no different. He sat at the coffee shop, sipping from his steaming mug, just like everyone else around him. Had he been wrong all these years? Just then, a mother screamed at a child. The kid had asked for a pastry and the woman berated him in front of everyone, making sure everyone knew she didn't have the money for a donut for her child. *Funny*, Dodge thought. She had the money for a five-dollar latte. She could've had a plain coffee and a donut and would still have been ahead. He shook his head. He had not been wrong. When you have children, they come first, and he wasn't willing to make that commitment. His priorities were work, coffee, bourbon, and him. Coffee and bourbon were interchangeable, depending on the situation.

The first police car sped past, its red and blue lights ricocheting off the surrounding buildings and windows, making for almost a circus tent atmosphere when the ringmaster comes out and all the different colored spotlights dance around the crowd. The siren only activated when a self-indulged pedestrian, nose buried deep in their phone, stepped off the curb and into the street—the whoop-whoop from the siren causing them to freeze in their tracks, then leap back onto the sidewalk before becoming a hood ornament. Then a second cruiser zipped by. And a third, followed by an ambulance. He watched as the emergency vehicles sped past and turned two blocks to the south, toward the fringe of downtown.

The phone in his pocket vibrated. Its jostling surprised him, causing him to jump in his seat. The caller ID showed the number for the state police post. It was Captain Blanchard.

"This is Dodge."

"Dodge, where are you at?"

"Downtown, having a cup of coffee. But I sense from all the racket down here that is about to change."

"You bet your ass it is. Do you know the Sunnyside Motel?"

"I do. It's a local flop house where some of the working girls in the neighborhood occasionally stay." His concern increased as he remembered Sarah lived at the motel and he knew the manager's past. "I had the manager on my caseload a few years back. He did a five-year stint downstate for a child pornography bust. Why, what's he done now?"

"Just get over there. Your old partner, Renquest, will meet you there."

Dodge clicked off and picked his coffee up from the table, placed a small tip under the saltshaker, so it wouldn't blow away, and then headed off toward the sounds of emergency vehicles. The motel was only a five-minute walk from the coffee shop, so he left his truck parked on the street. With all the cruisers, fire trucks, and ambulances that were likely to be on the scene, he would be forced to park a few blocks from the motel anyway. Easier to leave his truck where it was and come back for it later. Walking also afforded him the opportunity to surveil the surrounding streets for out-of-place vehicles and anyone paying too much attention to whatever was happening at the motel. He would be especially interested in any white, windowless panel vans with a ladder on top anywhere near the scene.

Police cruisers, an ambulance, and the coroner's van filled the tiny parking lot outside the motel's office. Ten cars in total. Guests stood in the doorways to their rooms, watching the scene unfold. Others viewed from behind windows and thin curtains, not wanting to be seen by law enforcement for one reason or another, Dodge guessed. It was a show and lights and sirens were a natural attractant for gawkers. He scanned the faces lining the sidewalks and motel doorways, but he didn't see Sarah's eyes staring back at him. A quick flash of his badge to the cop manning the door, and he stepped into the office. The heavy metallic smell of fresh blood filled his nostrils. Someone was dead. Certain things you never get used to; the smell of blood is close to the top, after decomp.

Renquest stood behind the manager's counter, the motel's guest register in his hand, its pages worn from use. Each corner discolored from the saliva used to wet the manager's finger before he turned every page. A disgusting habit. Also, a potential DNA goldmine. His partner placed the ledger into a clear plastic bag and zipped the top. He then signed the evidence log and passed the bag to a crime scene tech, before acknowledging Dodge.

"I don't remember calling you."

"I'm psychic. What have we got?"

Renquest pointed over his shoulder to the room behind the counter. "It's a real mess in there. The motel manager took the brunt of it. The coroner stopped counting the stab wounds at ninety-three. Most to the head and neck area. His spine is the only thing holding his head to the rest of his body."

"Crime of rage or passion," Dodge said.

"No passion in this one. The assailant was sure pissed about something. It looks personal."

"The guy was a first-class dirtbag. He had a thousand images of kids when they convicted him. The list of suspects could be a mile long. Parents. Victims. Hell, any of the girls living here could've done it."

"I don't think any of the hookers did this."

"Why?"

"Take a peek." Renquest pointed over Dodge's shoulder. "Did he have any family?"

"None that I am aware of, but I would need to check his pre-sentence report to be sure. If he has any relatives to contact, they should be listed in there, along with any previous addresses and a complete criminal history."

Dodge knew he would need to contact the clerk's office at the court to get access to the report for family information as the parole file had been purged years ago.

Before Dodge took a step toward the room, Renquest slapped him in the chest with a pair of rubber gloves and cloth booties. Dodge donned the protective gear then crossed into what looked like a scene from a horror movie.

Immediately, the veteran noticed two bodies sprawled out in the room. A male, the motel manager, with his head precariously hanging on by overstretched tendons and muscle tissue, and a young girl, maybe nineteen or twenty. Dodge couldn't be sure, but being she was at this motel with a half-naked man on the floor next to her told him she was likely a prostitute. The manager couldn't afford a high-priced call girl, and he certainly wasn't married. The pants pushed and bunched at his knees screamed this was a rush job. Sex for rent, as Sarah had mentioned to him and Beth the day before.

Blood was spattered everywhere. A pool formed on the floor under the head. The edges spilled out and spread across the uneven floor. Dodge bent down. A gash spread across the side of the neck. The jugular was severed. Causing an initial spray covering the walls. Nothing was spared. Not even the ceiling. Basically, every surface not blocked or shielded by something larger had the manager's blood covering it. The amount of blood meant his heart was still beating when the throat was slashed. But Dodge wasn't sure it mattered if he was stabbed or slashed first. Ninety-three wounds meant he would have died soon anyway. And no defensive wounds to the hands meant the victim didn't see the attacker coming. The initial blows came from behind.

Renquest had been right. This crime was all about rage and the killer seemed to get angrier the longer the attack lasted. In all his years working murders as a part of the task force, Dodge had never witnessed a scene quite like this. But it was the second thing he noticed that made his skin crawl, sending his senses into overdrive.

The dead girl, the prostitute, was clean. Even her clothes. Spotless. It was as if someone had taken the time to wipe the body down. The position of the body on the floor and the spatter patterns on the wall and sofa showed a scene that should have left the other victim soaked in the manager's blood, but the girl was clean. Dodge asked one of the crime scene techs to bring a portable black light to him. They used black light in combination with a chemical compound, called Luminol, to find trace evidence of proteins left behind after blood and other bodily fluids. Even cleaning with bleach wouldn't erase all the evidence.

The light came on with a click of a switch. A quick pass over the body and the skin on her arms and face lit up like a Christmas tree. The attacker had gone to great lengths to wipe the body clean, but the light illuminated evidence he couldn't hide. The clothes she wore had been washed, or the body stripped and redressed in new clean clothes. Using a pen from his pocket, he slid the metal shaft up and under the girl's clean shirt, lifting gently as not to touch the skin. An inch at first. Then two. He stopped after the third push. His heart raced and his palms warmed and were damp with sweat. A trace of red lipstick peeked out from under the bottom fold of her shirt. He didn't need to look any further. He knew what the letters would spell out. *The Savior.*

Pulling the shirt down, he looked at the room around him. Dodge noticed a small plastic utility sink jettisoned out from the wall next to a toilet in the corner. Dodge stood straight and made his way to the sink. He flashed the black light over the basin. Traces of blood clung to the dirty sides and pooled around the drain. The killer had washed up after the murders.

Renquest was standing in the doorway to the motel's office. He sipped from a cup of coffee he had poured from a pot sitting in the corner of the lobby, next to a couple of bananas and three stale muffins laid out for motel guests. Dodge stared at his partner. The scene somehow fit. A grizzled veteran sipping coffee from a Styrofoam cup with two dead bodies and a room that looked resembled a slaughterhouse. A scene from a fifty's detective novella.

Dodge stepped to his partner. "I take it you knew there was another body in the room."

"Yep." The detective took another sip of his coffee.

"You could have told me before I went in."

"You're a world class investigator. I knew you would figure it out."

"You see the girl's body?" Dodge asked, pointing toward the office.

"I did."

"Notice anything strange?"

Renquest nodded in the room's direction. "She was clean as a baby's ass."

"You find that weird?"

"Hell, Dodge, I find everything I see weird. Nothing about this job is normal, so you'll have to be more specific." The old detective paused for a second. "Unless you mean the writing on the victim's stomach."

Nothing gets by him, Dodge thought. "Yeah, I mean the writing and the clean body. There was enough blood in there to paint the ceiling of the Sistine Chapel. Yet, she was spotless."

"No oily substance this time, though. You think that's significant?"

"A crime of opportunity. No planning. It happened in the heat of the moment. But it's our guy. That's for damn sure. He even had a new set of clothes to dress her in."

"Wouldn't that suggest a plan? I mean, what guy carries around a new set of clothes with them for a woman?"

Dodge scratched his head and looked back toward the room. "It's just a guess, but I would say he always has clean clothes with him. We never checked to see if the clothes on the other dead girls belong to them. He has the clothes in his van and redresses the victim's postmortem. No trace evidence and he can dispose of the old garments."

"Probably burns the old stuff," Renquest said.

"That's what I would do."

"I agree."

"Who found the two?" Dodge asked as he scanned the room for witnesses.

His partner dug into his right front shirt pocket and pulled out a small wire-bound notepad. He flipped through the pages until finding the entry he was looking for. "A tenant. She just gave me her first name, Sarah." Renquest placed the pad back in his shirt pocket. "She came to the office to let the manager know her air conditioner wasn't working. After ringing the bell several times with no answer, she knocked on the door behind the counter and peeked inside."

"That door is concealed to keep people out. I mean, if a person knew what to look for, they might discern it's a door. But I have been in here a hundred times and never noticed. How did she know about it?"

"My guess is she had been in that room before," Renquest said.

Dodge thought back to his conversation with Sarah. She had

made a point of mentioning she never had sex with the manager. The other girls must have talked about what happened in that room.

"Where is the witness?"

"I had an officer take her down to the station. I thought I'd give you a crack at her before she disappears with the other night dwellers. But you better hurry. The girl is a witness, not a suspect. Once she realizes she is free to leave, she will bolt for sure."

"Roger that." Dodge turned to leave, but a man carrying a video camera blocked his path. The camera had an enormous light on top with a mic jetting out in front. Directly behind the cameraman stood Angela Cortez, microphone in her right hand and a smile on her face. She was staring straight into Dodge's eyes. He could not avoid her or the camera, which nearly hit him in the face when he had turned toward the door.

The parole agent was no rookie with reporters. He had been interviewed a hundred times over the course of his career and used the media twice as many times to get something he wanted. But he was not ready to talk about this case just yet. Especially to Cortez. His rule was: *if you know nothing, keep your trap shut.* That is what he did.

"Agent Dodge! May I have a word with you?"

Dodge brushed past the cameraman and reporter, throwing out a "No comment," as he started walking the three blocks to his truck. He would have to deal with Cortez at some time, but for now, the local brass or the state police post would handle any press inquiries. Fifteen minutes after leaving the motel, he pulled into the parking lot at police headquarters.

CHAPTER 11

SHIFT CHANGE HAD BEGUN by the time Dodge arrived at headquarters. Police cruisers jammed the parking lot, waiting for officers to claim one of the free cars after roll call, and begin the ritual played out three times a day. Sign in, patrol the streets, then sign out and go home. Rinse and repeat. The whole thing operated like a well-oiled machine. The city never sleeps, and neither do its protectors.

Sarah sat straight in the small metal chair; a large, cold steel-topped desk was bolted to the floor in front of her. The door to the room had been left ajar. Only a was small crack visible, but that was enough to make the argument that the witness was free to leave anytime during the process. Law enforcement used the technique for decades, with suspects brought in for interviews, but not charged with any crimes. This move was brought on because a legal strategy used in many cases by defendant's attorneys after incriminating statements were made would center around the claim that their clients were strong-armed into a confession and held against their will. Police had perfected it over the years. Going as far as making sure the detective or officer conducting the questioning left the room at least once, to take a phone call or get a cup of coffee while leaving the door partially open, all the while watching the suspect on a computer monitor in another room for nervous behavior or to see if they would get up and leave. If the person was eventually charged with a crime and decided to fight the confession during a trial, the District Attorney prosecuting the case could show the video of the door left open and unguarded in court. It was a legal gray area, but more times than not, the courts sided with the police.

Dodge watched her on the closed-circuit monitor in an adjacent room for a few minutes before talking to her.

"Good morning, Sarah. Would you like a cup of coffee or a soda?"

The attractive, young woman shook her head.

"I need to ask you a few questions about what you saw at the motel today. Do you think you are ready to talk about it?"

Sarah nodded.

"Good," Dodge said, setting his coffee on the table and sliding into the small chair opposite her. "Do you mind if I record this interview?"

Sarah shook her head.

"Sarah, I need you to say it out loud. The recorder doesn't pick up body language."

She said, "Yes," low and muffled.

Dodge spoke his name, stating the time and date. He then asked Sarah to say her name out loud.

"Ok, let's start at the beginning. What made you decide to visit the manager's office?"

Sarah hesitated, looking up as if trying to recall some distant memory. It was a normal reaction to a question concerning a timeline. "I woke up after sleeping in most of the morning. It was a late night, and I was more tired than usual."

"What time did you wake up?"

"Around two, I guess. It had gotten warm in my room overnight. He, the manager, had promised to fix my air the night before and obviously hadn't followed through. I was thinking about looking for another place to stay and thought I might be able to get a few nights free for the inconvenience. If he didn't agree, then I could find another place to stay."

"You were thinking about moving out because of his unwillingness to fix problems with the room?"

"I was. You had to stay on him to get things done around there. Money seemed to be the only thing he cared about, other than using some of the young girls for his own... you know?"

"The manager, he slept with his customers regularly?" Dodge

asked, full well knowing the guy was a sleazeball. He used people like it was his job in life.

"I wouldn't call it sleeping. He told the girls they could pay the rent on their knees or backs. Like he was doing them a favor by giving them a choice of which way to be humiliated. But not me. I paid my rent in cash. If I didn't have the money, I would stay on the street and work more to get the money."

"I'm not here to judge you, Sarah. You do what you need to survive." Dodge's tone seemed to relax his witness. She nodded and gave him a slight smile. "Let's move on to when you entered the motel office. What did you see and do? Think about the things you touched. What did the office smell like?"

"The office smelled like sweat and curry. The man was disgusting. I doubt he showered more than once a week." She shuddered before continuing. "The only things I touched were the countertop and the door behind the counter. The whole place gives me the creeps. I try to avoid going in there if I can. Just to pay the rent and complain about the air or hot water not working."

"How did you know about the door to the back office? You said you never paid your rent, *that way*."

"I don't! The girls all talk about it. That is, the ones that can't pay the rent, or just want to keep their money for drugs."

"It sounds like you are saying some women willingly go into the office with the manager?"

"I don't mean to make it sound like they had a choice. Addiction is powerful. Even more powerful than hunger. It will make people do things they wouldn't ordinarily do."

Sarah's eyes looked down at the table. The corners of her lips turned down, frown wrinkles exposed. He couldn't blame her for the indignation in her tone. The man was a first-class mope. Not too many, if anyone, would lose sleep over his demise. But that didn't matter. It was the task force's job, therefore Dodge's job, to find out what happened and bring justice to the victims, no matter how despicable the dead may have been in life.

"May I have some water, please?" she asked.

Dodge nodded and stepped out into the hall, leaving the door wide open, and filled a paper cup from a water cooler parked outside in the hall. He handed Sarah the cup and she took a long drink. Then another. The disgust eased its grip on her face. The frown lines diminished. She was becoming more comfortable with him.

"Let's continue from when you entered the office. What did you see? Was the door open?"

"At first, I couldn't see anything. It wasn't open, just cracked a little. Just enough to show where it was in the wall. I tried to peek through the slit but couldn't see anything. So, I pulled a little more. Real slow. I didn't want to wake him if he was sleeping in there."

"Once you were able to see in, what is the first thing you noticed?" Dodge asked.

"There was a smell in the air. It was heavy. You could taste it when you breathed in," she said. "Have you ever put a penny in your mouth?"

"No," Dodge answered.

"When I was younger, some of the girls I used to hang out with said you could beat a breathalyzer test if you put a penny in your mouth right before blowing in the tube. So, I tried it once," Sarah said.

"Did it work?"

"No."

Dodge paused for a second before continuing. Not wanting to get off subject, but also wanting to keep her talking. "Did you get a ticket?"

The young girl's head dropped, and her eyes settled on the table in front of her. She rung her hands.

"No. He wasn't interested in giving me a ticket."

As an experienced law enforcement officer, Dodge knew well that sometimes officers take advantage of young women in trouble. Renquest worked a case once where the suspect turned out to be a sheriff's deputy from a neighboring county. He had been forcing young girls to sleep with him instead of giving them tickets for minor traffic violations and misdemeanor drug possession. Sexual misconduct among officers was something he had no patience for. But that was for another day.

"You were talking about the smell in the air?"

"Yeah. It was like having that penny in my mouth again."

Dodge pressed on, diverting the conversation back to the case. "What did you see next?"

"Him lying on the floor. His eyes staring at me. Through me. Then I saw her. It looked like she was sleeping. But her eyes. Her eyes were almost purple. It was haunting. That's how I knew she was dead."

Dodge nodded. "Her eyes were full of blood. A result of strangulation and it tells us how she died before they even complete an autopsy. As for the manager, he was dead within minutes of the attack, most likely. There is nothing you could have done for either of them." He reached across the table and gently touched her arm. "What else did you see?"

She looked up. "Nothing. I got the hell out of there and went back to the room, locked the door, and dialed 911. I didn't come out again until the police arrived."

"You didn't see anyone else? No strange vehicles or other people hanging around watching the motel after the police showed up?"

"I didn't really look. I just hid in the bathroom until the officer knocked on my door."

"Ok. Are you sure you can't think of anything else you think I should know? It doesn't matter how insignificant you think it is. It may help us find who did this."

Dodge maintained eye contact. The eyes looking back at him were full of fear and uncertainty. She shook her head. He believed her and thanked her for her cooperation, then arranged for an officer to drive her back to the motel. He told the officer to stay with Sarah while she gathered some things as the motel would be closed for a few days. He would arrange for a room in a nicer hotel a few blocks away, but still a short walk to downtown where she made her living. The department would pay for the room for four nights. After that, she would be on her own. He also provided her with a few food vouchers to a local fast-food restaurant. Everyone needed to eat.

After typing up a quick report detailing his interview, a quick stop to fill up the truck with gas and himself with a fresh cup of coffee put him in the parking lot of the state police post in less than thirty minutes. He needed to bring Captain Blanchard up to speed on the events of the case so far.

Shift change had already occurred, and the parking lot was empty, apart from the night dispatcher's vehicles and Blanchard's cruiser. Inside, the post was much the same. A few evening employees to answer the phones and one or two troopers to take any walk-in complaints. The lobby was closed for the evening and visitors had to be buzzed in after announcing their business from an intercom attached to the outside wall beside the main entrance. The place reeked of cleaning chemicals and starched uniforms. It reminded him of the Air Force. Dodge hated that smell.

Captain Blanchard sat in his office at the far end of the main hall that ran the length of the building, dissecting it into two halves. A command half and a public half. The command half held the offices for the supervisors, training rooms, and interview rooms. The public half comprised of a large conference room used for training and press conferences, and a few smaller offices where station troopers could take reports from citizens. The overall building was not much larger than a single-story ranch home one might find in any of a hundred city suburbs.

Dodge's knock made a solid thump as his knuckles rapped the wooden door. Blanchard lifted his eyes, then waved him in.

"How was the scene today?"

"Messy."

"Was I right to send you out?"

Dodge nodded. "It's our guy."

"The writing on the vic?"

"Red lipstick."

Blanchard leaned back in his chair. "What do we do now?"

"Well, we have another problem."

"The reporter? I thought you were going to take care of her."

"No. Not Cortez. She will hold off on the story. We have another victim at the scene."

Blanchard shot up in his chair. "There were two dead girls?"

"One dead girl and one creepy motel manager."

"Wait. The second victim was a male?"

Dodge nodded.

"Are you sure this is our guy and not some copycat pawning for attention?"

"It's one hundred percent our guy. Remove the motel manager from the scene and it fits perfectly."

The captain slid his chair back, poured out, and crossed the room, stopping at a file cabinet next to the door. He rifled through the second drawer from the top until he found what he was searching for. Leaving the drawer open, he turned back to Dodge and tossed a file into his lap.

"I think you should see this," Captain Blanchard said.

A bold classification statement was stamped on the outside of the folder. It read: FOR LAW ENFORCEMENT EYES ONLY. LVPD, for Las Vegas Police Department, was printed in red below the classification declaration. Dodge glanced through the file.

"What's this?" Dodge asked.

"Once upon a time, I was a detective in the Las Vegas Police Department. I worked cold cases. Then one day a file landed on my desk. I wasn't sure where it came from or who put it there, but the serial number placed the start of the file three years prior. What began as a routine sexual assault cold case investigation soon turned into a public relations nightmare. For both me and the department. That file contains all the investigative materials from the original file. I copied as much as I could before I left the department."

The file lay open, on Dodge's lap. He began leafing through the sheets of paper. Everything appeared to be photocopies, as Blanchard had said. It wasn't uncommon for retiring detectives to make copies of files concerning cases they never closed. Old detectives often spent the remaining years of their lives reading and re-reading the files, trying to remove the burden of failure from their shoulders. Dodge did the same thing with parolees that had absconded or committed new serious offenses. He wasn't to the point yet where he copied entire files, but he also still had a purpose in his current job. The regret would come later.

Pretending to read the pages, Dodge spent five minutes

browsing through the file. Most of the details contained between its flaps were about what Beth had told him. He wanted to see what his new boss would add on his own.

"It appears someone had an admirer," Dodge said, waiving the file in front of him.

"The case you are holding in your hands is the reason I left." Blanchard moved back to his desk and fell back into his chair. "Things got complicated."

"How so?"

"He made it personal."

"Who? The Savior?"

Blanchard nodded.

"Things escalated, and we were looking at a body a day. He started leaving notes for me written in lipstick at first. Then blood. He was taunting me."

Dodge said nothing.

And the captain continued. "After about a week, we were five bodies deep, and the brass decided I needed to step away."

"From the case or the department?"

"From the case. They were worried about my safety. So far, the victims had been hookers and one homeless guy. The prevailing thought was that if a cop... a detective, was to get killed, the whole place would go into a panic. When your city's livelihood is based on out-of-town tourists dropping next month's mortgage payment at the craps table, the last thing you want is the cable news network vans parked in front of city hall and the reporters using the words serial killer and dead cop on the nightly news. So, I left. If I couldn't work my cases in Vegas, then I would find work somewhere else."

"And did he leave?"

"The murders stopped, and they buried the file deep in the archives where no one would find it."

"But they didn't know about your copy."

Blanchard nodded.

"Well, your troubles seemed to have followed you to my town. Now we are getting a body a day and nothing in this file seems to point to any suspects. What do you want to do now?"

"I could leave again." Captain Blanchard crooked his neck and gazed around his office.

"Then he wins. Again. And he'll just move to some other town once you set down roots again. He seems to have a real hard-on for you. That I can use."

Arms folded across his chest, Blanchard said, "Use how?"

"It's like throwing chum in the water. If you add enough blood, the sharks will come."

"So, I am to be used as bait."

"You got an issue with that?"

"Not if it ends all of this. I will do whatever it takes. You got a plan?"

Dodge stared at the folder in his hands for a moment. Then looked up. "I'm working on it."

"Can you hurry it up, please?"

"This is going to take some time. There will be more bodies," Dodge said, tossing the file back onto Blanchard's desk. "Nothing we can do about that right now. Let's concentrate on the things we can control."

"Like what?"

"The girl in the motel appeared to me to be a crime of opportunity. Something he hadn't planned out. The motel manager had so many stab wounds to the head he was nearly decapitated. The whole thing screamed of uncontrollable rage."

"He is escalating."

"Yep. And the way that killing played out, it doesn't look like he will be stopping anytime soon."

"So, you think the girl and the manager were not the reason he was at the motel?" Blanchard asked.

"They were certainly victims of his, but there was another purpose for him being there."

"What?"

"I'm not sure yet, but I'll figure it out," Dodge said

"You better hurry because I think he will eventually come for me. It began with me in Vegas and it will end with me here."

The veteran agent stood, bending slightly over the desk. "Not on my watch."

Dodge climbed into his truck and placed the key in the ignition. Only he didn't turn it. He just sat there, thinking about the murders earlier that day. Why was the killer at the motel? Why did he care if the motel manager was a perv that used his position to scam prostitutes in a sex for rent scheme? His mind sorted through a myriad of possibilities, but he kept coming back to the first question. Why was he at the motel in the first place?

The engine roared to life, and he eased the black chevy truck into traffic, beginning the brief journey downtown. The sun fell below the horizon and the night dwellers would soon be out. Whatever was going to happen that night, Dodge was certain it would happen downtown. And he would be ready.

CHAPTER 12

THE HEAT OF THE DAY WORE OFF as the blacktop and concrete covering most of the downtown area released its grip on the sunshine it spent all day absorbing. It was a strange phenomenon. One that happened all over the world in cities in tropical climates. The sun rose every day, slowly heating the asphalt in roads and parking lots. Baking, holding in the energy. Then, the sun set. The heat would release from the solid surfaces and the temperature would rise two to five degrees. It was constant and yet most people went about their business, paying no attention at all to the strangeness of the cycle. But the working girls noticed.

They noticed the temperature difference between the dark pavement and the light-colored sidewalks. For the first couple hours of their shift, the girls would stand farther from the street, welled up on the sidewalk, forcing them to yell louder and work their bodies harder to get the attention of passing drivers. As the night wore on and the pavement extinguished its heat, the girls moved closer, right up to the curb. Some even stepped out in front of passing cars to make drivers slow or stop. It was perfect choreography played out every night.

Dodge watched the scene unfold in front of him, amazed at how expertly the experienced girls were in luring customers. On the streets at night, classic gender roles were reversed. Cat calls came from the females, trying to attract attention. The construction workers who spent the day whistling and howling as women passed by became the targets once darkness fell over the city. While they ruled during the day, the night dwellers ruled the dark hours. A few of the girls even tried to get his attention. Calls of "Hey baby," and "Are you looking for a good time?" were met with a smile from the broad-shouldered agent, because tonight he was only interested in one girl—Sarah. Things kept happening around her and he just couldn't shake the feeling she was caught up in all of this. Albeit, unwilling, but none of the victims had been willing. He was sure she would need his help. And he planned to be there when she did.

A slight breeze cascaded through the streets, a rarity during the humid Virginia summers. The smell of the bay washed through the city, across sullen streets and through dirty alleys. Cleaning the air, if only for a moment. He loved the smell of open water. A sailing trip to the US Virgin Islands had ended only a short while ago. The trip turned out to be more work and less vacation, but the time away did him good. A sabbatical of sorts. Gave him time to figure out what was important to him. This life. This job. It was all he had, and he knew he would die doing it someday. A fact he now accepted which made things easier and the hard days more palatable.

The first glimpse of Sarah came after an hour of standing in the alley's mouth a block from her regular spot. She came in from the direction of the hotel the task force had paid for. A fifteen-minute walk. Not too far, but enough distance to separate working Sarah from personal Sarah. He thought she might like that distinction. At the motel, he imagined she was just another piece of street trash to the owner. One of fifteen or twenty hookers, all living in the same place, eating the same food, and talking about the same things. No chance to keep work at work.

A streetlight perched on the side of the building flickered before going dark, and the surrounding lights cast shadows across the corner. The scene had changed from the other night when he and Beth spoke with Sarah. That night, the lights in the street beamed so brightly that they were forced to slip into an alley to avoid looking exactly like what they were. Two cops and a hooker. Not good for business.

Dodge watched as the slim, attractive prostitute took up her position against the red brick wall of the storefront that spanned from one cross street to the next. The view was decent from where he stood, but he decided to move twenty yards down the sidewalk, positioning himself at a forty-five-degree angle across the street that ran parallel to where Sarah worked. His view was unobstructed for several blocks in either direction. If he took a few steps closer to the curb, he could make out the corner on which the third victim, Monica, had worked. Her lifeless body had been found dumped a few yards inside the alley next to it. He leaned back against the side of the building, pulled out a newspaper he had rolled up and stuffed in his back pocket, and pretended to read. His eyes scanned left to right—his head tilted slightly down to help hide his face.

The first car to make a run at Sarah was a rusted-out late seventies chevy four-door sedan. The car had one headlight out and an engine belt squealing like a cat with its tail caught in a screen door. After a brief conversation, the car drove away, and she returned to her spot against the wall. Dodge imagined the price was too steep for someone driving a car in such poor condition.

A second car approached from Sarah's right, Dodge's left, and rolled through the intersection; the driver's eyes focused on her. His gaze never breaking contact, he maneuvered the car through a U-turn. Its tires squealed as the tread tried to maintain level contact with the road surface. The passenger front tire climbed the edge of the curb, causing the front end to bounce as the suspension absorbed the shock of the tire as it rolled back onto the street.

This time the price must have been right because Sarah opened the passenger door and slid in next to the driver. The automobile swerved away from the curb, disappearing down a block-long alley, only to return about five minutes later. A smile curled on the driver's lips and at least fifty bucks less in his pocket, Dodge imagined.

For the next couple of hours, the cycle continued. Cars would stop, their drivers' bargaining for a deal. Others would pass by, their drivers' not showing any interest in participating in the oldest profession in the world. During one stretch, Dodge counted thirty-three cars cruise past Sarah's corner. Twelve stopped, just under a thirty percent engagement rate. Of those twelve, five solicited and closed the deal. He wasn't sure what a high success rate was for a corner hustler, but he could do simple math, and fifteen percent at between twenty-five and fifty bucks a pop might pay the rent at the Sunnyside Motel for a few nights, but there certainly wouldn't be much scratch left over for other essentials, like food. Add the risk of getting the shit kicked out of you, or worse, dead, and the work became less appealing to him. Addiction is a powerful thing, Sarah had told him. *Truer words may never have been spoken*, he thought.

As the clock ticked closer to midnight, fewer cars passed, and fewer stopped. Nothing unusual drew his attention. It was not a good night for either of them. The thought crossed his mind to call it quits and go home for a stiff drink before bed, when in his peripheral, something flashed two blocks to his right. He repositioned and dropped the newspaper at his feet. The pages separated and the breeze took a few for a ride. His eyes focused. He scanned each intersection like a quarterback checking off receivers. First intersection, nothing. Second intersection, same result.

A minute passed. Then two minutes. Finally, four minutes later, a white panel van pulled up and came to rest at the corner to Sarah's left. A metal ladder perched on the roof stretched from front to back. He noticed there were no straps or tie-downs holding the ladder to the van's roof and they didn't budge an inch as the vehicle came to a stop. Dodge moved closer, staggering as if he had too much to drink for effect. Not so much as to draw attention, but enough sway to make someone uncomfortable and look away. No one cared about a drunk stumbling home from the bar. Halfway down the block, he pretended to drop something, kneeling behind a car, peering through the side glass at the van, trying to get a good look at the driver. No luck, as the streetlight was throwing a glare on the windshield, making it impossible to see inside the cab.

The van was positioned right between him and Sarah. He could feel the air fill his lungs as he took a deep breath. In—out. In—out. The hairs on his neck twitched. His hand slid to the Glock holstered on his side hidden under his shirt, secured in an inside-the-belt holster made to help conceal a weapon by using the natural waistline to break up the boxy pattern of one of the most recognizable weapons in the world. His hand tensed, applying the exact amount of pressure needed to the back of the grip to disengage the locking mechanism holding the weapon in the holster. His eyes were laser focused on the driver's side window. Muscles tense, ready to pounce.

As quickly as it came, the van sped off, turning down a side street and out of view. He watched as Sarah sauntered back to the wall to wait for the next customer. Smart girl. No vans.

After the adrenaline dump, the muscles in his arms and legs ached. That's the thing no one ever talks about in training. If you neither fight nor run, your body must dispose of the energy that built up getting ready for the impending showdown. The result of holding all that emotion and energy in, is body aches and fatigue. Dodge now had both and was concentrating hard to shake off the effects. He had even closed his eyes for a few seconds and tried controlled breathing. He didn't notice Sarah cross the street in his direction.

She was on top of him before he saw her.

"Agent Dodge. What are you doing here? If I didn't know better, I would think you were spying on me."

The veteran agent's first attempt to answer came out as an awkwardly phrased stutter. Her catching him off guard, along with the effects of the energy dump he had just experienced, caused him trouble stringing more than two words together. He paused before attempting to answer for a second time.

"I couldn't sleep, so I figured I would come down and see what was happening downtown," was the best response he could muster.

"Have you tried going home to sleep?"

"What?"

A smile slipped past her lips. "You have been here since eight o'clock. I saw you standing at the corner pretending to read a paper. You weren't fooling anybody."

Dodge nodded. She had him figured out. "I wanted to see firsthand some interactions and how the deals work. Maybe even get lucky."

Sarah's head tipped to the side, and she smiled.

He blushed.

"I mean, get lucky with the case."

"Any news on when the motel might reopen?" Sarah asked.

"It's still closed. I would imagine the company who owns it needs time to clean up the mess and find a new manager. Hopefully, it will be open in a day or two and you'll be able to get back in. As for the manager, I am not sure anyone will miss him."

"I won't."

"Yeah, me neither. But I still need to find the person that killed him and the girl. Did you know her name?"

Sarah shook her head. "Just another girl on the street."

They each forced a smile, and she turned to head back to her corner to wait for the next man to fork over his hard-earned pay so she could have a warm breakfast.

"Sarah," Dodge said before she was too far away. "That last car, the van, what happened with that sale?"

"I don't get in vans," she said and kept walking.

The hour was getting late, and Sarah was right about one thing: he needed to get some sleep. His reactions were slow. His thoughts raced but were incoherent. He was tired.

He scanned the area once more before making for his truck parked out of sight. Turning onto South First Street, he instinctively dug into his pockets, searching for a cigarette. It was an old habit and one he struggled to break. Especially when he was tired, his brain mushed, and he needed the rush of nicotine to help him think straight. After not finding what he knew wasn't in his possession, his attention returned to the street in front of him as he turned the corner to the street where he had left his truck parked.

His keys jingled in his hand as he approached the black chevy truck. He stopped. Three car lengths behind his truck sat a van. It was white and Dodge didn't see any windows cut into the passenger side. And on its roof a metal extension ladder lay ready for a day's work. He wasn't sure from where he stood, but the van didn't appear to be the same one he had seen passing slowly by Sarah earlier. This van was in much better condition. There was less rust around the wheel wells. Dirt and grime covered its side panels, but you could still make out the faded outline where a decal had once been applied and then removed, likely when the van was sold.

He slid one step to his right, using the other vehicles on the street for cover. The tactical adjustment also distanced him further from the wall, making it less likely to be hit by shrapnel from a round ricocheting and fragmenting off the hard surface. He crouched and moved one step closer A shadow caught his eye behind the windshield. Movement in the driver's seat. It was too dark to see who or what was behind the wheel. Still crouched to keep his head below the roof line of the parked cars, he took another step forward and a slight bit back to his left for a better angle. The move placed him closer to the wall, but he needed to move to counter the glare on the windshield from the streetlamp overhead. He took one step forward.

The van's headlights flashed on. Full bright mode. The blinding light cut through the darkness, shining through the windows of the smaller cars in between him and the van, causing his pupils to dilate. His non-gun hand instinctively raised to block the piercing white light. His gun hand was busy rocking the Glock out of its holster. Two more steps forward and the headlights blinked as the van's engine roared to life. Dodge set out, running straight at the van. He closed to within two car lengths before the van shot out of the parking space, flipped a U-turn, and sped away. A city trash can lay spinning in the street, its contents scattered on the sidewalk and gutter.

After re-holstering his weapon, he heaved the trash can back onto the sidewalk, inspecting its sides for any paint transference caused by the van's front fender crashing into it during the driver's attempt to flee. He saw none. But he got a make and model and the last digit of the license plate as the van sped away. A rusty, late nineties Chevrolet Sahara with a license plate ending in seven. It wasn't much, but it was more than he had an hour ago.

Dodge took one last look around scouring the walls and rooftops for security cameras positioned to film the front doors of businesses in case they were ever robbed. Nothing. He then checked the street corners for traffic cameras mounted to signal poles used by city police to review accident scenes and determine risks at busy intersections. Strike two. While it was a long shot, he ensured no ATMs might have captured an image of the van and its driver on its camera. He went down swinging. There was no need for any of those in this part of town. No one cared about what went on down here.

The exhausted agent made his way back to his truck, hauled himself into the driver's seat, and leaned his head back against the headrest for a moment before starting the engine. His hands grasped the wheel and the engine purred as he pulled away from the curb and headed for home.

He was asleep the moment his head hit the pillow.

A low hum, like a cat purring, caused by his cell phone being set to vibrate, dancing across the glass coffee tabletop, rousted Dodge from his sleep. He rubbed his eyes to break up the crust formed overnight before slowly opening them and allowing time to adjust to the morning light blazing in through the living room window of his townhouse. He pulled himself upright on the couch, where he had crashed from exhaustion just six hours before. The phone continued to do its seductive dance on the table, beckoning its owner to reach out and snatch it from its samba. He watched as the phone slid to the edge of the table, his arm jetting out and the phone landing in his hand as it slipped over the edge and tumbled toward the floor below.

The name staring back at him from behind the reflective glass of the phone's face was Renquest.

"What could you possibly want this early in the morning?" Dodge asked.

"Are you still asleep? Man, you must have had a helluva night. What was her name?"

"It's too early for witty banter. What do you want?"

"First, that hurts. Witty banter is our thing. Second, it is nine in the morning, and I've already had three cups of coffee, all of which I had to buy myself. And third, I need you at the task force office in an hour. We might have caught a break in the case."

"Ok. I need a shower, coffee, and then I'll head your way."

"You know we have coffee here at the office."

"That's not coffee. It's recycled motor oil. Which is why your cheap ass actually paid for a cup."

"Hey! I made that myself. Insulting a man's coffee, not a good way to start the day."

"This is a balls and strikes game. I don't have the time or energy to brush you back from the plate."

"Which reminds me."

A moment of silence passed before Dodge answered. "Yeah?"

"Grab me a cup of joe when you stop. Two creams and..."

"And two sugars. Yeah, I know how you take it," Dodge quipped and rung off.

A shave and what amounted to a quick rinse shower, and the agent was out the door in less than half an hour. A slight detour for coffee and he pushed through the doors of the task force office before 10:00 AM.

Renquest sat in a black leather chair at a table that could accommodate over a dozen people in one of the smaller conference rooms, a street cop in uniform parked in a chair opposite him. A kid, really. Not over twenty-five years old. Dodge stepped into the room and squeezed into a seat next to the young officer.

"What's all the rush about?" Dodge asked, giving the uniform the once over.

"Dodge, this is Officer Simpson. He saw something last night while on patrol, and I thought you should hear it straight from him."

Dodge stared at the young patrolman, waiting for a response When none came, he spoke. "Well, what is it?"

The cop shifted his gaze to Renquest, who nodded. "Go ahead, tell him. We don't have all day."

The patrolman brushed his wavy blonde hair off his forehead and cleared his throat. "I was on patrol last night, around 22:00 in the area five or six blocks from the motel. You know, the motel where that double murder happened?"

"The Sunnyside Motel," Dodge said.

"Yeah. That's the one. Anyway, like I said, I was cruising the neighborhood, hitting license plates with my mobile plate scanner, and I get a hit."

"What do you mean, a hit?"

Renquest spoke up, "They mount the scanner to the trunk lid of the cruiser. It reads every plate that crosses its path, on the highway, on city streets, or on parked cars. If the computer program determines a plate number is a possible match to a stolen vehicle or a car associated with a wanted person, it sends an alert to the patrol unit's laptop. Most officers turn the alert off because it gets annoying, going off every five minutes on a ten-hour shift."

The officer continued after being interrupted by his superior. "I always keep mine on. You never know when you might get a hit on a high-value target. You know?" He paused and looked at the two old veterans at the table for approval. There was no reaction, so he continued. "So, I am driving along McQuery Street, near the intersection of Jackson Ave, and my laptop pings. I stop the car to check out the plate alert and I see there is an outstanding summons for traffic violations on the hit. I back up my unit until I match the plate with a vehicle."

Dodge leaned forward in his chair. His hands stacked one on top of the other.

"What kind of vehicle was it?"

"It's a little white four-door Toyota. Real clunker. Looked like it hadn't moved in months."

Renquest was getting bored with the story he had already heard at least once before. "Hurry up and tell him the rest."

"Yes sir. So, I ran the plates, and they came back registered to a stolen vehicle."

"Some foreign job that hadn't been moved in months. How does that help us?" Dodge said.

"That's the best part. Tell him Simpson," Renquest chimed in.

"The plates didn't belong to the Toyota. They belonged to a utility van."

The hairs on Dodge's arms tingled and stood on end. "A van? Like a work van? What make and model?"

"I thought that would get your attention," Renquest said. "A white Chevy Savannah. Late model from the nineties. Its owner reported it stolen in, wait for it... Las Vegas. The report was made nine months ago."

A rush of adrenaline coursed through Dodge's veins. His heart skipped a beat. It was almost a feeling of euphoria. "Are you kidding me?"

"Nope." Renquest said. "We caught our first break. The kid tried to make contact at the address the vehicle was registered to, but no one answered. I doubt they even know someone swapped the plates."

"So, I did good?" the young officer asked.

"You did great, son. Now go on home and get some sleep before your shift," the detective ordered. "Oh, and Simpson, say nothing about this. Not even to your sergeant. Understood?"

"Roger that."

Once the young patrol officer was out of earshot, the two men spoke again.

"How did you get him in here?"

"I put the word out that if anyone saw anything unusual in their zones and reported it to me, I would write their recommendation for promotions when their time came."

"They thought a rec from you would help them?" Dodge said, a smile creeping across his face.

"They're young and impressionable. I'll be retired long before any of them are ready for the promotion to Sergeant."

"Well, it was good work, and we may have caught a bigger break than you thought," Dodge said.

"What do you mean?"

"Last night, I was downtown watching the girl who found the motel clerk and the fourth victim."

Renquest interrupted his partner. "What was her name, Sarah?"

"Yeah. Anyway, I was keeping an eye on her and after a couple of hours of boredom, I figured I should go home and get some sleep. As I turned down the street where I left my truck, I noticed a white Chevy panel van sitting a of couple of spots behind me. As I got closer, the driver flipped on his headlights and spun the hell out of there. All I could get was one number from the plate before it drove out of view."

Renquest reached for a file sitting in the middle of the table. He rifled through a few pages, finding the one he wanted. "What was the number you saw?"

Dodge smiled. "It was the last one. Seven."

The detective looked up from the file. A grin stretched from ear to ear. "God Damn, I think we got him. The last number of the plate that was legally registered to the Toyota is a seven."

"Slow down, partner," Dodge said, patting his hands into the open air. "We haven't got anything yet."

"We know what to look for now."

"A white chevy panel van with a ladder on top? There are thousands in the county, tens of thousands in the state. And they stole this one in Las Vegas, so a search of local registrations would be useless."

His optimism quashed, Renquest tossed the file onto the table. Its contents spilled across the slick wood top. "So, what do we do now?"

"First, we talk to the owner of the Toyota. We find out how long they've owned it and when it was last moved. Then, we have your new friend, Officer Simpson, use his plate reader. Starting at the Toyota and moving outward block by block for three blocks in each direction."

"You think the perp lives in the same neighborhood?"

"I don't know what to think. But he felt comfortable enough to steal a license plate there, and my guess is, he will want to change the plate again as a precaution after last night. He must figure I might have gotten a read on his."

"So, why not go back to the same area you were successful in before?"

"Exactly. All his vics are from the same area. Why would his habit of stealing plates be any different?"

"Alright, I will have the boys canvas the neighborhood, looking for the plate from the Toyota."

Dodge spoke up. "Just Simpson. My guess is if the perp is staying in the area, he is aware of the number of patrol cars and how often they make their rounds. We don't want to spook him by flooding his neighborhood with black and whites."

"Sounds good. I'll keep you updated if we hit anything. Any predictions?"

"If he changed it, the plate from the Toyota will be on a newer model sedan. Within, say, two blocks of the Toyota."

"Twenty bucks to make it interesting?"

"Fifty is interesting," Dodge said.

Renquest laughed, and Dodge turned to leave. He stopped in the doorway.

"Say, let's keep this from the Staties and Blanchard for now."

"You'll get no argument from me."

Dodge took the quick elevator ride to the main floor and stepped through the front doors and into the parking lot. Time to do some research.

CHAPTER 13

THE HOUSES IN THE PART OF TOWN where the plate was taken from all looked the same. Most built in the early 1950s, during the post-Second World War boom when suburbs started sprouting up all over the country to meet the demands of returning soldiers with dreams of a quieter life. Rows of single story, two bed, one bath, thousand square foot homes, squeezed on a lot with enough front yard for dads to play catch with their sons after returning from the city and a long day at the office. White picket fences and carports. The American dream.

By the nineties, the suburbs had moved further out from the city center and the once family-friendly neighborhoods deteriorated into low-rent housing communities or part-time housing for new students drinking their way through the semester at the local community college. The owners paid little attention to the condition of the properties. Leaky roofs in need of repair. Instead of new shingles, blue tarps were spread across the peaks to keep the rain from getting inside. A green film of mildew covering siding hidden from the rays of the sun on the north side. Sidewalks cracked. And weeds choking out any chance of a return to yards full of lush green grass. Dodge didn't want to downplay the importance of rentals and low-income housing. They provided a needed service to the residents who couldn't afford to buy or didn't have the credit score to get a good rate. But it didn't mean the owners should neglect their responsibility to maintain the property and be good neighbors. It was a shame people had to live in those conditions.

The Toyota parked out front mirrored the condition of the property. Run down and neglected. A flat tire. Leaves and grime had gathered in the pocket between the windshield and the hood. He couldn't even see the wiper blades under all the refuse. Dodge used his hand to dig out a section of dried leaves on the driver's side. The VIN tag was missing. He checked the door and found it unlocked. Not surprising. Who would want to steal a car that would cost more to get rid of than it's worth? A quick check of the door frame revealed the rivets that once secured the chassis information tag, had been drilled out and the aluminum plate had been ripped from the door frame. That left only one place left to find the VIN, under the hood. Unfortunately, the hood latch broke when Dodge pulled the lever. The plastic handle fell to the floor and bounced under the seat. It would take a pry bar and a hammer to pop the hood latch now. Dodge shook his head.

Weeds enveloped the cement path leading from the curb to the portico. Only a sliver of concrete was visible, winding through the uneven edges created as the groundcover expanded its death grip on the once prominent sidewalk. The man-made expansion joints had been pushed to their limits, filled with roots and dirt, causing the concrete to buckle and up heave, making the sections uneven and treacherous to walk on. It ended at a front door in dire need of a fresh coat of paint. Whoever lived there covered the windows with newspaper to keep the light out, or to keep curious neighbors from seeing what lay beyond its dirty and soot-covered glass.

Dodge stood on the stoop for a minute before raising his hand to knock. He listened. No television or radio playing in the background. His knuckles rapped against the wooden door three times. No answer. He leaned in closer, his ear almost touching the door. No footsteps. No rustling. The only noise was a low hum. Maybe the air conditioner trying to keep up with the afternoon heat. His back foot slid one step back. He focused on the sound.

A memory flashed. He had heard that same noise before. A few years back, one of his parolees, who had an aversion to legal employment, got it into his head he could make money the old-fashioned way. By selling drugs. Neighbors complained to the police about a low hum coming from his house. Like, when a fluorescent bulb is going bad. A quick criminal history search revealed the owner of the buzzing house was on parole. Dodge was called to assist because parole agents don't need a warrant to enter an offender's home. Parolees are still bound by a strict set of rules they must abide by or risk being reincarcerated and serving out the remainder of their sentences encircled by cement walls, steel bars, and armed guards, along with one thousand of their closest friends. Some of which may want them dead. Not a good time.

The team arrived to discover the occupants used aluminum foil to cover the windows and condensation running down the inside of the glass. A common occurrence in grow houses. Since the subject they were looking for was on parole, Dodge led the entry team into the house. The front door crumpled under the force of a two-man battering ram. One hit two inches above the doorknob and the frame shattered. The door hit the inside wall with such force the doorknob lodged in the moist drywall, holding the door open. But this was a textbook entry and once inside the home, the source of the humming grew louder. A quick search revealed the house was empty of people, but there were hundreds of fluorescent lights used to mimic sunshine to help the marijuana plants grow inside.

The house in front of him appeared to have the same layout from the outside. He tried the door handle. It turned. The door pushed open easily and instantly the veteran agent knew the humming sound was not from grow lights or cooling fans. This house was not a marijuana farm. It was a mausoleum. The pungent odor smacked him right in the face. His eyes watered. Seconds later, he knew what the sound was. It was flies beating their wings. Millions of them. All moving in harmony.

Dodge stepped back and cracked the door to provide an escape for the flies and release the stench of rotting flesh. He propped the door open with a small decorative stone used to line what used to be a flower bed along the front wall of the house and stepped back into the yard and dialed Renquest's number.

"Hey, we are going to need a crime scene van down here."

"What've you got?"

"It's a maggot farm. Bring a couple of respirators and some

good gloves. Not the shitty kind the department provides, either. Bring your stash. The black ones. It's liable to get messy in there."

"God damn it," Renquest whispered. "I had a date tonight."

"Just give her an extra fifty and let her pick what she wants off the dessert menu." Dodge smiled, knowing his partner couldn't see him.

"Funny. I promised Custus we would have pizza and watch a movie on HBO.

"Stop and get him some takeout on the back. He won't mind."

Renquest sighed. "I'll be there as fast as I can. Don't go in there without me. That's an order, Dodge."

As he waited on the sun burnt sparce lawn, he wished he had a cigarette to flush the disgusting odor from his sinuses.

Once the crime scene techs arrived, Renquest, who had gotten to the scene minutes before, followed Dodge into the house. The two men donned respirators and rubber gloves, the black ones, and cloth booties to preserve the crime scene. Their weapons remained holstered. Unless the body morphed into a zombie, there was no chance of anyone alive living in the house. The two men cleared the front living room and the kitchen. The bedrooms and bath were at the end of a short hallway, which T'd into the living room. Dodge took the right side and Renquest the left. Two doors and one door, respectfully.

The bathroom was the first door the pair came to. There was no need to look any further. A cloud of flies pummeled their faces as the door swung open. Having gone to church as a child, he remembered stories about hordes of locusts and flies invading whole countries and devastating farms and food supplies. He imagined this was what it must have been like for people living through a swarm. The veil of insects forced the two men to stumble backward into a bedroom, where they slammed the door closed to escape the onslaught of winged bugs.

"Glad I brought the full-face masks now," Renquest said.

"Me too."

After a few moments, the noise outside died down and Dodge turned the handle, cracking the door far enough to peek into the hall. Most of the flies had disbursed. Even they couldn't wait to escape from whatever was in that room. The pair stepped into the hall, peering into the tiny bathroom. A vanity with a single sink and mirror sat against the wall to the right. A light bar with two bulbs suspended by electrical wires, perched precariously above the mirror. A round toilet, which Dodge imagined had originally been white ceramic, though years of neglect had stained it a deep brownish yellow, like a heavy smoker's teeth. A shallow tub filled out the room. It was a normal bathroom. Not unlike many you would find in the houses lining suburban streets across America. Except for the dead body floating in the tub.

The water surrounding the floater had morphed into more of a slurry than free-flowing liquid. Pieces of flesh and coagulated blood thickened the water into a thick soup-like consistency. A thin layer of maggots and flies covered the surface. It was all Dodge could do to keep from vomiting in his mask. He had seen a hundred dead bodies in different states of decomposition. Still, the addition of stagnant water gave the scene a movie-like quality he doubted any Hollywood special effects team could duplicate.

"We're not gonna be able to tell anything from that mess," Dodge said as he turned his head away from the gruesome scene.

"Whoever he is, he has been in that tub for days, at least. Let's get out of here and let the crime scene boys and coroner do the heavy lifting."

The two men left the bathroom and escaped into the clean, open-air of the yard, each taking off their respirators and sucking in a gulp of fresh air as soon as they were outside. Both were happy to be out of the house.

"I wonder how long he has been rotting in that tub?" Renquest asked.

"Did you see the water? It looked like stewed tomatoes. I don't know how long it takes for a body to decompose to that state, but..." Dodge felt the muscles in his abdomen contract. He couldn't hold it in. The acid in his stomach rose, burning his throat, ascending until spewing from his lips.

His partner laughed. "Rookie."

Dodge hunched over a moment longer, then rose straight, wiping his mouth with his sleeve. "Let's get some coffee."

"You go ahead. I'm going to stay here a bit longer. I want to see when the coroner's team removes the body if they find an easy cause of death. Like a gunshot to the head or signs of a drug overdose."

"A gunshot, maybe, but they won't find any signs of drug use. Not unless they recover a needle from that sludge."

"You want to meet later at the coroner's office for the initial autopsy?"

"I think I'll let you handle this one," Dodge said.

"What are you going to do?" his partner asked.

"I'm going to find our stolen van."

With one last glance at the house and the cars on the street, Dodge slid into the driver's seat of his truck, started the engine, and pulled out into the trafficless street, almost bumping into a red sportscar whose rear end was too far from the curb.

The veteran parole agent began his search by turning right on the next street, examining every vehicle parked along the sides. The decision to exclude vehicles parked in driveways came to him quickly. It was too bold of a move to steal license plates from a vehicle butted up next to a house. Motion sensors can activate garage lights, but only to about twenty feet. The thief needed vehicles the owners wouldn't know the plates had gone missing from. Immobile junk cars. The killer picked the Toyota for a reason. Its owner had all but abandoned it.

Nothing he saw fit the mold he had in his mind, forcing him to make a right at the next intersection. Just three cars parked on the street ahead of him. Two late models and a sports car. An eighties corvette. All of them were relatively clean. Washed in the past month. Not likely targets. He made another right, parallel to the street the dead guy lived on and continued for one more street before turning right again. Nothing. He repeated the pattern. Each time widening out the search area after circling back to the soupy guy's street.

Three blocks out and doubting his search plan, he saw the young patrol officer from earlier that morning. His cruiser parked in the road, back window lights flashing, next to a green ninety's American sedan. Dodge pulled up behind the police car and hopped out of his truck.

"Officer Simpson. What you got here?"

Simpson spun around. He was so engrossed in his routine task he never noticed the truck pull up behind him. "Agent Dodge."

"Sorry, didn't mean to startle you."

"You didn't."

He was lying, but Dodge let it slide. No need to embarrass a young cop for being too attentive to his work. "What's with the green sedan?"

"I was driving my cruiser around the blocks, just as the detective asked me to, when my plate reader went nuts. I turned around and pulled up next to the hit vehicle, this green hunk of shit. It appears to have not moved in months. Look here Agent Dodge, the rear plate is being held in by only one bolt," he said, pointing to the rear of the car.

Dodge kneeled behind the officer, examining the rear bumper of the vehicle. The license plate tilted catty-corner ended in the number seven.

A lump rose in the agent's throat, forcing him to swallow hard before speaking. "Did you run the plate?"

"Waiting on dispatch to get back to me now."

The two men stood silent, waiting for the crack of Simpson's radio signaling an incoming transmission. After a moment, the radio jumped to life.

Dodge knew the answer before the dispatcher spat out the results. The plate in front of him was registered to the white Toyota sitting three blocks behind him. An uneasy feeling fell over him. They had one car with a stolen plate registered to an address where they just found a soggy corpse. If the car in front of them now had the plates of the other vehicle attached to its bumper, where were the plates that belonged to it? He stared at the house the car sat in front of. If he knocked on the door, would he find its owner alive, or dead like the last one? There was only one way to find out.

Officer Simpson, two steps behind him, a cautious Dodge walked the path leading to the front door of the house. Every step the two men took, Dodge dreaded what he might find behind the faded red front door. He stopped just short, glancing back at Simpson, who appeared to be as nervous. He nodded at the young officer, who nodded in return. Dodge reached out his left hand and rapped on the door three times.

No answer. Dodge smacked the door again with the palm of his hand. The slapping sound reverberated through the metal door. Still no answer. Just as the pair was about to step away, the silver knob on the door jostled. Then a click, the deadbolt disengaging. The door cracked and a small gray-haired lady peeked through the tiny space created before the security chain caught, preventing the door from opening more than a few inches.

"Can I help you?" a soft scratchy voice said.

The reason the green sedan had been chosen became immediately clear. The old lady didn't drive. She was blind.

"Good afternoon, ma'am. My name is Agent Paul Dodge. We are working a rash of burglaries involving cars in the neighborhood. Does the green Chevy parked on the street belong to you?"

"Yes. Oh, my. They didn't take my car, did they?"

"No ma'am. I have Officer Simpson with me. He is one of the policemen who patrol your neighborhood." Simpson waved and Dodge gave him a look and shook his head. "The reason we are at your door is, someone stole the license plates off the vehicle, and I wanted to know when the last time was you drove the car?"

"I haven't driven in over five years. As you can see, I'm blind. But I have a nephew that sometimes borrows it."

"Do you remember the last time your nephew took your car?"

"It was some time ago. I needed some help with errands. He went to the store for me and picked up my medication from the drugstore. That was the last time I saw him, or the car was driven."

"Can you tell me your nephew's name?" Dodge asked.

"Oh my, is he in some sort of trouble? I told him he needed to stop hanging around that riffraff he calls friends. Now the police are at my door looking for him."

"He is not in any trouble, ma'am. We only want to talk to him to verify when the car was last used and if he remembers seeing if the plates were still on it when he used it. Can you tell me his name, or do you have his phone number?"

"His name is Arthur, but he likes to be called Art. I'll see if I can find his number for you. I've got it written down here somewhere." The old blind lady disappeared back into the dark house. She returned a few minutes later with a piece of paper and a number scribbled on it. The numbers were all out of line, like a child learning to write, or in this case, a blind person had written them down.

Thanking her, Dodge and Officer Simpson walked down the path back to the driveway and to the street. They stopped next to the green sedan. Dodge pulled his cell from his front pocket and dialed the number written on the piece of paper. The phone rang.

The voice on the other end appeared to be an older male. Maybe in his late forties or early fifties. His voice was gravely and low, like that of someone who had smoked for half their adult life. Dodge thought about his own voice and his past cigarette habit. Arthurs's tone implied he and his aunt were no longer on speaking terms. He told Dodge he used to borrow his aunt's car once or twice a month. He would use it to run personal errands and do grocery shopping for her. That all stopped around six months ago.

A little over half a year prior, the nephew needed to borrow his aunt's car for a job interview. The interview was a bust, so he stopped at a bar for a beer and to pick up some groceries for her on his way home. The old lady was so mad, she told him he couldn't use the car anymore. And he hadn't asked since. The nephew had since been employed because he told Dodge he now had his own vehicle.

"I don't need anything from the old hag anymore," and the nephew hung up.

The call forced Dodge to rethink his theory about the stolen plates and the dead guy a few blocks over. He now believed the cars with the stolen plates were chosen at random. The owners had no ties to the killer, and their vehicles were targeted because their owners didn't drive them. One blind old lady and a dead guy in a bathtub. Dodge guessed the autopsy of tomato soup guy would reveal a drug overdose as the cause of death. His original plan of using the stolen plates to track the killer down was a dead end. They would have to find another way to trace The Savior's movements.

CHAPTER 14

THE THIN SLATS OF THE PLASTIC BLINDS had a yellow tint to them, the kind of discoloration found in houses exposed to years of cigarette smoke. The carpet, walls, and cabinets all had a permanent film. The odor was strongest in the bedroom, where he had a finger wedged between two slats of the blind in the window. He applied enough pressure so he could watch the chaos across the street but not draw attention to himself. He imagined if he stood six inches from the edge of the sill no one would be able to see him watching them. He also kept enough distance between him and the wall to prevent an accidental brush-up and the disgusting film from attaching itself to his clothes. The smell made him physically ill. He wanted to throw up. Suppressing the urge was paramount. Getting sick was a sign of weakness and it was up to him how his body reacted. He must never lose control.

It had been a late night and he was exhausted when he returned to the house. The first emergency vehicle arriving rustled him from his slumber, its siren wailing and lights flashing, first red, then white. Repeating the sequence over and over, until the driver flipped the switch, killing the noise, but leaving the flashing lights on. The sirens' wails broke him from his slumber, but the steady stream of police cars, fire trucks, and ambulances kept him awake. He relished in watching emergency personnel do their jobs. A morbid curiosity. He thought about how easy it would be to kill them all with a few pipe bombs placed around the perimeter. Maybe in cars parked on the street. Another in the mailbox at the foot of the drive. A third hidden in the bushes in front of the home. It would be so easy.

He shoved the thoughts back, relegating them into the box he created inside his head for undoable fantasies, then focused his attention back to the scene unfolding outside. The fat cop was there. His partner, the new guy, was standing in the front yard. Puking. The Savior sneered. He couldn't imagine what had been in that house to make someone fold in that way. He imagined blood spray on the walls. Entrails spread across the floor. A body half devoured by vermin. Eyes gouged out. His thoughts bordered on the unthinkable. Even for him. The box in his head was getting full. It was harder to find room to repress the fantasies. If the box overflowed, he wasn't sure he would be able to stifle his urges.

The first taste he had of vengeance had been the motel manager. He knew killing him was an act of uncontrollable passion and that wasn't his mission. There was no saving the manager's soul from eternal damnation. His blood wasn't pure and as much as you try, you can't get all the oil out of water. There are always little drops tainting the entire supply, making it undrinkable. But secretly, he liked what he did. He had relished in it. The rush was like nothing he had ever felt before, and he already missed the euphoric high he experienced from running the blade across the fat motel clerk's throat. He knew one day he would need to revisit the concept. But not now. Not today. He had carefully planned out the next few days. No diversions. No distractions.

He wondered if his old friend, the State Police Captain, would show up.

"Look at them," he said to no one. "Like ants in the yard. Cleaning up someone else's mess." They would never tie the car and license plate to him. He didn't even know the house's occupant was dead. The car had sat abandoned for weeks. He had made sure of that before switching the license plates under the cover of darkness. Still, he wondered what had happened to the owner.

After a few minutes of standing in the yard and rinsing his mouth out with water, the parole agent left. The Savior watched as he drove away, making a right onto the next street. His heart skipped a beat as he thought about the second set of plates he had taken from the blind lady's car. There was no way the cops would ever find that one. He would check later, after the action across the street had dissipated. Right now, he would watch his ant farm. Busy little ants, all working for him.

—◆—

The sun occupied a space directly overhead by the time Dodge finished with Officer Simpson. Food was now a priority. He had planned on going downtown again after dark and realized he may not get the chance to eat again until late. He would park his truck in the same place, just in case The Savior wanted to find him. The killer had shown some interest in the parole agent the previous night when the van sped away from his truck parked in the alley downtown. *Why not feed that beast,* he thought? If the psychopath behind the prostitutes' murders had another target, maybe he would stop killing the girls and focus on him. It was a long shot, but one he was willing to take. He wasn't scared of the killer or dying himself. He always knew his fate would be a violent death. What kept him up at night was the idea of more victims. He could feel the fear in the city. It gave off an unmistakable vibe and he was in tune with the frequency. He needed to push things along by making The Savior play defense instead of offense. He could do this by releasing some details to the press. Things only the police and the killer would know. Dodge needed to talk to the reporter, Cortez, again.

Passing the downtown police station, Dodge stopped at the cart that stood just outside its main doors. He always liked to use the little guys as much as possible for snacks and coffee. Something about screwing over corporate America appealed to him. He ate his ketchup-slathered dog and drank his diet soda right there on the sidewalk. Wiping his mouth, he walked the six blocks to the Channel Six news station. It was always easy to find, with the enormous satellite dish mounted on its roof.

As he approached the building's entrance, he saw Cortez standing out front, talking with a city councilwoman. There were no microphones and no cameras. The interview was off the record or personal. The sun's rays had moved directly overhead and the mercury to the mid-eighties. Sweat built up under his ballistic vest, as he waited for the reporter to finish before approaching.

He remembered why he liked to watch her work. She was the best damn reporter he knew. Unfortunately, she knew it too. She spotted him watching her and walked toward him after finishing her conversation.

"Well, Paul Dodge, are you here to make my day or ruin it?"

"I would never dream of ruining your day."

"Except that one time."

The comment forced an awkward pause.

"I'm sorry. I don't mean to keep busting your balls about that. It's just easy and sometimes I can't help myself."

"It's fine. Hell, I deserve it. I know I have said it before, but I am sorry for the way things went down." It wasn't a lie, but he used the moment to his advantage.

The reporter smiled for the first time since they reconnected. "What can I do for you, Agent Dodge?"

"You know it's just Dodge. And this time, it's what I can do for you," he said. "You heard about the latest body they found downtown?"

"The guy found dead in his bathtub? Of course, I know about that. We have been monitoring the police frequencies, but frankly, it seems like a non-story. Probably some druggy overdosed and passed out. Drowned in his own bath water. Not a lot of viewers in that one."

"True. But what if the death turned out to be related to the other cases? Would that interest your viewers?"

The agent watched the reporter's eyes as she mulled over the concept he had just floated. It was a softball. Thrown right across the plate, chest high. A literal home run ball and all she had to do was take a swing. She didn't make him wait long as she tried to cover her excitement, forcing away any smile trying to form. Her brow furrowed, causing her to squint an icy stare. But Dodge saw through the ruse. His plan had worked, and no mask of false bravado would hide a reporter's excitement for a good story. Not even a reporter as good as she.

"Are you telling me The Savior killed the bathtub guy?" Cortez asked.

"I want to be clear. I am not saying that at all. What I'm saying is, the two could be related. There is a difference."

Dodge knew Cortez wouldn't see the difference, and he counted on it. She was already thinking up how to open her segment. A city gripped by fear as a psychopath takes his fourth victim, killing a local man, and today, police find his body rotting in a suburban bathtub. A good story gave a reporter tunnel vision. It was like a feeding frenzy. It would be all she could think of for the next few days.

After a few minutes, she shook off her initial excitement and narrowed the gap between them.

"Look, I have this thing I must cover for the evening news. But why don't we have drinks, or maybe dinner, later tonight? You can fill me in on the details."

"Strictly off the record?"

Cortez smiled. "Of course."

She was lying, and Dodge knew it. It wasn't the first time he had done this dance. He knew nothing was ever really off the record with a reporter. Anything you say can and will be used against you in the court of public opinion. He had a rule for talking to reporters. Say nothing to the press that you don't want your grandma to hear about you on the news. Rules were important, and this was a gold star one. Cortez said she would text Dodge later with a few places they could meet up.

He watched her saunter away. He knew she knew he was watching her. There appeared to be a little more wiggle in her step than usual. Once again, he remembered why he had been so attracted to her in the first place. He took a quick glance at his watch before making his way back to his truck. He didn't know if the bathtub guy's autopsy was still in progress but he wanted to stop at the coroner's office and let Renquest in on his conversation with Cortez.

The coroner's office was not busy by the time Dodge arrived. There were no police cruisers in the parking lot, and he didn't notice Renquest's unmarked unit as he drove into the parking lot. He found a parking spot next to the entrance. As he approached the front desk, a young man, probably an intern from the local college, looked up from the book he was reading.

"Can I help you?"

"My name is Paul Dodge," he said while flipping open his badge wallet. "I'm with the sex crimes task force and I was hoping to get a word with the doc."

"I'm afraid he is gone for the day, but he left something for you, Agent Dodge." The young intern reached under the desk and pulled out a file folder, handing it to Dodge, then returning his attention to his book.

Once back in the confines of his truck, Dodge spilled the file contents onto his lap. He read the file in order, front to back. He made a point to never skip to the end. It was important to come to his own conclusions, and to remain objective. Knowing the cause of death before looking at the evidence made an investigator prone to bias. Nothing killed a homicide faster than an investigator trying to feed a self-fulfilling prophesy.

The coroner's report read like a book. It told the same old story. Years of trauma and substance abuse. The man in the tub, Vern Banski, age forty-six, had several healed breaks to his arms. Spiral fractures, the telltale signs of abuse suffered as a child. It was caused by the twisting of the arm in two different directions. Kids used to call it an Indian burn. The victim's liver was less of a filter now and more of a toxic sponge. Years of alcohol abuse along with prescription pain med abuse forced an end to its biological purpose years ago. Banski had contracted Hepatitis C and was HIV positive. Dodge didn't know the man's sexual orientation but guessed his HIV-positive status came from intravenous drug use. Sharing needles was still a problem and caused illnesses and disease to spread amongst the user population at higher-than-normal rates compared to non-drug users.

When he came to the back of the file, the part with the pictures, he skipped looking at them, for now. He had seen the body in real life and no picture could capture the horror of what he saw in that bathtub. Next came the section with the breakdown of the cause of death. Drowning, likely caused by an overdose of opioids. No surprise there.

He picked up all the papers spread out across his lap and seat and placed them back into the file. The coroner's report had provided no new information. The condition of the body made it impossible to calculate a proper time of death. Dodge was nowhere closer to finding a connection between the newest victim and the others.

For the moment, Dodge had nothing to do. Any reports from the officers canvasing the dead guy's neighborhood wouldn't be ready until tomorrow morning at the earliest, and he still needed to meet with Cortez before driving downtown to keep an eye on Sarah. The day hadn't been as productive as he wanted, but it was what it was. It was time to head home for a drink. He shuttered. It may take two bourbons to wash away the memory of bathtub soup guy.

It was about a fifteen-minute drive home and he thought about the case the entire trip. He couldn't put it all together yet. Captain Blanchard, Vegas, The Savior, bathtub guy, and the dead hookers. It was like a jigsaw puzzle with missing corner pieces. Impossible to build the frame and lock in all the pieces. Before he knew it, he sat, parked in front of his townhome, the truck still running, staring through the windshield at nothing. A passing car backfired and broke his concentration.

He killed the engine, slid out of the cab, and made his way to the front door. A small table inside the front entryway caught his keys and wallet. Once in the dining room, he removed his weapon, still in its holster, and placed it on the dining room table he used as a desk. Next, he lifted the lid from the globe bar in the corner by the kitchen, pulled out a lowball glass and a bottle of Blantons, and poured a double of the brown liquid. He turned back to the table, covered with papers and files, and plopped down in the straight-backed wooden chair, designed to help force him into better posture.

He began by reviewing the files of the first three victims, looking for any additional similarities to the victim found at the motel. The girl's fingerprints returned zero hits, meaning she had no arrest history. A quick search turned up no addresses other than the motel. The girl was invisible. Dodge took another long pull from his glass and dug for the picture of the young girl in the file. He held the photo up, gazing at her lifeless face.

"Who are you?"

There was nothing he could have done to save her. Hell, he didn't even know she existed until she was dead. But he knew the motel manager. He could have stopped him. A sense of failure crept over him. His mind wandered, second-guessing every conversation with his former parolee, every visit to the motel, and not finding the hidden office. One more search of the motel before his supervision ended may have turned him on to the secret room. One more scan of his mobile phone might have revealed pictures or text messages. If Dodge had done anything to send him back to prison where he belonged, she might still be alive.

Lifting the glass, he swallowed the last of the Blantons and placed the glass on top of the girl's photo. He didn't deserve to look at her face. He couldn't stand to see his failure in her dead, grey eyes. The brown liquid burned as it traveled down his throat and into his stomach. Even his faithful friend, alcohol, knew he had failed.

A vibration against the side of his leg snapped him out of his self-loathing state. It was a text message from Beth. Suddenly, he felt a jolt of energy, but before he could read it, there was a knock on his door.

CHAPTER 15

SHE STOOD ON THE FRONT STEPS of his townhome. A skintight blue dress exaggerated her curves and revealed a tasteful amount of cleavage. A sneak peek at what he could get if the night went the way she wanted. What he wanted didn't matter.

"Cortez, what are you doing here?" Dodge said. An honest look of surprise on his face.

She stared at him, her green eyes fixated on his. "I finished my interview early and thought, why not an early dinner?" A bottle of wine rested in one hand and a plastic bag hung from the other.

The aroma from the food in the bag wafted in through the front door. It was an unmistakable odor, and it was his favorite, Chinese.

"It's a little early for dinner, don't you think?"

"We can have dessert first." She said as she slid past him and into the house. "That's what's great about being an adult. You get to choose when and who... I mean, what you eat."

Dodge shut the door, following her into the living room, watching her every move, not sure what to make of what was happening. The reporter paused, and scanned the room, looking at the medals and awards on his walls. She had been here before and he was sure she saw the same scene the last time she had spent the night.

"I almost forgot how many of these things you have." she said, picking up a plaque from the bookshelf next to the bedroom door. She peered over her shoulder. Her right hand sliding under one of the shoulder straps of the blue dress she was wearing. The silky material slipping over her shoulder and down her toned arms. Without another look back, she disappeared into the bedroom.

Dodge stood by the makeshift desk in his dining room peering into the dark room. He had been down this road before, and it had ended in a train wreck. He wondered what she was up to. What was her angle. The only thing he knew for sure was she didn't come out of the bedroom, and him standing in the next room with a confounded look on his face wasn't going to get him any answers.

The pair sat on the bed, eating Chinese food from the containers. Dodge in an old t-shirt and boxers—Cortez wore nothing. She was proud of her body, and who could blame her? She had all the right parts in all the right places and knew exactly how each one worked.

"I forgot what a caring lover you are," Cortez said, taking another bite of Kung Pao chicken.

"I'd say you did most of the heavy lifting this time. I was just along for the ride."

She shook her head and smiled. "You never could take a compliment."

"I'll work on that."

"Make sure you do, or the next girl might not find her way in here."

The two finished eating in silence.

Once Cortez had finished her food and drank the last of her wine, she rolled over on top of Dodge. He wasn't sure he could take the beating but turning her away didn't seem like much of an option. At least not a reasonable one. She must've noticed his hesitation because her hands moved across his chest slowly, more deliberately than before. The sway of her hips choreographed like a dancer, and less like a horny teen. She was incredible.

After the second session, Cortez slipped out of bed and walked into the bathroom, picking up the little blue dress and heels on her way. He watched through the open door as she touched up the makeup around her eyes, which had smeared and formed thin tear-like lines in the corners of her eyes. After a few minutes, she reappeared, looking as perfect as when she had arrived a few hours earlier.

"How do l look?"

"The same as always. Like a big city reporter."

She smiled and kissed his cheek.

"l hope you enjoyed that, because it won't be happening again."

"That's a shame."

"l just felt we needed to get the tension out of the way so we can focus on business. And besides, a good release helps me focus on the story. Kinda unclogs the mind."

"Among other things," he said.

"Don't be crude."

Dodge held his hands up, signaling his submission.

With that, Cortez went into the living room. Dodge got out of bed and used the bathroom and washed his face and brushed his teeth. He heard the front door open, then close. An engine revved to life outside his window and taillights cast shadows on the blinds as the vehicle pulled away. A second car passed a few seconds later. He stood in the living room in his t-shirt and a pair of athletic shorts he picked up off the bathroom floor, contemplating what had just happened. Everything about this night caught him off guard. The confidence Cortez oozed made him crazy. He couldn't help himself. After a few minutes of going back and forth on the matter, he felt it was best to just let the whole thing drop. She had taken him for a ride, literally, and that was all it had been. His mind drifted to Beth. Now he needed a drink.

He poured some more Blantons into the glass he has used earlier. His phone perched on the edge of the table, balancing half on and half off. As he reached for the device, it toppled over and bounced on the hardwood floor. Landing with the screen facing up. Beth's earlier text message was no longer pinned to the home screen. Knowing that the text notification only disappears if the phone's user unlocks the device, accessing the home screen, he rewound the tape in his head. When the doorbell rang, he placed the phone on the table next to his laptop and answered the door. The pair then ventured into the bedroom, where she never left his sight. Until she left and he used the bathroom. Could she have had enough time to sneak a peek at his phone? He was loose with his security PIN. He always used the last four of his phone number. It was easy to remember. It would've been easy for someone with her talents to guess it. It would be the first one he would have tried.

She had gotten what she came for, and it turned out not to be him. While the realization was a hit to his ego, he remembered he had once used the same tactic against her. Shaking his head, he couldn't help but smile. Smart girl. She used his weakness against him. Just how he would have played it, if he had been thinking with the head mounted on his shoulders.

He did not know if Cortez had seen any actual information about the case on his cell. Or if she even tried to access it. The case may be that he might have unlocked the phone and simply didn't remember doing it. It wasn't out of the realm of possibility. More important things slipped his mind every day.

The burn from the bourbon had dissipated and he decided, until he knew for sure what had happened, his instincts were to play it close to the vest. No need to blow it out of proportion before knowing if there had been a leak at all. He made his only call about the incident to Renquest. The reaction from his partner was predetermined. Renquest hated reporters. Especially Cortez. Their verbal sparring sessions during task force press conferences were legendary. She pushed him to the edge and the seasoned detective pushed back with the same ferocity. Dodge loved to watch the two do battle in a packed press briefing room. That was why he wanted to make sure his partner would be ready for any coming fight.

Renquest picked up on the first ring.

"Yeah."

"Hey, it's Dodge."

"I know. Your number is right here on my phone. I was just getting ready to call you. The coroner sent over some more test results. The blood tests on the stiff in the tub came back positive for opiates and cocaine. Apparently, he had been speed balling and decided to…"

Dodge cut him off.

"Look, I've got to tell you something."

"Oh, for Christ's sake, what did you do now?"

Dodge envisioned his partner falling back into his chair. One hand holding his cell phone and the other brushing back through his thinning black hair.

"Why do you just assume I did something wrong?" Dodge asked.

"That's fair. But..."

"But what?"

"But what did you do?"

Dodge hesitated for a moment. Then he said, "I fell for it again."

"Fell for what?" A pause. "Wait a second, not the reporter again. Is this a joke? Please tell me this is a joke."

"I'd love to say no, but... Yeah, the reporter," Dodge sighed.

"God damn it, Dodge! You are the most stubborn son of a bitch I have ever met. Didn't you learn your lesson the first time?"

"I know, I know. I messed up."

Dodge heard his partner take a deep breath. Then silence. But he could feel the icy stare, even though he couldn't see him.

"What does she know?" Renquest asked.

"I don't know how much, or what she knows. I think she snooped on my phone and all the calls and text messages about this case were on there. She could have seen all or none of them. I just don't know right now."

"How the hell did she get your phone?" Renquest's voice dropped a level. "You know what, never mind. I don't care."

Dodge nodded, though his partner couldn't see him. "We will know what she found soon enough."

"You think she will go on air with it?"

"I can't imagine any scenario where she wouldn't. Cortez is *the* reporter, so it will take her a few days to nail down all the details. If she tries to talk to the staties, I'll hear about it. But my guess is, her first call will be to Las Vegas."

"That's what I would do," Renquest said.

"Me too."

"I had better be your first call if you hear anything about this."

And with that said, Renquest hung up.

The parole agent's next call was to Captain Blanchard to see if Cortez had left the good captain any messages yet. The phone rang directly to voicemail and Dodge left a brief message for the captain to call back tomorrow. If Cortez was poking around, Blanchard would call Dodge immediately as he was under the impression his new investigator was handling the reporter. Professionally, of course.

The last thing he did was answer Beth's text from earlier that evening. His fingers pounded out a reply as he thought about the mistake made earlier that evening. He wasn't as worried about anything Cortez had seen on his phone as he was about the lapse of self-control. He and Beth were not exclusive. Hell, he didn't know what they were. Two people separated by careers and two thousand miles of farmland and desert. He wasn't sure what any of it meant. But he still felt guilty and angry with himself. Never lose control. It was the rule he had trouble following.

It would be great to see you again. Plus, I could use someone to watch my six. Things are getting dicey here- Dodge.

After pressing send, he stuffed the phone in his front pocket, slid his weapon into the holster resting in the small of his back, and grabbed his keys from the entryway table with a quick glance back to see if he forgot anything before shutting the door behind him.

The sun dipped below the horizon. Streetlamps flickered on and light emanating from store windows tried to overcome the encroaching darkness. But shadows still ruled the spaces in between. Dodge parked his truck in the same place as the previous night, where the white van had made a hasty getaway. He wouldn't make the same mistake twice. Tonight, he would walk a block in the opposite direction, circling the back to the street he parked on, putting him behind the van if the driver returned and parked in the same location as the night before.

His finger flipped the little red switch installed under his driver's side dash to the ON position. The camera had enough memory allocated for about four hours before it reset and began recording over the footage to make room for another four hours.

He took one quick look around before heading to the corner to keep a watchful eye on Sarah. Nothing caught his eye, and he headed down the street toward the four blocks comprising the working girl's district.

As he turned the corner from the side street and stepped onto the curb, Sarah noticed him before he saw her. The two made eye contact and Dodge patted his hands down low by his waist, signaling his intention to be discrete. Sarah leaned back against the wall's brick face.

Dodge pulled a ball cap out of his back pocket, donned it, and pushed back into a vacant doorway, watching as the first car approached. The young prostitute didn't move, ignoring the car completely. The potential payday sped away, to the next corner, where he found a more welcoming face. It was the same scene repeated for the next two hours. Johns pulling up to the curb and the inattentive prostitute giving a half-hearted performance. A few drivers accepted the deal, and she got into the car, pulling around the corner, conducting business and returning a few minutes later. The same look on her face. Total subjugation. Dodge had seen that look many times over the course of his career. Women beaten down by the system, wanting to get out of the life, but not knowing how. It always saddened him.

When the clock on his phone flashed midnight, he had had enough. The night was quiet, and he didn't notice any white vans, or any vans at all, pass by. He began to wonder if he would catch the perp in time. Before he killed again.

As he made his way back toward his truck, he felt his phone vibrate in his pocket. He thought of the text he had sent Beth, and his heart skipped a beat. He dug deep into his pocket, trying to retrieve it before the call went to voice mail. Once the device was free from his pocket's grip, he saw the number on the screen. It wasn't Beth.

CHAPTER 16

HIS LUNGS ACHED AS HE RAN flat out for two blocks before seeing the flashing red and blue lights bouncing off the buildings, reflecting endlessly from window to window down the empty side streets. His pulse raced. The woo-woo hairs on his neck stood at full attention and sweat ran down his back. A piece of yellow crime scene tape stretched between two patrol cars just inside the intersection of the two roads. Two uniforms stood guard and took a step in Dodge's direction as he lifted the yellow tape to slide under.

"Sir, I am going to need you to step back from this area."

Dodge lifted his shirt over his waist, exposing the badge that hung on his belt loop. "My name is Paul Dodge. Where is Detective Renquest?"

"Sorry sir. The detective is just up the street, by the body," the second cop said.

Dodge stopped dead in his tracks and turned to the officers.

"The body?"

"Yes, sir. Just up there," the first officer said. His finger pointed up the street towards the mass of the emergency vehicles lining the street.

He could see the outline of his truck straight ahead near the end of the street. Its chrome grille flashed from the blinking lights all surrounding it as he approached. Any cars that were parked in front of the truck had either been towed or the owners drove away before the police showed up. He slid under the second tape line surrounding his truck and the sidewalk and stared at the scene in front of him in bewilderment. The usual players were there. The coroner, Renquest, the crime scene team, and now, him.

Renquest locked eyes with his partner. Dodge recognized the look.

"Dodge, I need you to stop right there."

The confused agent moved closer, getting within five feet of the now visible body. "What the hell is going on here?"

His partner stepped between Dodge and the dead girl, sticking out his arm, and placing his hand on Dodge's right shoulder. "I need you to stop and take a step back."

"I need to get my truck out of here," Dodge said, using his weight to push against his much heavier partner's arm.

"If you don't stop, I'm going to have two officers come over here and stuff you in the back of a patrol car and take you downtown."

Dodge saw the seriousness on Renquest's face. He raised his hands level with his chest, signaling his surrender. "Somebody better tell me what the hell is going on? And why can't I get to my truck?"

The detective's gaze shifted to the scene over his shoulder, and then back to his partner. "It's more than a body this time."

Dodge looked past Renquest's shoulder at the crime scene techs shuffling about, picking up and bagging trash and anything they thought might be evidence.

"Was it him? Is it the same as the others?"

"Not exactly."

"What the hell does that mean?" His frustration mounted. Eventually, someone would have to let him have access to his vehicle. He preferred sooner rather than later.

"I'll let you into the scene, but you can't touch anything."

"Ok."

"I mean it, Dodge. You can't leave anything from you behind that wasn't already here."

Dodge was confused by the personal nature of the request. He understood how crime scenes worked, and Renquest knew that. Dodge nodded and his partner stepped aside to let him pass. One look and he immediately knew why his partner's warning had seemed so personal. Against the wall, bordering the sidewalk opposite his truck, partially obscured by a trash can, was the body of a young girl lying propped up. Eyes open, staring, empty and black. Like a child's doll's eyes. Her skin was shiny and smooth. Apparently lathered in the same oily substance as the previous victims. Ligature marks ran the span of her neck, like the others. A bruise could be seen under her eye and a swollen lip rounded out the damage to her face. The wounds looked partially healed, likely a day or two old.

Dodge donned a pair of rubber gloves. He stooped down next to the body. He reached out and turned the girls face toward him. The wound to the eye appeared to be older. The same held true for the busted lip. Both maybe a day or two old. The lip had already begun to heal. He could see scabbing around the edges and the surrounding tissue still had some red tone. A sign of a slight infection. Bodies don't heal after death. This didn't make any sense. The killer had always seemed to go to great lengths to take care of his victims after strangling them. He wondered if the damage to her face wasn't inflicted by a pimp or customer that enjoyed rough sex and beating on women. Either way, she didn't deserve to be treated that way. Nobody did.

"Doc, can you lift her shirt for me? I need to see something?"

The coroner turned to Renquest, who nodded, then carefully lifted the shirt from her stomach high enough to fold it over and expose her entire midsection. No message. There was no lipstick. No claim to the work that had been done.

The agent turned to see his partner had taken a few steps back and was now standing next to the passenger side door of his truck.

"Looking for this?"

It was like being hit in the face with a sledgehammer. Dodge's heart dropped like a rock to the pit of his stomach. He couldn't move. Just staring at what lay before him. *The Savior*, smeared across the passenger glass. Streaks ran down from the letters. As if the message was crying. No way this was drawn from lipstick. It was more liquid, thick enough to stay on the glass, but thin enough to run. He knew it could only be one thing.

"Is that blood?" Dodge asked his partner.

"We haven't tested it yet, and the Doc doesn't have a black light in the van."

"I don't need a black light and neither do you. We've both been exposed to enough blood to know it when we see it."

His partner looked at the writing and nodded.

Dodge continued to stare at the substance on his truck window. This new development changed everything. A moment passed before he turned his attention back to the victim. He noticed no blood on the ground around the body and no open wounds, other than the busted lip, which couldn't produce enough blood to create the message on the truck's window alive or dead.

"It didn't come from her," Dodge said, his eyes darting back to his truck. "Not enough damage to the body."

"Let's let the Doc do his job before we jump to any conclusions."

"I don't need an autopsy to tell me that amount of blood didn't come from this victim. There are no major wounds anywhere visible on her body big enough to produce that much blood," Dodge said.

Renquest stepped closer to the victim, leaning in and examining it. "Could have drained her slowly," pointing at her arms. "Those look like needle marks to me."

Dodge didn't bother to look at her arms. He didn't need to. "Those are track marks. She was a Hype. The difference in the size of the needles used to draw blood and shoot heroin is discernable from the marks they leave on the body. Those scars are old and healed. No bruising. The veins in her arms haven't been used for a while. She probably was shooting between her toes. Forced to find a vein that won't collapse upon itself. The blood isn't hers."

"So, there's another victim out there?"

Dodge said nothing.

After the realization of what lay before them wore off, the pair scanned the surrounding area. There were no dumpsters. Only trash cans. All of them owned and maintained by the city. Renquest ordered the crime scene officers to empty every trash can in a two-block radius and have their contents examined for butchered animals or anything big enough to have once contained enough blood needed to leave the message smeared on the trucks window.

At the same time the techs dispersed to collect the trash from surrounding streets, Dodge remembered his backup camera. He had set the device to record while he was surveilling Sarah. He walked to the back of his truck. There were no immediate signs of damage and the little fisheye camera lens, no bigger than the eraser end of a pencil, was still intact. Built into the plastic housing surrounding the release latch for the tailgate. He leaned in closer and examined its glass lens. No scrapes or paint covering it. A lucky break.

"Renquest, come over here."

The old detective made his way to the rear of Dodge's truck. "What ya got?"

Have your guys processed anything on my truck yet?"

"Not yet. I wanted you at the scene before we towed it to the lab for processing. Why?"

"I had the backup camera set to record while I was downtown."

"Recording what?" his partner asked. "And those things record while parked with the engine turned off?"

"No, not from the factory. I had the tech guys at work reconfigure the software in mine, allowing me to control the recording function of the camera with a switch under the dash."

"Why would you need, or want, to record anything from a camera on the tailgate of your truck?"

"A couple of years ago, I had a suspicion I was being followed home from work. I took all the precautions. I watched from the windows at work before heading out to my vehicle. Planned different routes home, using side streets to help me more easily spot a tail. I even reviewed the security camera footage of me leaving the office for a week straight. I found nothing, but I couldn't shake the feeling I was being tailed."

"So, you were paranoid? It happens to the best of us."

"Turns out, I wasn't paranoid. After the techs fixed up this little sucker, it enabled me to record my drives home, from behind anyway, and I ran a few of the license plates of vehicles I thought looked suspicious or followed me for too long."

"And you found one car belonged to a parolee you put in prison once," Renquest boasted.

"No. Turns out not that exciting. It was an old girlfriend that had been tracking me down. She wanted to get back together but was watching me to see if I was married now."

His partner smiled. "You nailed her, didn't you?"

Dodge ignored the comment and continued examining the area around the rear of his truck. After a few minutes, Renquest broke the silence.

"What did it record this time?"

"Everything. Everything from the time I parked until right now. It still has about a half hour before it overwrites the hard drive to make more room."

Renquest's arm snapped out, his hand extended, finger pointing at the small camera. "Can you stop it?"

Dodge nodded. "I can, but I need to get inside. The switch is on the driver's side, so I don't need to go near the passenger door."

His partner dug into his jacket pocket and fished out a new pair of black latex gloves. Worried about transfer of trace evidence from one area of the truck to another, he removed the old gloves and placed them into an evidence bag. With the new protective gear donned; he retraced his steps to the driver's door. There was no guarantee the killer hadn't approached on this side of the vehicle, but it was clear The Savior knew who the truck belonged to and didn't need to circle it to make an identification before dumping the body and defacing the trucks window. Plus, carrying a dead body, even at one-hundred pounds, takes strength and time. He would have wanted to position the body as quickly as possible. No witnesses. No reports of strange men lingering suspiciously on darkened sidewalks, paying a little too much attention to any particular vehicle. The whole thing, from parking, to staging the body, to writing on the truck's glass, couldn't have taken over five minutes.

The lights flashed twice as he pressed the button on the key fob with the little unlock pad. His right hand outstretched, fingers grasping the smooth plastic door handle, then pulling it until the lock mechanism released. The door opened smoothly and silently. Dodge reached inside and flipped the little red switch under the dash. He backed away, leaving the door open. No need to contaminate the scene more than necessary.

Renquest made his way back around to the rear of the truck, stopping for a moment to inspect the lens to the camera mounted in the tailgate.

"Do you think he noticed the camera, or tried to avoid it somehow?"

"I don't know. He would have no reason to think a backup camera would be recording. They are standard equipment on almost all new vehicles, and I hope he didn't pay any attention to it." Dodge paused.

"Buuut..."

"No but. It's that he has been one step ahead of us throughout this entire investigation," Dodge said. Contempt in his tone. "So, I'm not sure what to make of this entire scene." His knees popped as he kneeled to peer under his truck.

His partner remained standing. "Do you think he knew he targeted your vehicle?"

"Well, he was here the other night, so I have to say he knew what he was doing." Dodge returned upright.

"This is where you parked last time?"

The agent nodded.

"You put it here on purpose?"

Dodge said nothing.

"You wanted him to find you."

Again, Dodge said nothing.

"Damn it Dodge, talk to me. Why would you want him to make this personal?"

"It was already personal. He is killing women in my city. Dumping their bodies like trash tossed out a car window.

"Our city," Renquest quipped.

"What?"

"You said your city. It's my city too."

The look on his partner's face told Dodge he crossed a line. Renquest was right. The city didn't belong to just him. Every cop, firefighter, EMT, and all of the people that lived there had a stake in this case. Even if they didn't know it or didn't seem to care because the victims *were* trash to them. Safety is a concern for all. The lowliest homeless person to the wealthiest resident living high on the hill should be able to feel safe when walking the streets. Either in the light of day or the darkest of night. Murders have a way of eroding that feeling. Serial killers expedited the process.

"I needed to move things along. To change the focus of his obsession to something new."

"To you? But what was he focused on before? Besides all the dead hookers."

"What was the one thing each crime scene had in common?"

Dodge watched as his partner worked the cases over in his mind. He could see the wheels turning. It wouldn't take him long.

Renquest eyeballed his partner, who had started slipping the protective gloves from his hands. "Captain Blanchard."

"There it is. I knew you would get it with enough time," Dodge said.

"You're such a dick."

"That's the prevailing opinion."

Renquest shook his head. "But why make the killer focus on you? Isn't it just as easy to keep him concentrating on Blanchard and follow him? I mean, why interject yourself into his sick little fantasy?"

"I don't know enough about Blanchard yet to make things happen. With Blanchard, I'm just a spectator. Forced to sit on the sidelines and wait for the next move, which means waiting for *another* victim. If he fixates on me, it changes everything. I can start calling the shots and moving things along at the pace I want."

"So, you are pushing up his timeline?"

"Exactly. Pushing him out of his comfort zone might cause him to make a mistake, act on emotions."

"Or kill faster," Renquest said.

"He was going to kill again, anyway. There was nothing we could do about that. But now, his focus is on me. He will make a move. My guess is sooner rather than later."

"I wish you would have run this by me. We're supposed to be partners." Renquest's outstretched a finger, a foot from Dodge's chest.

"Put that thing away. I wasn't moving forward without you. My parking in the same spot as the other night was a fishing expedition. I wasn't sure if our perp had targeted me or if it was a coincidence that he parked on the exact street right behind my truck. I needed to know."

"I would say you know now."

Both men peered over the hood of the truck at the crime scene techs, who were winding up their work.

"Yeah, I'd say he knows who I am. The question now is, did he see it on the news or has he been watching?"

Both men turned and faced the far end of the street. Then they looked back at the opposite intersection. A crowd had gathered. The media would arrive soon and if The Savior wasn't watching at this moment, Dodge was certain his adversary would monitor the television and radio stations for coverage of his latest triumph.

The parole agent glanced back at his truck and then at his partner. "Have the crime scene boys take the license plates off my truck. And get a tarp down here to cover it. We don't need me to be the story."

"I called a tow truck earlier. It should be here any minute."

"Call them back and get a hauler. Easier to hide the vehicle under a tarp on the flatbed."

Renquest used his radio to call the impound yard and instructed the tow truck driver to return to the shop and swap out his normal ride for a flatbed big enough to haul a pickup truck. The radio cackled with the sound of the driver's voice. He expressed his displeasure about the change in plans but did as the detective instructed.

"You need a ride home?" Renquest asked.

"No. I think I am going to head back downtown. I want to check on the girl from the motel. Make sure she gets back home safe."

His partner smiled.

"Shut up." Dodge said. "Beth is coming back to help me with some things I need to get done. She will be staying with me for a few days."

Renquest, his smile growing bigger, made his way around the truck to finish overseeing the scene's processing.

Dodge took one more long look around before making his way back to the street corner where Sarah worked. By the time he arrived, she was nowhere to be found. In fact, most of the girls were gone. Then he looked back over his shoulder. The red and blue flashing lights. Cops had a way of driving away business. The incident with his truck had ruined more than one person's night. He waited for a few minutes, scanning the nearby stores and alleys to make sure Sarah hadn't just turned a trick or taken a bathroom break. Once satisfied she was not returning, he hailed a cab for the ride home to get some sleep. Alone. At least for tonight.

CHAPTER 17

A SINGULAR RAY OF SUNLIGHT broke free from the tight grip maintained by the curtains. The solitary beam danced across Dodge's face. The clock read six-thirty in the morning, and he began the day the same as the hundred before and likely the hundred after. A shave, then a shower, followed by a cup of coffee and a quick read of the news on his phone or computer. The news's conveyance depended on what room of the house he was in. A cursory scan found no mention of his truck being used as a macabre whiteboard, or his involvement, whatsoever. Whatever Cortez had planned, it wasn't going down today. He had another twenty-four hours at least. A sigh of relief escaped his lungs as he sipped coffee at his dining room table.

After closing his laptop, he checked his phone for messages. After entering his PIN, the screen lit up, showing a new message from Beth. The time stamp showed he had received the text a few hours ago and her flight would arrive around two in the afternoon. She had tried to book an earlier one, but a storm over the Midwest had delayed many of the crossover flights to the east coast. The travel agent put her on the first available flight out of Phoenix with one layover in St. Louis. Eight hours of travel, factoring in time zone changes. The feeling in the pit of his stomach returned, as it always did when he thought of her.

As he sipped his coffee, his thoughts returned to Sarah. There was no point in lying to himself by acting like he wasn't worried about her. A psychopath was cruising the city, waiting for his chance to strike again. He also knew the killer had taken an interest in the young woman with the last three killings being within eyesight of her corner. That was no coincidence. Add to that whoever was committing these murders had fixated on him now. It was planned, but still moved his worry meter to ten. In fact, the only person benefitting from the change was Captain Blanchard. If part of this was personal, some sort of a vendetta against Blanchard, Dodge hoped the staging of the body at his truck meant The Savior's attention had switched to him. Most serial killers focused on one victim at a time. The two possibilities, in this case, were a parole agent and Sarah. Dodge planned to keep it that way. It was time to talk to the girl again.

The hotel the task force placed her in was nice enough. It wasn't the Four Seasons, but it had room service and a security staff capable of handling most situations. Other than being under twenty-four-hour police protection when she wasn't working, her overall safety was adequate. Much safer than at the no-tell motel she previously called home.

He thought about last night and all the things that could go wrong over the next several days as he rode in the back of an orange and black taxicab. The unpredictability of The Savior was foremost. Last night proved how bold the killer had become and these things never deescalated. It was always one more step on the ladder of insanity. Then there was Blanchard. He was the wild card in this whole thing. How would he react to the news from last night? Was the state police captain somehow entrenched deeper in this mystery than Dodge had imagined? And what about Sarah? What would her role in all of this be? His fingers combed through his short sandy hair as he pondered all the open questions remaining. He had no more answers than yesterday. He shook his head and watched as the buildings zipped past.

The driver pulled up in front of the main doors to the hotel and stopped. Dodge pulled a twenty from his wallet and passed it through the small opening in the glass that separated the driver from his passengers. As the driver reached for a stack of bills to make change, Dodge waived him off as he slid out of the back seat, closing the door behind him.

"Keep the change."

He watched the taxi pull away and nodded a hello to the doorman as the man in the red trousers and jacket pulled the heavy glass door open as he approached. Once inside, he spotted the front desk which sat directly across the room from the main entrance. A quick check to make sure he remembered his badge, and he made his way to the check-in counter. A young man about Dodge's height, but a good forty pounds lighter, was standing behind a computer screen, his fingers tapping away at the keyboard. The young clerk raised his head as the parole agent approached.

"Good morning, sir. Are you checking in with us today?"

"Good morning. No. I am looking for a guest that's staying at the hotel."

"Do you know what room the guest is in?"

"I'm afraid I don't. But her name is Sarah and she's been staying here for a couple of days now."

The man began typing again and after a minute he looked back up at Dodge.

"I will ring her room and tell her she has a visitor, sir."

The always security-conscious parole agent liked the clerk following the rules. Rules were important. He gave the clerk his name and then found a high-back chair with views of the elevator bank and the front entrance to his right. If she came from the room or the outside, he would see her.

Five minutes passed, and no Sarah. His mind wandered to a dark place. What if she didn't make it home last night? What if the scene at his truck was merely a distraction? A way to get him and all of the other cops away from his hunting grounds. He would then have been free to snatch Sarah while no one was watching. He pushed the thoughts back and focused on his surroundings. Cameras adorned the ceiling in all four corners of the lobby and an additional three behind the counter where guests check in and out. There didn't appear to be any areas where the camera's view couldn't reach. From the moment a person entered the hotel, they were on full display. The camera sees all, recording all that pass before its lens for posterity.

The second hand on Dodge's watch ticked forward. He could hear the tic, tic, tic as the seconds passed. It sounded like hammers pounding in his head. Never stopping, maintaining a steady, slow pace. Tic... tic. His eyes flashed between his wrist and the elevator bank. First the wrist, then the door. Back to the wrist, then the elevator bank. The sudden ding of the bell when the elevator reached the lobby snapped his attention back to the two silver doors as they slid apart. Still no Sarah. The usually steady parole agent's anxiety swelled.

Dodge stood from his chair, took one last look around the lobby, then made his way to the check-in desk. The same young man was at the counter.

"May I help you?"

"I need you to ring the room I you asked about earlier," he said.

"What was the name of the guest?"

Annoyed, Dodge's patience wore thin. His badge clanked as he slammed it on the counter. The sound of metal against a hard surface. "Call the same number you called earlier and tell her the police are here to see her."

The man behind the counter jumped back, the badge resting on the stone countertop in front of him. His voice cracked as he answered. "Sorry, sir. I didn't know you were a police officer. I will call her right away." Hands shaking, his fingers fumbled across the numbers on the phone.

Dodge watched him dial, making a mental note of the sequence, 0402. Her room was 402. The clerk avoided eye contact and stared at the monitor on the desk in front of him as he held the phone to his ear, waiting for a voice on the other end. Finally, he lowered the receiver and shook his head.

"She isn't answering, sir."

"Give me a room key," Dodge said as he found it harder and harder not to reach across the counter, grab the clerk by the tie and use it to slam his face into the desk's hard surface for wasting time. "Has she had any visitors?"

The clerk raised his head, peaking at Dodge from under the locks of hair draping his face. "Umm, I'll have to check the visitor's records."

"Son, I know what she is, ok. I'm not here to jam anyone up, especially not a kid who makes minimum wage, who might have taken an unreported tip for agreeing to keep a visitor transaction off the books."

The nervous clerk nodded.

"Good. Now, do you remember what the man looked like?"

"He looked, well, a lot like you."

"What do you mean, like me? Was he, my height? Did he have the same hair color?" he said, pointing to his head.

The boy shook his head but said nothing.

"Son, my patience is growing thin here."

The clerk raised his hand and pointed at the badge on the counter. "He had one of those and told me not to tell anyone he had been here. He tipped me fifty bucks!"

Dodge stared at the silver piece of metal lying on the counter. On its face, the words State Police imprinted in black. He snatched the key card from the clerk's hand and turned toward the elevator.

The clerk yelled, "Room 402."

Dodge ignored him and jumped on the elevator as the door opened. A tall man wearing a windbreaker and baseball cap slid past him and stepped off. Bumping shoulders as they passed.

"Excuse me," Dodge said, as he turned and pressed the button for the fourth floor. "Asshole."

The man didn't answer and didn't look back. He kept walking and Dodge watched him exit the lobby, on to the sidewalk, as the elevator doors slid shut.

The elevator bank was conveniently centered in a long hallway. A sign on the wall pointed guests in the direction based on their room number. Rooms 421 to 440 were to the left, with 440 being at the end of the hall farthest from the elevator banks. Room 402, Sarah's room, was at the far end to the right. He exited the elevator and looked in both directions before proceeding to Sarah's room. The long hall made him nervous. It was like a shooting gallery. If someone appeared from a room and began popping off rounds, anyone caught off guard would be in a bad spot. He tried to maintain a twelve-inch distance from the sides. It wasn't the stray bullets ricocheting off the wall you had to worry about. It was the scattering debris broken loose from the round impacting the soft construction material that made up mass produced American buildings. Splinters and drywall fragments sprayed into the eyes could blind a person, giving the shooter time to take careful aim and make the next round count.

His pace quickened. Each step was more deliberate. More resolute. Once past the door, he slid his Glock from its holster. The normally calm agent's hands shook. He dropped to one knee, his back against the wall. The door handle within reach of his non-gun hand, meaning the door would swing in and to the right. A brief thought of leaving and waiting for Beth to arrive and back him up crossed his mind. It would be smarter to set up near the entry to the stairs, five feet away, at the end of the hall. Using the opening as concealment if things went south. Dodge took a deep breath, then exhaled. Another deep breath. Exhale. His hands steadied and his focus cleared. There would be no hiding and no waiting. He needed to be in that room.

With his left hand, he passed the keycard over the reader. The light turned green as the locking mechanism released. The door was metal, heavy and not well balanced. He had placed himself in an awkward position—his back to the wall forced him to push back against his body and the strength of the hinges. The door only opened a few inches as the springs pushed back. His efforts hadn't produced enough space for the two-hundred-and-ten-pound parole agent to slide through. He had tried to be discrete but failed. The element of surprise was lost.

When in doubt, use excessive force. It was a rule he believed in. And it was always better to be sued than dead. Taking one last deep breath, he spun to face the door. His right foot raised to waist height. He swiveled on his left foot away from the door, doing a 180-degree turn and released all his weight, through his right thigh, down to his foot, connecting with the door inches below the handle and locking mechanism. The kick was solid. The metal door slammed against the wall, breaking a mirror strategically placed on the inside of the door to give guests one last look at their outfits before heading out for the night.

The room was divided into a common area with a couch and television and a bedroom. A small mini fridge sat below the desk on the right as he first entered. A microwave oven rested on top, taking up one corner of the already crowded desktop. As Dodge cautiously moved further into the room, he noticed glass from a coffee tabletop lay shattered on the floor. Like a million little diamonds, sparkling in the light coming through the open curtains. A lamp lay on its side, its shade caved in. His stomach clenched. There had been a struggle in this room. A violent one.

As he moved through the living area and toward the bedroom, his Glock at the ready position, its muzzle aimed at a slight down angle about five paces in front of him, he noticed a small red smear on the doorjamb of the bedroom. It was blood. His front sight raised to chest level, and he slid to the left side of the doorway. He could see the bed and the entry to the bath. The rooms appeared to be empty. A quick scan of the bathroom from his position in the hall, using the mirror above the bathroom sink, confirmed no one was hiding in the shower. He knew one thing for sure. Sarah didn't leave the room on her own. Someone had taken her. And she put up a fight.

Dodge holstered his weapon and pulled his phone from the front pocket of his jeans. Using speed dial, he called the task force. Detective Renquest answered on the first ring.

"Dodge, where have you been?"

Dodge checked the time on his watch. It was half past nine in the morning. "I'm at the hotel where we placed the witness to the motel murders, Sarah."

Renquest interrupted his partner before he could finish. "Damn it, Dodge, do you ever check your messages? We have been calling and texting you for an hour."

Dodge looked at the screen on his phone and the little speaker symbol had a line through it. "I must have forgotten to turn my ringer back on this morning. Sorry about that. But before we get into that, I called you because I'm here at the hotel and the girl is gone."

"Like moved out?" Renquest asked.

"Not unless she threw a killer rage last night. The furniture is in pieces, and I found some blood."

"Do you think it is hers? I mean, does it look like she left alive?"

Dodge scanned the room, then ripped the bedspread off,

revealing the mattress beneath. "I don't see any other blood stains. My guess is she left alive. Whether she was conscious, I can't say."

"Well, we have ourselves a pickle here," Renquest said.

"What do you mean?"

"The task force received a call this morning from the State Police. Your friend, Captain Blanchard, is missing."

It hit him like a brick to the back of the head. Dodge sat on the edge of the bed, ignoring everything he had learned over his career about crime scene integrity. But his mind wondered. He knew there had been something off about Blanchard, from the first time he and Renquest met him at the crime scene of the third victim. His gut had spoken to him then. He ignored it. It was a rookie mistake and may have just cost a woman her life. The anger built. Starting in the pit of his stomach and working its way to his chest and up to his head.

"It was him," Dodge grumbled.

"What was him? The guy who took the hooker? Hell, Dodge, we don't even know if it's related to our case. She could have had a John up to her room and things got a little out of hand. Maybe she cut herself shaving her legs and had to go to the pharmacy for a box of band-aids. The bottom line is we don't know what happened yet. Besides, why the hell would a State Police Captain kidnap anyone? What could he possibly want her for?"

"It was him. The clerk downstairs saw his badge. He pointed to mine and said the badge the man who visited her showed him was identical to mine. Jesus Christ, it was all right in front of me this whole time. I was just too blind to see it."

"Too blind to see what?" his partner asked.

Dodge's silence was as loud as a screaming baby as he mentally worked through the details of what he thought he knew about Blanchard and The Savior to this point. After a moment, he spoke.

"Get the crime scene team over here. I will bet the only things we find in that room belong to Sarah, even the blood." He could hear Renquest breathing on the other end of the line.

"Why would he take her?"

"This thing has been personal to him since Vegas. He has been reading my reports and the notes I put into the system after

I talk to witnesses. It wouldn't be hard for him to put two and two together. The girl is important to our suspect and therefore important to him. He will use her to get The Savior to come to him," Dodge said.

"Two birds, one stone, huh?"

"Sounds about right. Blanchard is putting this psycho's two obsessions right in a row. One shot, one kill."

"Two of three obsessions," Renquest said.

"Three?" Dodge asked.

"He has three obsessions. The captain, the hooker, and after last night, you."

Dodge's mind was working overtime, trying to decipher random details he recalled from his talks with Blanchard. So much so, that he had completely forgotten about his truck. The Savior using the parole agent's truck to stage a crime scene had been a statement. It was personal, like in Vegas with Blanchard. This gave Dodge some leverage, though he wasn't sure how to use it yet. But it's always better to play offense than defense.

Energized again, the parole agent checked his watch again. It was almost a quarter after ten, and he needed to get to the airport to pick up Beth. She would arrive in a little over an hour. "Can you send a patrol cop over here to guard the room until the crime scene team gets here?"

"Sure. There is always a uniform in that part of town. You got somewhere you need to be?"

"Got to see a friend for a bit."

"Alright but keep your phone on this time. We will probably need to brief the brass on the recent developments."

"I'll call you later today. I need to figure some things out before we make our next move," Dodge said, and rung off.

The uniform officer arrived at the room about ten minutes later. He told the officer to stand at the door to the room and not to let anyone in, except for the crime scene team. He closed it behind him, and he handed the key card to the officer.

As he approached the small nook on the left where guests got on and off the elevators, he stared at the ceilings. He noticed there were no cameras. No way for him to see who exited on this floor last night or this morning. Or ever. He then glanced down the hall opposite the room where the officer stood guard. No camera. It appeared the lobby was the only place the hotel management was concerned about crime. They were more concerned about their own employees. The other cameras in the lobby were just for show. To provide a sense of safety to the guests as they entered the building. A façade.

Dodge hustled back to the end of the hall. The officer watched him pass but didn't move. A lighted exit sign hung from the ceiling, pointing to the entry to the stairwell. As he approached the door, a spot of blood caught his eye. It was on the outside edge of the door trim. He used the bottom of his shirt as a makeshift glove to push the door handle, then forced the door open using his foot, doing his best to try not and contaminate any evidence left on the door and its framework. He took one step into the stairwell. First, he looked up the stairs leading to the roof, then down toward the lobby and basement. He saw another blood smear on the railing leading down. Peeking his head back out into the hall, Dodge instructed the officer to use his radio and call for four additional uniformed officers to assist at the scene.

"I want one officer on every floor to make sure no one uses these stairs until the crime scene team goes over every inch of the room and this stairwell."

The officer tapped the mic pinned to his shoulder and spoke quietly. There was a short pause before the radio cracked back to life. "They will be here in about five, sir."

"Good. What's your name, son?"

The officer tapped the name tag attached to his right breast pocket. "Murphy, sir."

"Well Murphy, you can stop the sir shit. Just call me Dodge."

"I know who you are sir... eh, I mean, Dodge."

"How long have you been on the force?"

The officer looked down at his watch as if it were a calendar that could reveal past historical events. "It'll be four years this December."

"Where was your first beat?" Dodge asked.

"When I was with my Field Training Officer, right out of the academy, I worked the downtown district. That is where most of the action is, on the night shift anyway."

"Where did the brass assign you after they cleared you for solo duty?"

"A little of everywhere, really. People were quitting every day back then, it seemed. I became a sort of swing guy. If there was a shortage of officers in a particular area, I would fill in for that district until they could bolster the ranks," Murphy said.

Patrol officers boasted a more intricate knowledge of the streets and their players than even a seasoned parole agent could ever hope to possess. He could use that.

"So, let me ask, where would you take someone that you needed to hide? Someplace quiet and where people wouldn't ask questions."

"Is this about the girl staying in this room, sir?"

Dodge nodded. "Where would you go?"

The officer scratched his head and looked over Dodge's shoulder. Not at anything, but into a distant void. Then he looked up.

"If it were me, sir, I would take her down to the warehouse district. There are plenty of abandoned buildings down there. The only people that hang out there are homeless folks and neighborhood kids who use the buildings as a place to drink and smoke pot."

"Don't you all patrol that area?"

"Sometimes, but no one cares about kids and pot. It's the dealers officers want to bust. Dealers are the career makers. Addicts are just dirty disease-ridden mopes. No one wants to wrestle some heroin junkie to the ground, get pricked by a needle, and maybe get AIDS."

Dodge said nothing.

"Oh, and there is a pretty shady self-storage place down there, too."

Dodge felt a surge of adrenaline. "Storage units?"

"Yeah. But, not like the nice places you see in town with electricity in each unit and air conditioning. Basically, it is an old warehouse lined with used and rusty shipping containers. The owners only take cash, and no names are required. They assign each unit a key and a number and if you cannot pay, the owners cut the locks and sell off anything valuable, then dump the rest in the trash to be taken to the landfill."

"How do you know about this place?" Dodge asked.

"All the beat cops who work that area know about it or have at least heard of it. There was a raid at the warehouse about a year ago. The State Police found a missing girl chained up inside a container. Her stepfather had taken her from her mother and kept her there for a couple of days. He finally cracked under questioning and admitted he took her and hid her in that shithole. His plan was to sell her to some pervert for drugs and cash. What a sicko, you know what I mean? Who would do that to a child?"

Dodge vaguely remembered the case from the news. It happened right after he had returned from vacation. The task force didn't get involved, as police considered the case custodial interference and not kidnapping. The state police and sheriff's office usually handled cases where the perpetrator was a parent or guardian, so he only checked the news to see if they found the girl alive. He never thought about it again. However, it was the words State Police coming from the officer's lips that caught his ears.

Did Blanchard know about the makeshift storage units? It was only a month after the incident with the girl when the Staties hired him. There was still a buzz in the air and the news conducted follow-up stories on the young girl during the trial of her stepfather. Dodge's gut told him Captain Blanchard knew about the warehouse district, its shady owners, and that it was where he would find Sarah. But first, he needed to make it to the airport before Beth's plane landed. Renquest would be busy in the hotel room for most of the day and if a State Police Captain were involved in the kidnapping of Sarah, he would need backup he could trust.

CHAPTER 18

THE UNMARKED POLICE CRUISER Dodge requisitioned from the police motor pool looked like a million miles of pavement had passed beneath its wheels. Hard miles. The once shiny paint was now faded and chipped. The tires, well past their usable life, looked more like racing slicks than factory street tires. But the mechanics must have figured there was another six months of tread left on them. Dodge guessed none. The air conditioning worked, but the passenger's side window did not roll down. In fact, the only thing that appeared to operate flawlessly was the engine. It fired up at the slightest turn of the key in the ignition. Its internal combustion components sparked the fuel and the V-8 roared to life with the hum of a race car. A mechanically sound engine and air conditioning. It would do. At least, until he got his truck back.

The well-tuned cruiser got him to the airport just as Beth's plane was scheduled to touch down. He swung the car into a parking spot reserved for police close to the entrance and pulled a small white sign out of the glove box with the words "OFFICIAL POLICE BUSINESS" printed on its face, placing it on the dash in the front windshield. He reached into his front pants pocket and felt around as he had done so many times before when stressed or nervous. But the pocket was empty. There was no small box. No plastic lighter. No way to get the fix he craved. He hated not smoking and always knew he would start again once he proved he could quit whenever he wanted. The words of an addict.

The sign on the wall inside the arrival section of the terminal showed the only flight from Phoenix had arrived five minutes early. When talking to Beth about coming back for another visit, he never mentioned he would pick her up at the airport. In fact, he hadn't planned on it. Four days ago, on her last trip, she rented a car. Secretly, he wondered if she had gotten the rental in case things didn't go the way she planned with him. A vehicle allowed her to come and go on her terms. He pushed the thoughts out of his mind. She had come back. To see him. There was no chance to overthink the situation. Anything that might go wrong was a future Dodge problem. Current Dodge was going to live in and enjoy the moment.

As soon as he entered the arrivals gate, he could see the rental car counters to his left. The usual agencies were lined up along the far wall. Only one employee manned the counters. The rest had been replaced by self-serve kiosks where the customer could check in and go directly to the vehicle they rented, without having to talk to a living, breathing person. He turned back to the luggage carrousels lined in front of him. Dodge questioned whether he had made it before she could get through the rental process and into a car.

He hustled down the long corridor until he saw the sign that flashed the fight number and "Phoenix" above a carousel. The belt was already spinning clockwise, and luggage was dumping out of a conveyor onto the racetrack-shaped retrieval system. Some people huddled around the contraption waiting to glimpse their bags being dumped onto the moving belt, others were physically checking the tags on every piece of luggage that passed as if they didn't know what their own luggage looked like.

He had a nervous knot in the pit of his stomach as he scanned the travelers. He looked at every face, hoping to pick Beth out of the crowd, which was now growing larger by the second. Then the hairs on his neck stood up. An icy chill ran the length of his spine, his arms sprouted goose pimples. Someone was watching him. He could feel it in his bones. Screenwriters and directors love to build up cops for the dramatic effects a theatre audience expects. But the truth is, a cop's second sense was the only accurate thing portrayed in police-related movies and shows. Then he felt a hand grab his shoulder.

—∿∿—

The inside of the container smelled of burnt oil and animal feces. It was dark. The darkest she had ever experienced. She remembered being a child in rural Kansas and her mom covering the widows in her room with aluminum foil, slamming the door and stuffing a wet towel into the gap between the bottom of the door and the floor. Even then, a few rays found their way through the cracks, sneaking into the room against her mother's attempts to control the light. Some were big enough that she could make them bounce on her hand. Her mother had told her the dark room was to protect her. To keep the bad people outside from getting to her. But she knew it was all a lie. By the time she was ten, she figured out her mother was really a meth cook for a local drug dealer. As had the authorities. One night after a police raid, Child Services came and took her and her sister. It was the last time Sarah saw either of them.

It was hauntingly quiet in the darkness. She could hear the muffled squeaks of rats scurrying outside the metal walls. Were they trying to get in? Rats didn't scare her. They had been a part of her life since she was a baby. One of her earliest memories was of opening her eyes in her crib and seeing a large rat chewing on the rubber nipple of the bottle her mother had given her to get her to go to sleep. The fury animals had already taken up residence in almost every house or motel she had ever stayed in. One time, she even started supplying her whiskered roommates with names. She lovingly applied the name Charlie to the rodent that visited during the night at the Sunnyside Motel. He had a blonde patch of floppy hair on top of his head and it reminded her of the boy in *Charlie and the Chocolate Factory*. She tried to think about a name for the rat outside her container but couldn't come up with one. Her eyes closed as she slid down the wall until she was sitting on the cold floor. Her head was buried in her knees. She thought about crying but couldn't muster any tears. Her eyes closed as exhaustion overcame her.

The squeak of the metal doors opening to the building pulled Sarah out of her slumber. How long had she been asleep? She could make out the sound of footsteps in the distance but couldn't tell how far away they were. The clacking of heels on the concrete floor became louder with every step until the noise stopped just outside the container. Then silence. Not a sound. Not even the rat she had heard scratching at the sides of the metal container before she fell asleep. After a moment, she heard a second pair of shoes clicking against the concrete floor. The sound was off in the distance but coming toward her direction. Then they stopped outside the steel walls of the container.

Sarah stood and stepped back from the wall and kneeled, somewhere near what she imagined was the middle of the container. There was no reason for her to choose that location, other than it put her more than an arm's reach from the door, but not so deep into the box she would find herself backed into a corner. She tried to make out what was being said. It was certainly two men—their voices muffled by the metal walls and stale void air. Raising to her feet, she crept toward the voices outside, trying to keep her balance while walking on the uneven floor.

Her outstretched hands finally touched the end of the container. There were doors—she could feel the steel bars that slid and locked the doors into place. She now knew if anyone came for her, they would have to enter from that end. She began to plan an escape. When her kidnapper opened the door and stepped inside, she could conceal and attack. She moved slowly about the container but discovered nothing she could use as a weapon. Even worse, the container was empty. Just her. Nothing to hide behind and leap out from to surprise her attacker. Her mind went back to that dark bedroom. The way the light flooded in when her mother opened the door the next morning. The sudden flash of light as the doors swung open, temporarily blinding her. She shook her head. Any attempt to surprise someone coming at her from the outside was impossible. Then, out of the corner of her eye, she saw a speck of light flickering from the door.

Light was penetrating the spaces between the shaft of the bolt and the door's metal walls. Any light, no matter how small or dim, was a welcome reprieve from the isolation and blackness. She moved her hand and the speckles of light danced across her skin. The voices outside were louder, but she still couldn't make out what they were saying. At that moment, she didn't care. It somehow seemed less important than the freedom from blackness the light brought. Her attention now focused on the sliver of light. She felt hope again.

Should she try to remove the bolt? The hole would be small, but she might be able see outside. It would be like looking through a keyhole. Her fingers manipulated the nut on her side of the steel wall. If she could slowly loosen it, the bolt would fall to the floor. She doubted anyone would even notice. At least, she hoped.

As she gripped the nut between her fingers to twist it, the voices quieted. Replaced by the sound of footsteps. Not walking or running. Those sounds were distinct. It was more claps and shuffles. Like dancing. It sounded as if two people were dancing, but that couldn't be true. Then silence again. No talking. No dancing. Absolute silence. Her body shook as the fear boiled in the pit of her stomach. She needed to get that bolt out of the wall so she could see what was happening outside.

The nut turned slightly, but her hands were sweaty, and her fingers kept slipping off the rusty metal. Sarah tugged on her shirt, using it like a glove between her fingers and the slick metal. The nut moved. Just a quarter turn at first, then more. Finally, the nut reached the end and fell into her hand. Unfortunately, the bolt did the same on the other side. A sharp clack echoed as the metal hit the concrete floor outside. She froze, but silence filled the air once again. After what seemed like an hour, she built up the nerve to place her eye up to the hole. The light blinded her, forcing her to back away. But after a few seconds of staring at the shimmering rays coming in through the holes, her eyes adjusted, and she tried again.

The hole was small, but with her cheek pressed against the cold steel, she could make out some details of the building her metal prison was in. A wall with windows stood about fifty feet in front of her container. The light in the room appeared to be from the sun shining in through the windows at the top of the far wall and some hanging industrial lights. She smashed her cheek harder against the container's side, moving her head right, then left to see if she could get a better view of either side. It was no use. It was impossible to have peripheral site lines from her makeshift peephole. She stood on her tiptoes and peered down through the hole and saw the soles of two shoes. Running sneakers. The kind she had seen displayed in store windows downtown on mannequins dressed in workout clothes. Only in the store windows, the mannequins were standing up. The person wearing these shoes was flat on the ground. She shuddered.

At that moment, the light from the hole went black, and all she saw was an eye staring back at her. She fell backwards onto the cold, hard floor. Her whole body shook. Tears came this time as she screamed. *I hate you, mom*, she thought. *This is all your fault.*

CHAPTER 19

DODGE SPUN TO HIS LEFT. Using his right hand, he cupped the hand on his left shoulder. Turning into the arm, he twisted the wrist to the right and lifted straight up, heaving the arm and the person attached to it up to their tiptoes. He turned slightly to face his attacker. The entire encounter was over in less than three seconds. It was instinctual. A reaction based on years of training. A deep recessed part of his brain took over, forcing his body to react. Only this time, he stopped before popping the arm out of its socket. The hand and arm he had a tight grip on belonged to Beth.

"Ouch!" she yelled. "What the hell are you doing?!"

Dodge, embarrassed and shocked, released her arm and took a step back. "Sorry, but you startled me."

"No shit. That hurt, God damn it."

"I'm really sorry," Dodge said. Head hung; his chin tucked into his chest. "I've been on edge the past few days."

Beth glared at him, rubbing her hand and wrist. "What the hell is going on, anyway?"

Dodge looked around, scanning the crowd still gathered at the baggage carousel. He saw no one staring back at him. Not a single person looked out of place.

"What is it?" she said.

Dodge refocused on his friend. "Nothing, I guess. I'm just a little jumpy." He looked at the ground around her feet. "No bags?"

"I only brought one suitcase, because I didn't know how long I would be staying. It should come around on the carousel in a minute," she said, pointing at some of the luggage making the round trip around the carousel.

"Thought you might stay a little longer this time, huh?"

Beth smiled. "Depends on how good the company is." Then she motioned to a black plastic suitcase that had tumbled from the chute and onto the conveyor. "That's mine right there."

Dodge stepped past several people and squeezed his way to the front of the growing group of people waiting for their belongings. As he reached for the suitcase, a faint odor breezed past his nose. The smell was oddly familiar. He looked up but saw nothing no one he knew. After pulling the black plastic luggage off the conveyor and placing it at his feet, he peered around at the faces all around him. He took a deep breath through his nose. The smell was still there but had faded. The investigator part of his brain, the part that never shut off, processed the information. The smell was metallic, like from a junkyard, or the way a container full of old change smells. Part musty and part oily. His lungs expanded as he took another deep breath. But the smell had dissipated, and he picked up nothing.

"Dodge?" Beth said. Careful not to touch him this time.

The sound of his friend's voice snapped him out of his trancelike state. "Yeah," he said as he started moving through the crowd. "Let's get out of here."

"Are you ok? You're kinda freaking me out."

Dodge nodded, then continued pushing his way through the growing group of passengers until they reached the less crowded main aisle of the departure terminal. Still unable to shake the feeling of being watched, he glanced around the baggage carousels and the escalators for anyone paying too close attention to the pair. Or anybody that seemed out of place. He saw nothing. Chalking the feelings up to paranoia, he pointed to the exit and followed Beth through, guiding her to the left once outside and to the cruiser parked nearby. Beth slid into the passenger seat while Dodge placed the suitcase into the trunk. He still felt strange. One last scan of his surroundings before closing the trunk lid. Trust your gut, he thought. If it feels wrong, it probably is.

As Dodge got into the car, he noticed Beth was staring at him. Her eyes were narrowed and her face was void of any smile. Her expression told him she was going to ask questions he didn't want to answer. Although he wanted, needed, her help, the idea of placing his friend in the middle between him and a serial killer concerned him. He wasn't worried about jurisdictional issues. Getting the task force to grant her legal status after the fact wouldn't be too difficult. It is not uncommon for police departments to bring in outside help to solve crimes. What bothered him was Beth's safety. What if the killer's attention shifted to her? Throw in the wildcard of Blanchard, and the giant red flag with skulls and crossbones went up the pole, flapping in the wind. In the end, he trusted her as a partner and a cop. He had to. She could take care of herself.

"You need to tell me what is going on right now, Dodge," Beth said. "What have you gotten yourself into?"

Dodge started the car and backed out of the parking spot. He turned toward the exit, saying nothing until they were up to speed on the highway.

"Things have really taken a turn for the worse. I'm sorry, 1 can't ask you to help..."

Beth cut him off mid-sentence. "Are you freaking kidding me? You think 1 took time off work for a twenty-five-hundred-mile booty call?" The corners of her mouth edged. Smile lines were twisted. A frown formed. "Now tell me what the hell is going on here. And if you pull that shit again, you can take me right back to the airport Paul Dodge."

"You wouldn't get a flight back to Phoenix until tomorrow," he said. His eyes trained on the road ahead.

"I'm not messing around here, Dodge. You tell me right now what's going on. And where are you taking me?"

The fact that Beth used his full name only solidified what he already knew. Her irritation with him was growing. His mother used to do the same thing when he was in trouble as a child. Some things never change. He didn't like it as a child and the practice didn't become more amenable to him with age. There was one more thing he didn't care for as an adult. When people close to him kept things from him. Especially if the sole reason was, *for his own good*. It was time he told Beth everything. He looked over at her. Her eyes were fixated on him.

"You remember that girl we spoke to last time you were here? The one in the alley downtown?"

"Sarah? Of course, I remember her. She had real street smarts. Did something happen to her?"

Dodge turned left at the next intersection.

"We were concerned she may have unknowingly seen the killer when he murdered two people at the motel she lived in. After I interviewed her, we moved her to a safer location. A hotel in the business district. Then there was another murder last night, so I went to see her this morning. When I got to the hotel she was gone. The room was in shambles. Broken furniture and I found small amounts of blood, both inside the room and in the stairwell."

Beth's eyes widened. "Do you think it was the suspect? What are they calling him, The Savior?"

"It wasn't him," Dodge said.

"How do you know?"

"I just do."

"That's not an answer."

"It's the best I have right now."

"Well, if the killer didn't take her, who did?"

Dodge turned right at the next light. "It was Blanchard," Dodge said. "He knew where the task force stashed her and he has a badge, so the desk clerk told him what room she was in. He walked right up to her room and snatched her."

"Why would she let him into her room?"

"Why wouldn't she? The police have been nothing but helpful to her. And if he used my name, she would certainly feel safe to open the door."

"But what would he..." Beth stopped mid-sentence. Her bottom jaw dropped, and she sat there staring blankly out the front windshield. "He's going to use her, isn't he? He wants to use her to see if he can get The Savior to come to him."

Dodge nodded. "End it all right here in one final showdown."

"But why? I mean, I knew it was personal, but to put an innocent girl at risk is a different level of stupid. But how did he know The Savior would know he had the girl?"

He shook his head. "I'm not sure about that part. There must be a connection between the two of them. Something other than both men were in Vegas at the same time."

Beth's gaze turned back outside her window at the passing buildings, then back to Dodge. "What else are you not telling me?"

Mired in thought, Dodge didn't answer immediately. He didn't want to tell her about his truck and the last dead girl. And he didn't want to tell her about his plan of making himself the bait. His friend was right about one thing, making it personal was a new level of stupid.

"Dodge?" she said again.

"There was an incident the other night."

"What do you mean, incident?"

Dodge explained how the killer staged a crime scene, using his truck as a prop to get his attention. He told her about the bodies in the houses and the use of stolen license plates to throw off police if a witness from any of the crime scenes recalled the plate number and a white panel van. By the time he finished filling Beth in, they had reached his house. He pulled up to the curb and shut the engine off.

Beth reached over and placed her hand on his. "This is all a bit terrifying."

"Yeah."

"So, it's a good thing you called me." The smile returned to her face.

He returned the smile, then nodded.

Once inside the townhome, Dodge gathered two glasses from the globe-shaped bar and poured a shot of Blanton's for each of them. Then the pair began hashing out a plan. Getting Sarah back would not be easy. They were up against a seasoned cop and a methodical murderer. Dodge guessed Blanchard planned that Dodge would figure out he was the one that took Sarah, and the task force would come for him. The only play he had was to stash her someplace. Somewhere off the beaten path. A place patrol cops don't pay much attention to. An abandoned lot lined with empty warehouses, as it was described to him. A final showdown between Blanchard and his Las Vegas nemesis.

Dodge had mixed feelings about the move by the State Police Captain. He respected the guts it took to force a one-man lives, one man dies face-off. He himself had used the same strategy in the past. The difference was, he never used innocent people as bait. He was almost always the cheese on the trap. There are some lines you don't cross. To protect and to serve; try to reduce the chances of collateral damage. Rules are important.

"So, if you know where she is, why not call the task force in to take Blanchard down? Renquest and a small shoot team could handle it just fine. Toss a couple of flash-bangs in the building and breach. The whole thing would take less than thirty seconds," Beth said.

Sliding out a chair next to her at the dining room table, Dodge sat down and placed a small Smith and Wesson 9mm pistol in front of her on the table. "Your right. Renquest and a TAC team could handle Blanchard and probably even get Sarah before he kills her."

"You think Blanchard wants to hurt Sarah?"

"I don't know what he is thinking. He knew about Sarah and my concerns about her safety because I told him. I can only guess he believes she is somehow important to The Savior, whether it's as a witness or a target, I couldn't say. But what if The Savior is watching? We all go to the warehouse, and he uses the time to strike again. There is only one of me..."

"Two," Beth said, reaching for the semi-auto pistol.

Dodge smiled. "Ok, two. We can only cover so much ground and he may toss the next victim right on my front steps."

"That'll hurt the resale value."

"Probably get some new neighbors as well."

The two let out an uncomfortable laugh. After the incident with his truck the other day, the idea wasn't out of the realm of possibility. He had considered all the responses he could think this killer might use next. The idea of him dropping a strangled half naked hooker in his doorway wasn't that farfetched. After a moment, Dodge's seriousness returned.

"I say we go to the warehouse and deal with Blanchard. I'll get Renquest and all the boots he can muster to beef up patrols tonight downtown. Beat walks and structured patrols are what I am talking about. When one black and white turns a corner, another takes its place."

"That's a lot of cops and a massive amount of budget expenditure. Do you think the department will go for it? The brass love a scapegoat and it looks like Blanchard has set himself up perfectly," Beth said.

"Renquest will figure it out. He lives to screw over the seventh floor at headquarters."

Beth glanced at the clock on her phone. It showed 3:30 pm. "When do you think this should all go down?"

"I say we hit the warehouse before dusk. There will be fewer prying eyes looming."

"Do you think he will keep Sarah alive until then?" Beth asked.

Dodge shrugged. "My best guess is, he will. He did his little hotel snatch and grab early this morning so he could take her there under the cover of darkness. I can't imagine he would risk doing anything until nightfall. If anyone were to call in a tip about something wrong in the warehouse district, Staties would swarm the place. They have a history there. It would all be over in minutes. He wants The Savior. And this may be his best and last chance."

"You better call your detective friend and let him know what's going on."

Renquest was not happy when Dodge filled him in on the plan to use Beth as his backup at the warehouse. "Jesus Christ, Dodge. How many times do I have to save your ass before you trust me?"

"This isn't about trust. You know damn well I would go to war with you. But this time, I need you to get as many cops as you can and canvas the downtown area. This whole thing could be one big distraction meant to catch us off guard," Dodge said.

Beth shook her head. Dodge lowered the phone from his ear and said, "Not you, of course." She punched him in the arm. Hard.

"If it is a con, it means our Captain Blanchard is in cahoots with this nut job," Renquest said.

"It would leave me to believe one hand is washing the other, for sure. But we won't know anything until I get Blanchard into custody."

"I don't like it when people blow into my town and cause trouble. And I don't like it when they murder my people. Hookers or otherwise," Renquest said.

Dodge liked it when his partner got angry. It made him give in to his irrational side. Act with a little more emotion. The heavy-set detective had been on the job for the better part of two decades and had seen a lot of blood and guts. He could shoot a suspect with his duty weapon in his right hand while eating a hotdog with his left. Even the soupy body in the bathtub didn't seem to bother him. Dodge shuddered as the thoughts of putrid water and maggots rushed back into his head. Secretly, he wished he were capable of the emotionless statue-like façade his partner put forward. He also dreaded ending up that way.

"You will only be about ten minutes away. If I need you or think it may be a trap, I'll call you. You can rush down and save the day. Hell, I'll even let you do the media interviews."

"Screw that. You can deal with the media, good or bad. Just refer to me as the Hero Detective, or some corny shit like that," Renquest said., chuckling at his own joke.

"I got a few names for ya."

"Amazing, dapper, sexy..."

"For God's sake, man. You're going to make me throw up again," Dodge said. "Seriously though, I will call you at about eight tonight. I plan to hit the warehouse a half hour after you begin your patrols. If you see any white van, run the plates. If the registration comes back to another vehicle, grab the driver, and call me."

"Will do partner," Renquest said. "Dodge, you be careful out there. Blanchard put himself in a tight spot by taking this girl. He may not be happy to see you."

Dodge nodded, even though his partner couldn't see him, then disconnected the call.

Next, Dodge disappeared into the bedroom for a minute and returned with two plastic cases and a small metal box. He handed one case to Beth and placed the other on the table in front of his chair. The metal box contained six extra magazines for a Smith & Wesson 9 mm and four for his Glock. He placed the empty magazines and several boxes of ammunition from the box on the table.

Beth didn't speak. She opened the plastic case, which contained a series of short aluminum rods, small wire brushes, little pieces of cotton cloth, and a bottle of gun oil. Then began disassembling her weapon, laying the parts on the table in an orderly fashion, so that when finished, they resembled the shape of the gun.

Dodge smiled. He liked this woman.

CHAPTER 20

THE SKY SHIMMERED shades of orange and red as the sun headed for the horizon. The man looked at his watch—he hadn't carried a cell phone in years. Not since he found his calling in life. Those little computers are easy to trace. Since the events of September 11, all manufactured cell phones sold in the US had GPS built in to make it easier for the government to track its citizens. Even if you turned the phone off, the device continued to ping towers, just not as frequently as a phone that is powered on. There was no escaping the government if you owned one of those devices. Use the internet on one of those phones and the big tech companies would sell your information to the highest bidder. All too often that was the government or proxies of big brother. The thought of people knowing things about him, intimate details about his routine, enraged him.

He took a deep breath. *Expel the distractions*, he thought. It was going to be an important night. The State Police Captain was going to pay for meddling in his work. He didn't mind the chase. They both had a job to do, just like back in Vegas. But intentionally interfering with whom he chooses as his next saved soul, was something he wouldn't tolerate.

The Captain had been good. The two had almost met once in Vegas. Then he left and disappeared, and everything changed. It wasn't the same when he didn't have a cat to chase his mouse. When he found him again, working on the other side of the country, it was like fate had intervened. His cat was back, and things were good for a bit. But the Captain broke the rules. He was supposed to do things the right way. His mind wandered to the new guy that showed up at the third crime scene—the one they called Dodge. He was a rules guy. Someone who would play the game right.

New stolen plates hung from the bumper of his van. This time, the plates came from a neighborhood next to the one he had been pilfering from. He needed to make the change. The cops had figured out his plan quicker than expected. He was sure he could get another month or two out of the houses around where he set up his workshop. The streets were littered with transient renters, invalids, and drug users who never left their houses and kept the curtains pulled tight—that neighborhood should have paid off for months. But the new cop was an X-factor he hadn't counted on, ruining the hunting grounds before he had been able to finish his work.

The new cop was clearly smarter than the rest, *but not smarter than me*, he thought. He watched the warehouse from inside his van concealed inside one of the abandoned buildings, its bumper nestled up to an exterior wall with a row of small windows. Dirt and grime caked the glass and made it difficult to see, but he guessed a freshly cleaned window in this area would draw more attention than a random van parked in a building. His eyes strained to make out shapes through the filthy glass as he concentrated on keeping count of the people going in and out.

He watched as three people had entered the building over the past several hours, including a skinny man with ratty shoulder-length brown hair and a large hoop of keys swinging from his belt. The man wore tattered clothes about five sizes too big for his frame. His best guess was the frumpy man was the manager of the storage company. Who else would saunter around with five pounds of metal keys, jangling and clapping with each step, tugging on their belt line? With the baggy clothes and greasy hair, he looked like someone who exchanged meth balls for rent payments. Who would place this man in charge of anything?

He focused on the front door, waiting for the manager and the others who ventured into the warehouse to come back out and leave with their poison. After a few minutes, a man and woman exited, and stopped to look around before dividing up whatever they must have just purchased or bartered for. He couldn't see what the couple was passing between each other. And it really wouldn't have mattered if he had been able to make what they carried. He didn't know the first thing about drugs. He had never used illegal substances. He saw how crack and meth and even marijuana took hold of people's minds. Turning normal men and women into sheep. Controlling their every thought, mood, and action. He personally knew of straight men that traded blow jobs for one needle of heroin. If a drug could make a straight man perform sexual acts on another man just for the fix, then that was something he wanted no part of. He shuddered at the thought of being under something with that amount of control over a person's thoughts and actions.

The drug couple turned left and walked down the street. He watched as long as he could before they disappeared from sight into one of the other rusting empty buildings. He returned his attention to the front door of the building housing the storage units. The manager had still not returned. Anxiety began to creep in. He couldn't make a move until the captain and the girl were alone. The plan only accounted for one person to die to get to the girl. The police captain. The manager was a different story. He was an innocent. And he couldn't dispatch an innocent. Sure, he had killed innocents before, but only when the ends justified the means. Like that disgusting motel manager who interfered with his work. That was easily justifiable. And he didn't want to lie to himself—it was fun slitting that pig's throat. It was so freeing. He didn't even remember plunging the knife into his body over and over. As the thought of the motel manager flashed through his mind, the odor from the fat man's sweat crept into his senses, forcing him to fight back the urge to vomit. He wasn't an innocent and deserved what he got. But he knew nothing about the building manager.

As the daylight faded, the lights from the radio's digital clock cast an eerie glow upon his face. Highlighting his prominent nose and chin while forcing shadows to occupy the space around his eyes. He looked in the mirror and was reminded of an old black and white horror movie he saw as a child, where a man waited, lurking in the shadows for his prey. The man's eyes almost glowing in the dark recesses of his face. Just enough light bouncing off his features to show the moviegoers the outline of a face. But those eyes had haunted him ever since. He grabbed a roll of duct tape he kept in a bin next to the driver's seat. Tore off a section and covered the face of the radio. Then he looked at his reflection in the mirror before turning his attention back to the building across the street.

It had been an hour since the manager entered. His impatience grew with every tick of the clock. Every second that passed caused a rush of anxiety that made his head hurt and muscles ache. It was as if the muscles in his body were working collectively. Trying to force him to climb from the van and rush into the building. He dedicated every ounce of energy to fighting the urge. But he weakened. Not sure how much longer it would be before the monster inside gained control. It happened for the first time at the motel, and he could feel it clawing at his insides, ripping, and tearing through the wall of his soul. The anxiety was too much to contain. It was time. He needed to move before darkness took over.

Mud squished under the soles of his boots, and he soon had a thick layer caked to his feet, He stopped, stamping his feet to loosen the wet clay from his boots twice before making it across the alley that separated the buildings. Looking back, he noticed the indentations he left in the soft, wet clay. Not the best idea to leave a trail back to his van. Once finished inside, he would have to double back. He could drive his van over the footprints, using his tires to crush any evidence left behind. He smiled at his own genius.

The building's interior was dark. Much darker than he had imagined. He needed shadows to hide in, but darkness bothered him more than it should have. It was a weakness and weakness ate at people little by little, until there was no strength left and they became a quivering mass of Jell-O, mired in their own fear. Unable to think. Too scared to venture out of their own homes. There was a time when he swore it would never happen to him, but he could sense the weaknesses inside him growing, trying to take over. The more he pushed back against the fear, the more it swelled inside him, making it harder to concentrate on his work. Even the monster in him couldn't quell the growing irrational phobia. That's why he was here, in this town, in this building, to finish it.

Two offices sat directly inside the entrance and looked unused. Each one contained a few old filing cabinets and large wooden shelves lined the outside walls. The manager didn't look like the sort of person who would use a traditional office for keeping track of rentals and income and expenditures. The building appeared to have been retrofitted for many purposes over the years. Once he passed the first two rooms, lights sporadically lit the halls and side rooms. Some flickering, their florescent bulbs emitting a low hum. Other fixtures hung from the walls and ceilings by the very wires meant to bring the power of light. His attention wandered as he tried to spot a pattern. Many stores at night only turn on every other row of lights to try and save on electricity and lower expenses. There appeared to be no organized effort to maintain a lighting sequence. Many of the bulbs' ends had blackened—a sign of bad ballasts. He imagined no one cared enough to change the fixtures or bulbs as they stopped working. Again, a sign no one used this area of the warehouse.

He crept through the hallway, stopping only to orient himself and to listen for the voices or sounds of people moving about. Caution would keep him from being surprised. He heard none. In front of him to the left, a stairway ascended providing access to a series of catwalks suspended high above the main warehouse floor, appearing to run the length of the building. His face wrinkled as a smile formed. A perfect place to lurk in the shadows and out of sight. The higher vantage point provided an unobstructed view of the two entrances to the complex. If the police approached, he would know.

The stairs were solid, but an overabundance of caution forced him to tread the edge of the steps, the part closest to the steel support stringers, to reduce metal flex and squeaking beneath his feet. He slid his hand up the railing as he ascended to lessen his weight's effects on the steps. Once at the top, the warehouse sprawled in front of him. Lights hung from electrical conduit over the floor beneath him, obscuring anyone's vision attempting to look up. *Perfect*, he thought.

As his eyes took in the sheer size of the surrounding space, he kneeled, took a deep breath, holding the air in his lungs, listening for any sounds of life. At first, there was only silence. Broken only by the sound of pigeons in the rafters above. He slowly allowed the oxygen to escape his lungs. He took in another deep draw of the cool musty air and held it. Then, in the distance from behind, he heard shouting. He was too far away to make out what was being said, but he was sure there were two people involved.

Knees cracking as he stood, he made his way across the metal span walkways, turning left at the first intersection, toward the direction of the voices. His feet moved faster than he wanted, a result of adrenaline flushing through his veins, making it difficult to control his pace. But even at this quicker pace, his movement was fluid and efficient. Each step was engrained with purpose. His ears scanned for subtle noises and his eyes scanned the floor for his targets. Then he stopped. His body, motionless, as he glared at the two people on the ground below him. Only one person was lying on the floor. Dead. Or at least dying.

Traffic was light for a Thursday afternoon. Dodge didn't find it necessary to use his lights and siren to help him maneuver through normally busy intersections on the way to the warehouse district. Beth sat beside him. She had removed the magazine from her weapon.

"You know, the experts say you shouldn't load your magazines all the way. You should stop one round shy of full," Dodge said. "They say it damages the spring inside."

"Yeah, well, the experts all work in offices in an office building somewhere. Security manning the entrances with armed drivers to take them for their morning cup of coffee."

Dodge nodded.

"Besides, I never want to be one bullet short in a shootout. That seems like poor planning to me and completely avoidable," Beth said as she jammed one more shell into the magazine and slid it back into the receiver until a clicking noise emanated from the S&W semi-auto. Then she slipped the weapon back into the holster on her right hip.

"I'll double check mine before we make entry," he said and smiled.

The sun had fallen below the rooftops, and streetlights took over where the sun's rays had once ruled by the time the pair arrived at the sprawling warehouse complex. Paved roads turned to a mixture of gravel and mud. Dodge could hear the rocks and clay grind under the weight of the cruiser's tires. He pulled over; parking between two of the rusted metal framed buildings. The engine cut off. And they sat silent, taking in their surroundings. He then slid this finger down the right side of his weapon and felt the little tab sticking out from the slide. A neat little way to check if a Glock has a round in the chamber without removing the weapon from the holster. If the chamber was empty, the tab would be flush with the frame. He took the keys from the ignition and dropped them on the floorboard.

Beth broke the silence. "Do you know which one Blanchard has the girl in?"

"I vote for the spooky one."

His attempt at humor seemed to cut some of the tension, which hung heavy in the air. The pair laughed for a moment, then looked at each other.

"You ready for this?" Dodge asked.

"I never liked the son-of-a-bitch, anyway. Smug little prick. You ever notice he wears sneakers all the time? Who the hell wears sneakers with a suit?"

Dodge said nothing.

"Don't worry, I'm ready. This is the thing I do well."

As a badge, he was fine with what was about to happen. As a man who cared about the woman sitting next to him, he worried about her safety. Trusting her was not the problem. The skill set she brought to any fight was as good as any partner he had ever had, including Renquest. This was about him, and a deep-rooted chauvinistic attitude pounded into him by his father and then the military. Men must protect women. It was their primary job in life. It was all macho bullshit, and he fought to destroy this demon inside of him every day. Sometimes he won. Sometimes he didn't. Today would be a win, he decided.

He leaned across the seat to kiss Beth. Bits of glass and vinyl sprayed onto the front seat, peppering him in the face and arms as the windshield exploded. Instinctively, the veteran agent threw his arms around his partner and pulled them both down to the floorboard, between the seat and the dash.

Adrenaline pumped through his veins as he focused on where the shot might have come from. What did he know? He rolled his head toward the back of the car. The rear window was still intact. A shot from straight on should have continued its trajectory, and passed through the back glass, which it didn't. This meant the shooter was positioned much higher than the vehicle, forcing a downward line of sight.

This revelation carried both good and bad news. He now knew where the shot came from. The road they sat on ended in a T-intersection bounded by another warehouse building roughly twenty yards directly in front of their position. The bad news was their position kept them in the line of fire.

It was just then—he realized he was still on top of Beth. She was struggling and cussing at him to get off. He rolled over toward the back of the seat and pushed her to the dash, where there was more plastic and metal to absorb any impact from another round.

"Are you hit?" Dodge asked.

"No, I don't think so. How would I know? I've never been shot before."

Dodge laughed and said, "You would know."

"Where the hell did that shot come from?" she asked, her voice rattled and shaken.

"Second story of a building about fifty yards straight away."

"Are they still there?"

"I don't know. Wanna stick your head up and check?"

"Not really," Beth said, driving an elbow into his gut. "But we can't just stay here either. We are sitting ducks."

Dodge knew she was right. His eyes scanned the car for anything they could use as a diversion or protection. Another shot rang out. The bullet rang through the steel plating of the hood.

"That was too close," Beth said.

"Yeah, the next one might make it through the dash. We need to get the hell out of here. Now!"

With the door handle to the passenger side in his left hand, and his left leg pulled tight against his body, the 220-pound agent released a monstrous kick. Glass shattered under the force of the heel of his boot as it smashed into the center of the driver's door. Simultaneously, his left hand pulled the latch to the passenger's door. He pushed Beth out, crawling closely behind her, landing on the damp, muddy ground. The pair crawled around to the back of the car, hunching down behind the rear bumper.

"What do we know?" an anxious and out-of-breath Dodge said.

Beth's head twisted, looking for anywhere else to be. "There!" she yelled, pointing at an open door in an adjacent building.

Dodge turned and saw the door. It was a more than twenty-five feet away. On the other side of the alley. "Shit."

"We can't stay here."

The desperation in his partner's voice was clear. And he agreed.

"A cigarette would be good right about now. I always think better with a smoke."

Beth said nothing, leering at him.

Potential scenarios ran through his head. It was at least twenty-five feet across open ground to the door. The first person might make it, but the second one to try would be a sitting duck. What they needed was a distraction.

Mud clung to his hands. He wiped his palms on his pants leg and felt a bulge in his pocket. It was the key fob for his truck. That gave him an idea. He crawled on his stomach to the open passenger door. Sliding into the car's floorboard, he stretched his arms out, grabbed the keys and turned the ignition to the ON position. Then he reached under the steering column and turned on the headlights and pulled the lever to engage the headlight's bright setting. He pushed the button on the dash, turning on the red flashers installed in the front grill of the vehicle. As he climbed back out of the passenger side using the metal door for concealment, he opened the glove box and pushed the trunk release button before returning to the rear of the car and Beth.

"Good distraction. It will probably draw some attention too," she said.

"It'll sure as hell make it harder to see us."

Beth nodded. "Ok, then. What's next?"

His right-hand rooting around in the now open trunk, he used his left hand and pointed at the open door. "You're going to go for that door?"

Beth's head swung to the door across the alley. "Ok." Her eyes turned back to Dodge. "I didn't come all the way here to take one for the team. I'll make it. What're you going to do?"

With a road flare from the vehicle emergency kit in his left hand, and a can of commercial tire sealant in his right, he said, "Make sure you get there."

He used his knife to cut the release valve from the clear plastic hose protruding from the top of the aerosol can. Then jammed the end of the hose under the back of the cruiser, between the rear tire and the gas tank. The flare sparked to life when he slammed the butt end of the long red cylindrical tube against the ground. The top burned deep red. Dodge raised is off hand to shield his eyes from the chemical flame.

"When I say run, you run like hell. Don't wait for me, just get to that door."

"I'm not leaving you here to take a bullet. You can cram that idea right—"

Another shot rang out. The round ricocheted off the ground between the cruiser and the building, throwing dirt and debris into the air.

"Damn it, Beth. I need you to listen to me. Can you do that?"

"I don't..."

"Yes or no!"

She paused before answering, staring into his eyes. Finally, she said, "Yes."

"Good. When you get inside the building, head straight for the far wall. Wait exactly two minutes, then make for the end of the building, toward the shooter's position. Find the door on that side and try to make your way to the front of the building at the end of the street. If you hug the wall, you'll be below him and he shouldn't be able to get a bead on you."

"Where will you be?"

"After I light this thing up, I'll be in the building next to us here," he said, nodding at the wall next to them. "Once inside, I'm going to make my way to the shooter's nest. He can't track both of us, and my guess is, if it is Blanchard, he will focus on me."

As he returned his attention to Beth, he noticed she was glaring at him. "It's not that. I qualified a few days ago for the troopers so I could carry a statie badge. He's seen me shoot, so I'm the obvious threat here."

Beth turned away, pulling her weapon from the holster. She took in a deep breath. Dropped as low as she could to the ground without lying flat on the ground. Readied and waited for Dodge's command.

With his duty weapon in one hand and the lit flare in the other, he sprang up from behind the trunk of the cruiser, flailing the hand with the flare in the air above his head as he moved away from Beth. Then he fired two rounds at the building across the street.

"RUN!", he yelled.

Beth shot to her feet. The Smith & Wesson pointed in the direction from where the shots came. Dodge watched her as she sprinted across the muddy alley. Her ponytail rocked from side to side with every stride. Twenty feet away. He put two more rounds into the windows lining the top of the wall, directly below the roofline. The building was too far away to see if any windows were open, or busted out, providing a good shooting platform. His eyes darted back to the alley. Beth was still running. Ten feet to go. With all the might he could muster, he dove back towards the rear of the police cruiser. His left-hand thrusting under the rear bumper of the car, jabbing the shaft of the half-burned flare into the tire sealant, which by that time had expanded and coalesced into a sort of super glue. The flare's flaming end pointed directly at the rubber tube that carried the fuel from the gas-filling spout to the tank. Dodge knew the tank contained only half its capacity, creating plenty of room for fumes.

People think it's the liquid gas that explodes. It's not. It's the fumes. Fumes are always more flammable than the liquid it emanates from. He once attended a training in the Air Force, where a fireman tossed a lit cigarette into a five-gallon bucket of gasoline. Twenty-two Special Security Officers scattered to the wind. Some dived onto the concrete runway and others ran for the safety of the hangers. The fire marshal never moved. "It's the fumes that get you," he said, after busting out in a laugh heard all the way across the tarmac. Dodge always remembered that day. He reminded the new recruits at the corrections academy to be aware of surrounding smells before discharging a firearm. The clue was right there in the name. *Fire*arm.

The smell of the flare's flame burning through the rubber hose filled his nose. Thick black smoke poured out from under the driver's side wheel well. It was time to get out of there.

Dodge sprang to his feet, pointing his weapon over his shoulder and firing three rounds. He glanced to his right and saw Beth leap through the open door and into the building across the street. His head tucked down into his chest, creating a smaller target as he ran for the only door he could see leading out of the line of fire. It was closed. Stopping to open the door would leave him vulnerable, so he veered to his right, creating a more direct angle of attack. The last thing he needed was to bounce off the door frame and knock himself out.

His feet pounded against the damp ground, gaining speed as he closed the gap. The 220-pound agent lowered his shoulder at five feet. About one second before making contact, he pushed off his right foot, aiming at the weakest point on the door, the door latch side. His shoulder hit first. Directly above the door handle. The door frame splintered into a thousand smaller shards of itself. The latch assembly, along with the door handle, shot across the empty warehouse floor, bouncing and sliding until coming to rest twenty feet inside the building.

Dodge was thrown off balance by the impact. He tumbled to the cold hard floor, following nearly the same path as the door handle moments before. Arms and legs flailed in the air as he spun and rolled, eventually winding up on his back. His feet pointed toward the now open door. Through the windows at the top of the wall, he could see flames and smoke rising into the air. The car hadn't exploded as he hoped it might. But it didn't matter. Fire and rescue would be on the way soon. Police would follow shortly after. Though he knew the response time would be a bit slower based on the location. He needed to get out and to the building at the end of the street.

As he reached into his pocket, he began to worry his phone might have been damaged in the collision and ensuing floor routine. He stared intently as the device slid from his pants—his fingers rubbing the face, feeling for cracks or chips in the glass. His thumb depressed a button and the face lit up. The agent let out a sigh of relief and his fingers tapped a message out to Beth.

Are you ok?

I'm good. Where are you?

His fingers slid across the keyboard.

I'm in the building across the road. Make your way to the far end and wait for my signal before entering.

kk.

His phone was secured in his pocket; Dodge pulled himself off the ground. As he righted himself, he knocked the dirt from his pants and shirt. A plume of dust surrounded him making him sneeze. Instinctively, his head spun to see if anyone had seen or was in earshot to hear it, even though he knew he was alone. Then he sprinted for the end of the darkened warehouse. Once at the wall, he looked for a door. There was only one. Positioned in the middle, facing the building the shots were fired from. The hinges squeaked as the rusted metal scraped and clawed against years of weather and age. Looking up, there was no view past the overhang of the roof. Anyone using the roof for a shooter's perch wouldn't have an angle for a clear shot down at the alley. The threat now was when he and Beth entered the rusty structure if the shooter had repositioned on the ground floor. Waiting. Lying in ambush for the pair to burst through the front door. That was always the trouble with entries when the bad guy knew you were coming. The exact reason why Dodge sent Beth to make entry at the opposite end. A single shooter could only cover one door at a time. A flip of the coin on which door the shooter guarded. When in doubt, follow the rules—only worry about what you can control and focus on the mission.

Dodge peeked around the corner. A quick glance left, then right. One more up toward the roofline. He saw nothing. A deep breath and he glanced at his watch. Time was running out. Once in the alley, he immediately veered left. He could see Beth exiting her building and heading for her door, in the same spot as his, on opposite ends of the warehouse. Exactly what he had hoped for. It took him four strides to cross the alley, spinning a hundred and eighty degrees on his last step, ending with his back pressed tight against the wall. The door on his right. Again, he glanced in Beth's direction. She mimicked his every move. Only it took her about seven steps to cross the alley. Shorter legs mean more steps. A two-to-one ratio. A simple math equation concerning height and distance. But, because his partner was quicker than him, she covered the same distance in a shorter amount of time. Speed was the X-factor.

After a deep breath and the two were in place, Dodge gave the signal. The pair rushed through each door, into the unknown.

CHAPTER 21

AT THE EXACT MOMENT Dodge and Beth made entry into the warehouse, Renquest sat in a patrol car downtown with a rookie street cop named Boynton. Boynton was a corporal, only a year into his tour. Promoted right out of the academy for graduating first in his class and showing exceptional leadership skills during the twenty-six weeklong police academy. One reward for finishing at the top of your class was getting a choice of what unit you wanted to join. Availability and scheduling needs are taken into consideration, but the top recruit usually gets their pick. The practice is both an incentive and reward meant to push the best to be their best. Normally, it could take an officer ten-plus years to get assigned to a task force And even then, they had to interview against a hundred other cops vying for the same position. Boynton was tops in his class, not hesitating for a second when asked where he wanted to be assigned.

"The Sex Crimes Task Force," he told the academy commandant during the graduation ceremony.

Renquest noticed early on the young officer seemed to have a knack for the work. Add to that, his hesitancy to engage in idle chit-chat while on a stakeout, along with his willingness to follow orders, made him an instant favorite of Renquest for long nights of sitting side by side in the front seat of a police car.

The team had been working the downtown area for two hours. There had been no reports of any creepers hanging around and officers reported no white panel vans carousing the area. To this point, the entire evening had been a waste of money and resources.

"l hope Dodge is faring better than this shit show," Renquest said to his partner for the night.

"Detective," Boynton said, in between sips of an energy drink. "What's up with Agent Dodge?"

"What do you mean?"

The young cop bit at his bottom lip. "I mean, he always seems to find the action. First it was that parolee, Heller, I think his name was. Then there was that business down in Colombia."

"How do you know about Colombia?" The detective watched as Boynton shifted weight from one side of his butt to the other, expelling nervous energy.

"I hear guys at the station talk. Some say he killed a CIA agent in South America. I don't know if I believe that, but he has shot more people than anyone else I know on the force."

Renquest said nothing, hoping the conversation would end. But his rookie partner was unusually talkative tonight.

"You've known him longer than anybody, detective. That's all I'm sayin."

"That's probably true. When I found him in that house, the one Heller had kept that poor girl chained up in for weeks, the place looked like someone butchered a hog inside. There was blood everywhere. Dodge took a knife to the gut, a real nasty wound. Yet he managed to make his way to that room and found the girl." Renquest took a sip of coffee from the foam cup he had been nursing for an hour. "Even a knife thrust into his innards couldn't stop him. A few hours after being stitched up, that crazy bastard checked himself out of the hospital and, and like a bloodhound, he wouldn't stop until he found his prey. I don't know many people like that. Do you?"

The rookie cop shrugged. "No."

"Exactly. I would follow Paul Dodge into the fires of hell if he asked me to come along for the ride." Renquest took one last sip from his coffee and tossed the empty cup into the back seat.

"You want me to get you another cup?"

The detective shook his head. "No. I'll already have to piss every fifteen minutes."

Boynton sighed. "So, we just wait?"

Request's watch showed it was nearly a quarter after nine. If he was being honest with himself, he was tired of waiting around for something to come across the radio. Eyes and boots on the street are what he wanted. He looked at his watch again, as if time would somehow defy the laws of physics and leap forward to a more desirable place.

"You want to take a walk? Maybe see some things for ourselves?" Boynton suggested.

"What the hell. I gotta take a leak anyway," Renquest said.

They parked their cruiser where South First Street converges into downtown. The two men stepped out of the car and made their way to the center of Hooker's Row, a name many of the old heads on the force used when referring to the blocks the prostitutes used for business. He never cared for the name. It made everything sound so dirty. He found no pleasure in demeaning people that had already experienced a bad run-in life. Who'd that benefit? His eyes scanned the streets and sidewalks as men came and went. Cars of all different makes and models slowed, cruising the merchandise. Black high-end Mercedes and rusted out heaps. Twenty-dollar blowjobs were a currency for all socioeconomic backgrounds apparently.

"What time is it?"

"Sir, you have a watch."

"I'm aware. Just tell me what time it is," Renquest snapped.

The young cop pulled his phone out of his pocket and said, "Nine twenty-five, detective."

"How many units you see drive by since we've been standing here?"

"The whole time? Including while we were in the car?"

"No. Just since we have been standing here, on this corner."

"None, detective."

"How many beat cops do you see right now?"

Looking right, past Renquest and then left, the rookie cop said, "One, sir."

"Exactly," the stout detective said, as he glanced up and down the sidewalk and at the corner across the road. "Where is everyone? I could have sworn I said to blanket the area with black and whites. Does this look like blanketing to you?"

"No, detective," Boynton said.

"Get on the radio and locate Sergeant Hopkins. Tell him I want his fat butt standing in front of me in two minutes."

The corporal reached to his belt and turned a knob on the top of the radio, making a clicking noise. The detective's head spun toward the sound. He had been a cop long enough to know the sound of a radio being turned on.

"Was your damn radio off this whole time?"

Boynton stuttered, "I must have clicked it off in the car."

"Why in the hell would you shut your radio off?"

"My earbud doesn't work, sir. And this mic blasts calls right next to my ear," he said, pointing to the handset attached to his left shoulder. "I can't hear a thing with this thing going off all night. I turned it down and must have turned it too far."

"Turn it back on. Would you please?"

As the embarrassed officer turned the volume knob, the radio waves filled with chatter from police and fire units. A dispatcher was liaising between police and fire units heading to a vehicle fire in the warehouse district.

"Isn't that where Agent Dodge is?" the Boynton asked.

"God damnit. This whole thing was his idea and now I'm stuck down here babysitting a greenhorn who can't work a freaking radio."

The radio blunder was a major misstep for the aspiring rookie, but he quickly returned to form and showed why he graduated first in his class. Good instincts and just the right amount of butt kissing. "They will need a command presence who knows the case, sir."

Renquest said nothing, just turned and the pair hustled back toward the cruiser. Boynton two steps behind. Once in the vehicle, he hit the emergency lights. The cruiser's tires squawked on the pavement as they broke free under the powerful engine's torque. The rapid acceleration pushed both men back into their seats.

"Take it easy. No need to kill us on the way," Renquest belted out.

"Sorry, detective. I just thought you would want to get there as quickly as possible."

"Every cop and fire rescue unit are on the way, so no need to endanger anyone else's lives."

The car slowed as Boynton eased off the accelerator. Renquest nodded. The incident with the radio aside, Boynton took orders without question. He still liked the kid.

He'll be a good cop one day, he thought.

CHAPTER 22

AS SOON AS THE DOOR CLOSED behind him, Dodge realized his tactical error. The other buildings had been wide open. An endless cavern from one end to the other. Straight shooting lines. Good for seeing someone coming. This building's layout was different. Altered to fit its occupant's needs. Businesses needed offices. And that is what he encountered as soon as he made it inside the main entrance. Desks pushed neatly against the wall. Old metal file cabinets and chairs stacked in the center. While the offices may have once bustled with staff—computer keyboards clicking and phones ringing, it was clear the spaces hadn't been used in some time. A thick layer of dust blanketed everything. Undisturbed for years.

His mind wandered to his partner. Had she encountered offices? Or did her door open onto the main floor? Dodge imagined the building must have had a separate employee's entrance. It seemed impractical for all the warehouse employees to travel through the maze of offices to get to the floor. Then, another question popped into his head. If her door opened onto the warehouse floor, would she find Blanchard before him? Would he remember her? His grip on the Glock tightened. He moved quickly through the first office. Scanning from left to right. The room was dark, the only light coming from a small window set in the door he presumed led deeper into the building.

The handle on the steel door turned silently. Unused door handles squeak and clank when turned. This one was smooth and quiet. Dodge eased the door open and slid through the space stepping into a hallway beyond. Each side of the wall was lined with windows. Behind the glass were more empty offices. The rooms were pitch black. A thick layer of dust had settled on the ledges and the glass was hazy with grime. These spaces hadn't been used in the past decade. Still, he checked every door to be sure no one was lying in wait to put a bullet in his head as he passed, or worse, a knife in his back. Once at the end of the hall he faced the last door and a set of stairs leading up.

Squinting, he tried to see up the stairs into the black void, but the light hanging from the ceiling of the hallway blinded him. His left hand felt for the small flashlight he normally carried on his belt but came up empty.

"Shit."

As his front foot eased onto the first step, his Glock rose to eye level. Front sight in a fight. At this close distance, gaining a sight picture and aligning the little white dot on the front sight between the little white dots positioned on the rear sight wasn't necessary. There wouldn't be enough time. All you could do was place the front site on the target and squeeze the trigger.

He paused as he neared the top of the staircase. One more step would expose his head. The one place you try to avoid a bullet hitting. One shot to the noggin and its lights out. The big sleep, or worse, living the rest of your life breathing through a tube, having underpaid, begrudged nurses' aides wipe drool from your chin and change your colostomy bag.

Not today, he thought as his right foot moved back and down one step—his head centered slightly to the side so he could watch the door below him for anyone trying to sneak up on his six.

An industrial-style light hung by a chain with an electrical cord wrapped intermittently around and through the links, fifteen or twenty feet above his head to the base of the light a few feet below him. After switching his Glock to his left hand, he stretched out to reach the chain supporting the light. As he leaned into the railing, the L-shaped metal bar digging into his side, a sharp pain shot through his abdomen. He winced. The railing pressed directly upon the scar left from a knife wound while working a case early in his career.

His fingertips brushed the chain as he tried to tap it to force it to bounce into his outstretched hand. The effort was having little effect. The chain was too far away. Or his arms were too short. He leaned back, relieving the pressure from his abdomen. What he needed was something he could use to hook the chain and pull it to him instead. A quick scan of the floor below only confirmed what he knew to be true. He had seen nothing in the hall on his way in that would be helpful. His hands felt around the duty belt strapped to his waist. The only thing he had on him was his weapon. Using a firearm for anything other than its intended purpose broke every safety rule in the book. There were always stories of people getting shot with their own weapons by using the butt end of the grip as a hammer to break a lock on a door or the barrel as a makeshift pry bar. Dodge taught this exact lesson in the academy to new recruits. He even showed graphic videos of officers' heads being blown apart through "accidental discharges" while instructing weapon safety courses. But he needed the light below him and as he looked around, he could see nothing else he could use to help him reach it without backtracking into one of the abandoned offices and rummaging around, looking for a broom or metal rod he could fashion into a grappling hook.

Never going back was a rule. Always advance.

The index finger on his right hand pushed the magazine release button on the frame of the Glock, ejecting it into his palm. He slid the magazine the rest of the way out and stuffed it into his back pocket, where he could reach it and jam it back into the weapon if needed. Next, he ejected the round from the chamber into the air, catching it with his left hand. He placed the round in his front pocket.

After locking the slide back and checking the loading port to ensure the weapon was safe, he gripped the weapon by the barrel and used the L-shape of the frame to hook the chain securing the light to the ceiling, pulling it toward him. Once he had the light in his hands, he secured it to the railing and removed the magazine from his back pocket, replaced the round from his front pocket, and slid it back into the receiver. He kept his hand on the rail of the weapon as it actioned and loaded a round back into the chamber to keep the noise to a minimum. A technique called riding the rail. It's frowned upon and can cause the weapon to jam when fired.

Unnecessary under usual circumstances. If a bad guy is breaking into your home, you want the intruder to hear the weapon being readied. Most people have seen it in movies or heard the sound before in real life. It serves as a warning. If people are too stupid to heed it, then a cleaning of the gene pool is the next step.

The light bulb was warm. Too hot to unscrew with bare hands. Sliding his shirt over his head—he folded it onto itself several times, forming a sort of oven mitt he could slip his hand into and twist the bulb free of its base. Once the bulb was out, he pulled his shirt back on and waited for the bulb to cool enough to handle it. The metal base cooled first. It needed about two minutes before it was warm to the touch, but not hot enough to burn the skin. He placed the bulb in the middle of the step, careful to make sure it didn't roll off. If anyone came up the stairs in the dark, they would kick the light bulb and it would crash to the ground, giving away their position.

He once again slid his weapon, from its holster. He took a deep breath. Then exhaled. Another, and then a third. His hand steadied more with each exhale. It was time. Dodge pushed off the stairs with his off hand. Launching him over the top two steps, his Glock punched out from his chest in perfect shooting form. The front sight settled on a darkened shape ten feet in front of him, crouched, but facing the opposite direction on the catwalk. His finger moved from its extended position along the frame of the weapon to the trigger, applying enough pressure to engage the trigger safety, but not starting the firing sequence. The shadow in his sights spun, facing his direction. Dodge noticed a hand raising, but he couldn't see if there was a gun in it. Then he saw the hair. It was shoulder length and extended like a rope from the back of the head. His finger was steady on the trigger.

"Beth?"

There was a moment of silence. Then, a voice came back to him.

"Dodge? Is that you?"

His muscles relaxed as he released the trigger. "How did you get up here?" he whispered.

She crept toward him until he could see her face. She had

sweat dripping from her nose and her eye makeup had streaked down her cheeks. "What the hell. You scared the crap out of me." Beth used the bottom of her untucked shirt to wipe sweat from around her eyes and mouth.

"How did you get up here?" he asked again.

She pointed behind her and told Dodge how, after entering the building, she found herself in a set of offices. It was dark and none of the offices appeared to be in use. When she got to the end of a hall, she noticed a staircase leading to a catwalk system above the main floor of the warehouse. She thought if she had the higher ground, she might spot Blanchard before he saw them.

"Besides, anyone looking up would be blinded by the lights between my position and the floor," she said.

Dodge stared at her, mesmerized by her cop-ness and good instincts. She was perfect.

"Have you seen anyone?"

"No. It was quiet. Too quiet," she said—her eyes peering into the emptiness around the pair. "Do you think he is still in here?"

"Blanchard? My guess is he is long gone. If he was the one taking shots at us, he knows the one thing that draws police to a place like this is gunfire."

He could now hear sirens wailing in the distance.

"Or a car on fire," she said

Dodge had completely forgotten about the cruiser he set on fire as a distraction to give them to escape, and he laughed.

"I don't imagine your boss will think a burned-up squad car is hilarious," Beth said.

"No, he won't." The smile still spread across his face. He couldn't help but find humor in the situation, knowing he might be the only person who did. Then he turned back toward the staircase. "Let's get down to the floor and see if we can find Sarah."

"Do you think she is still here? And why would Blanchard shoot at us?"

His right hand combed through his short hair. "I don't think he was the shooter."

Dodge moved down the stairs, careful not to step on the

lightbulb he placed there earlier as a booby trap, and through the door to the warehouse floor—Beth tight on his heels. Both holding their weapons at the ready position, out front, elbows slightly bent, and the muzzles angled down.

It didn't take long to find something. For lying on the floor in front of a rusted steel shipping container, its doors secured with a padlock, was Blanchard. The front of his shirt was stained red and his body lay in a pool of dark, almost black liquid. The dark blood was a sign of a liver laceration. He bled out in a matter of minutes.

"Shit," Dodge said. "How the hell are we going to find Sarah now? He was the only one that knew where she was."

"Not the only one," Beth said, staring at all the steel containers around them.

Dodge knew what she was thinking. The person who killed Captain Blanchard also knew where to find Sarah.

"I need to get Renquest out here and some dogs," he said, reaching into his pocket and pulling out his phone.

The sound of sirens grew louder until they could see the reflections from the flashing lights coming through the windows lining the top of the walls. After Fire and Rescue showed up to deal with the burning squad car, Renquest arrived on scene. He had a young corporal in tow. The detective stood over the captain's body, silent, only a shake of his head to show his displeasure.

"Well, isn't this an immense pile of shit?"

Dodge said nothing. There was nothing to say. Blanchard had strayed outside the lines. He took an innocent girl hostage and tried to use her as bait, and it ultimately cost him his life. But he was still a cop. And no one took a cop's death more seriously than other cops. Even if the officer might have deserved it. The badge meant something. It was a symbol of a bond civilians couldn't understand. A collective of men and women with shared experiences. Death always hovered around the corner, ready to strike. It is one reason a good deal of ex-military types joined the force. It was a way to keep a bond forged through combat.

Renquest gazed around the room at the hundreds of steel containers. "Any idea where the girl is?"

Dodge shook his head. "I suppose we should get the bolt

cutters in here and start going through these containers. At least the ones close to the body."

"I'll get working on the search warrant application," Renquest said.

"No need. Who is going to complain down here? People use this place because they don't want the police to know what they are keeping hidden away. Just open the containers and if you don't find the girl, close it back up. You can start with this one," Dodge said, pointing to the container closest to the dead cop's body.

Renquest nodded at the young corporal, who appeared to be champing at the bit to do some actual police work. Or maybe he wanted to find out what was inside that container. All new cops wonder what it is like to shoot someone for the first time. And all new cops wonder what it will be like when they find their first dead body. Dodge remembered both, because for him, it was the same person. The first time he fired his weapon on duty, the round found its mark and tore through the man's chest. He died slowly, painfully, as Dodge rendered aid attempting to save the life of the man he had just shot. That was an irony that had stuck with him. Having experienced both in one day, he didn't envy anyone's first time shooting or corpses.

Corporal Boynton returned from outside with a set of bolt cutters.

"Where did you get those?" Renquest asked.

Proud of his haul and with a big smile on his face, the corporal said, "Took them off one of the fire trucks parked around the corner."

Dodge and Renquest nodded their approval of stealing from the fire department. The pair's approval of his thievery only seemed to embolden the rookie more to prove his worth to the veteran officers. He stepped over to the container and placed the shaft of the padlock between the steel cutting blades of the bolt cutters and squeezed. It was over before any of them had time to yell.

CHAPTER 23

THE POPPING SOUND ECHOED through the warehouse, bouncing off the walls and ceiling, eventually returning to its point of origin. The initial shock wave snapped the door's hinges like toothpicks, turning it into a three-hundred-pound piece of shrapnel moving at one-hundred miles an hour. Corporal Boynton took the full force of the explosion and the door that came after. He was dead before he hit the floor. But Dodge doubted anytime he heard those words. Violent deaths led to violent pain. Even if just for a split second.

He wondered if Boynton knew what was happening to him. Did he realize he was going to die, but could do nothing about it? That's the part that scared cops and soldiers. The idea of dying at any time was always in the back of your head. The unknown was, would you know what was happening to you?

His ears rang, and his typically sharp vision became black and tunneled. Dodge stumbled as his equilibrium reset, attempting to stand. The blast had picked up him, Beth, and Renquest like rag dolls, tossing them about ten feet across the hard cement floor. A few windows lining the ceiling from east to west of the old warehouse blew out; some remained intact. The cavernous interior of the building and its contents acted as a soundboard for the noise, reverberating from one end to the other, until the echo wasn't louder than an average person's footstep.

Renquest was sitting up, at arm's length, from where Dodge fell. The detective's hands were busy rubbing his eyes—his head tilting to one side, like a swimmer desperately trying to get water to drain out of their ear. His partner's lips were moving, but it was no use. The battered parole agent couldn't hear anything. Then he felt a pressure on his shoulder. He turned and saw Beth's face. She was talking to him. He waved his hands in the air to let her know he couldn't hear anything she was saying. His brain was on overload. Unable to process all the information coming in. He found it hard to focus on one singular event. His whole body needed a reboot. A hard shutdown.

Dodge closed his eyes, trying to concentrate on nothing. The way a pitcher on the mound in baseball can drown out the opposing fans' screams and stadium noise. He counted. One, two, three. At first, he couldn't even make out his own words, but slowly, the surrounding sounds crept in. Just noise at first. So, he focused on a single point: Beth. His eyes squeezed tight. He heard words. Then sentences.

"Are you ok?" she yelled at him, kneeling next to him.

He opened his eyes and peered up at her. Other than being clearly rattled by the explosion, she appeared to be unharmed. He let out a sigh.

"Check on Renquest." Dodge shook his head. "I'm fine."

Beth turned and crawled over to the older detective, who was pulling himself up from the floor. A little shook. Temporarily hearing impaired. But alive. And angry.

"What the hell happened?" the Detective asked. His hands visibly shaking.

"He had the fucking thing wired to explode when the door opened." Dodge managed to rise to his feet and pointed at the twisted steel that used to make up one of the container's doors.

All three stared into the emptiness of the steel box. Then, the three cops' attention switched to the crippled metal door and the arm still donning the dark blue uniform sleeve worn by city police. Dodge kneeled and tried to slide the door, but it was too heavy to move alone.

"Give me a hand and let's get this off of him," Dodge said.

Renquest moved closer to the body part protruding out from under the door. He bent over, placing his index finger on the bloody wrist. He found no pulse.

"Leave it. He's gone."

"Does he have any family?" Beth asked.

"I really don't know. We never talked about it." Renquest opened his mouth wide, shifting his jaw from side to side to get his ears to pop. "Once the evidence team and the bomb squad boys get in here and clear the place, the coroner will do his thing. Then I'll make the call," Renquest said, staring at the steel door and the only part of Boynton visible. His bloodied hand. Then he turned and walked toward the door and the trove of firemen and police that had made their way to the building after the explosion.

Dodge turned to Beth, who still appeared shaken by the blast. He reached out and placed his hand on her shoulder, squeezing slightly. The touch broke her concentration.

"You alright?"

"Not really."

His hand slid from her shoulder, down to her forearm. "Why don't you go find Renquest?"

She nodded, taking one last look at the tangled steel at her feet as she turned and walked away.

"Don't forget to have the medics check you out. Better safe than sorry."

She nodded again.

Firefighters and medics had entered the building, and one of them asked whether she was hurt. She shook her head and glanced back at Dodge, then walked out of sight.

He watched her until her she disappeared into the mass of emergency personnel gathered outside the entrance. The explosion knocked one of the rollers from its sliding rail, causing the door to tilt and crash to the ground and leaving an opening large enough to walk through. He thought about how lucky the three of them were to be alive. He turned to the rescue personnel and began barking orders.

"I want that container," pointing at the container now open at one end, "and all the ones in this row checked for explosives and booby traps."

Two of the firemen looked at each other before returning to their truck to don the bulky Kevlar lined suits made for examining explosives, then began examining the damaged shipping container. After about five minutes, the all clear was given.

"Ok. Now get the explosives dog in here and check the rest of 'em."

Dodge walked over and peered into the mangled container. He took out his cell phone and turned on the flashlight. The container was empty. Nothing had not been inside when the explosion happened.

Police dog handlers ran the dogs around every container in the immediate area, taping a red flag taped to the steel doors after clearing them to mark it, the team had completed their check for explosives. Soon after the flag went on a container, Dodge cut the lock and opened it, examining its contents, and moving to the next one when finished. After fifteen minutes and ten units, he told the team to take off. Sarah was nowhere to be found. The little hope he had of finding her alive faded. He slammed his hand against the side of the last container he searched.

"Damn it!"

Outside, the fire department had finished dousing the flames from the police cruiser. As Dodge approached, he could see Renquest staring at the burned-out shell of the department vehicle he personally signed for.

"You do this?" he asked, as his longtime partner sidled next to him.

"I needed to get your attention."

"You could have called," Renquest said, still staring at the totaled remains.

"I needed a distraction, and I knew smoke from the warehouse district would get the fire department down here in a hurry." He turned to Renquest. "What the hell took you so long, anyway?"

Renquest shook his head and looked back at the building bustling with emergency personnel behind them. The coroner had arrived, and two men in white lab coats were unloading a gurney. "The rookie turned his mike off."

Dodge said nothing and simply nodded. It was a mistake, but there was no need to walk all over a man's grave. He was also sure that Renquest expressed his disappointment to the young cop over the error. Which might explain why he was so eager to open the container to impress his mentor. Guilt like that sticks with a man. Dodge had felt the same guilt and it never goes away. He decided to let that dog lie.

The two men walked back to the building where Blanchard and Boynton still lie after watching the tow truck driver load the cruiser onto the flatbed transporter.

"Where is Beth?" Dodge asked.

"The paramedics looked her over then cleared her. I asked her if she wanted to stay, and she said she was going to get some air. I had a patrolman take her to your place."

Dodge nodded.

"Do you think she will be there when you get home?"

"I wouldn't be."

The two men continued the last few feet before entering the building in silence.

Once inside, Dodge told Renquest about the shooter on the roof of the building and how he had used the flare as a distraction, allowing him and Beth to get to safety. The pair ducked under the yellow crime scene tape and as they approached the police captain's body, he detailed how they came to find Blanchard, lying in a pool of blood. Dead from a stab wound to the abdomen.

"The blood was black. Most likely lacerated his liver," Dodge said.

"Painful way to go. Any luck on finding the girl?"

"Not so far. I had the dogs clear every container in this area for booby traps and then searched each one myself. No sign of her."

Looking at the scene around him and then at his watch, Renquest said, "We could go back to her place and get a piece of her clothing, maybe give the scent dogs a go?"

"Why, so they can lead us to one of the other buildings and a set of tire tracks that will match the set we have on file from the first victim's crime scene? No, that won't get us anywhere."

Two men in white lab coats loaded Blanchard onto the coroner's gurney and pushed the cart toward the exit.

"I'll have the report to you as soon as I can," the medical examiner told Renquest as he passed. "I'll make sure they move him to the front of the list."

"Thanks, Bob," Renquest said.

In all the years they had worked together, he had never heard his partner use the medical examiner's first name. Dodge wasn't sure he even remembered his given name. Funny how death can bring out the worst and the best in humanity. The pair watched the sheet covered gurney as it rolled past.

"You think it was him? The Savior, I mean?" Renquest asked.

"It was him," Dodge replied.

"You think he was the one shooting at you as well?"

"I do."

Renquest shook his head in disbelief. "Why would he kill Blanchard?"

Dodge looked around the room. Studying each fire personnel and paramedic. He quickly ruled out the medical professionals and focused on the fire department personnel. Specifically, one woman. She had taken most of her gear off. Her mask and oxygen tank lay at her feet. The heavy fire-retardant jacket she was wearing was unbuttoned and Dodge could see she was wearing a t-shirt under her protective gear. More than that, he could make out a pocket over her left breast. The only people who wore t-shirts with pockets these days were smokers.

After bumming a smoke, he just held the cigarette in his hand for a few minutes. It felt good. He felt a rush of energy go through his body. His brain started running scenarios as he lit his crutch, then took a long drag, exhaling only after feeling the burn in his lungs. Oh, how he missed that burn.

A moment passed before Dodge realized all eyes were on him. Renquest shook his head.

"Well, that lasted a month longer than I thought it would," the detective said. "Now, put that out before you contaminate my crime scene."

Dodge snuffed out the glowing ember on the sole of his shoe and stuffed the extinguished butt in his pocket. Then he walked back over to where the Blanchard's body lay a few minutes earlier. His eyes combed the scene. He knelt, stood, and knelt again. His mind working like it used to. His thoughts cleared and his senses were keen. He knew in that moment he would be a slave to his addiction. He couldn't work without the nicotine, and he gladly accepted the reality.

Turning to his partner, he said, "Blanchard was no use to him anymore once I became his new obsession. That's why he gutted Blanchard and took the girl. This is now about me and him."

Renquest had a puzzled look on his face. "Ok, I'll bite. Let's say the psycho tired of Blanchard and set his sights on you. Let's say Blanchard knew this, and he took the girl as bait to lure in the killer, which obviously worked. But none of that explains how this god damn lunatic got the drop on an experienced State Police Captain, who was expecting someone to show up. He took a blade to the gut, Dodge. It's not like they stabbed him in the back. I mean, just look around. He would have seen anyone coming from fifty feet away. Why didn't he just shoot the cock sucker in the face as soon as he saw him?"

Dodge said nothing. He didn't have the answer to his partner's question. He didn't know why Blanchard opted not to plant a round between The Savior's eyes. The idea of letting a threat get within arm's length only served to confuse him more. Who would let a known killer walk right up to them? Close enough to drive a blade into his gut and never even get off a round. Whatever the answer, Dodge knew he wouldn't find it there. He needed to think. Alone. As he pulled the set of car keys from his pocket, he realized two things he needed: a ride home and a new car. He wasn't sure if Renquest would supply either. He was mad about the fire and two dead cops. And rightfully so.

Dodge shook his head, staring at the keys in his hand. *Not every plan is good*, he thought.

CHAPTER 24

DODGE LEANED AGAINST THE SIDE of the warehouse. The cool metal soothed his aching back. Reaching into his pocket, he pulled out what was left of the crumpled cigarette he snuffed out earlier on his shoe as he contemplated his next move. First, he asked Renquest for a replacement vehicle. The request received less than an enthusiastic response. The reluctance shown by his partner was understandable. As the head of the task force, the budget fell within his purview and therefore it was his responsibility to face the brass downtown and explain the demise of the forty-thousand-dollar vehicle.

So, with what Dodge guessed was an easy choice, his partner decided the department had kept Dodge's truck long enough and called the impound lot, where the black Chevy truck had sat since the crime lab finished processing it for evidence. The detective had planned to tell Dodge he could pick up his property that afternoon, but he had forgotten it amid all the excitement of the day. A civilian employee was tasked with driving the truck to the warehouse, where Dodge waited patiently, smoking another cigarette he bummed. This time, the cigarette came from a paramedic caught sneaking a smoke behind one of the fire trucks.

While he awaited the return of his property, Dodge thought about the day's events. He was happy he didn't have his truck that day. He shuttered at the idea of bullets piercing the steel exterior and shattering its windows. And he was sure he wouldn't have set his truck on fire as a distraction, allowing him and Beth to escape. Renquest had done him a favor by not returning it.

The drive home took fifteen minutes. He was on the opposite side of town but had avoided the chaos and stoplights of downtown and detoured through the neighborhoods surrounding the center of the city. He had lived there for years, and as a parole agent, became familiar with the side streets and back alleys. Knowing which streets had stop signs every block and which were thoroughfares made conducting home visits more efficient. It allowed him to claim back some lost time from busy days, by not spending countless minutes waiting at lights and traffic from the left-hand turn lanes of busy intersections.

Cars lined the curb from one end of the street to the other. It took two laps around the block before he spotted an empty spot a half block over, just large enough to squeeze into. The hitch protruding out about a foot behind the rear bumper stopped only a few inches from the front of the tiny sports car nestled in behind him. Dodge laughed, wishing he could watch as the owner of the car came out in the morning and curse him for parking so close.

As he crossed the street, and onto the sidewalk, he looked at the cars lining the curb in front of his house. A red midsized caught his eye. Dodge knew every car on his street. Memorizing the vehicles owned by his neighbors was a habit born out of necessity. Parole agents were the same as any other citizen when it came to public property records. A quick search of the county's website would reveal the name and address of anyone who owned property in the county. An angry parolee could find his address, lying in wait until he returned home from a long day and shoot him before he was even able to get the keys out of the ignition.

He touched the hood, and the cool surface told him the car hadn't been driven in hours. A quick glance at the license plate, which was local, eased his mind some. He trudged up the walkway and climbed the steps to his front door. His body was overwhelmed with tiredness from the day's events. The adrenaline dump earlier at the warehouse had run its course and now his body and mind were reeling from the aftereffects. He was having trouble focusing. So much, it took two attempts to get the key into the lock to open the door.

Once inside, he slipped off his shoes, pulled his shirt off over his head, and dropped his pants on the floor of the living room, heading for the bathroom and a hot shower. As he stood in the shower, the hot water running over his head and down his chest and legs, he thought about Blanchard and the warehouse. Why would an experienced cop let a serial killer get so close to him? It made no sense. He was missing something. And why choose that warehouse? How would The Savior know where to find Blanchard and the girl? Blanchard's death complicated the entire case and in his current condition, Dodge couldn't get any of it to make sense. He wondered if he had put too much faith into the magical powers of hot water.

Dodge turned the shower nozzle and grabbed a towel from a hook on the wall. As he dried himself off, he ran the scene through his mind. Blanchard taking Sarah to the warehouse, probably stuffing her in the container for safe keeping. Dodge knew if he dug deep enough into the warehouse's finances and records and interviewed the manager, he would find a connection between one of the shipping containers and Blanchard. It would take some time, but the link would be there. One call to Renquest, and a criminal analyst would have the information within the week. The fact the killer and Blanchard were in the same building with Sarah was enough circumstantial evidence to make the connection. But the State Police Captain's death made that point moot. The lead wasn't going anywhere, and the task force could circle back to it after Sarah was safe.

He needed to switch gears. It was time to think about this from Blanchard's point of view. What if Blanchard knew he was being followed? He could have set the whole thing up as a giant rouse. A trap to corner the killer, but something went wrong, and The Savior got the drop on him. Dodge thought hard, but he couldn't sell it to himself. Blanchard was too experienced, and even though he acted irrationally by taking Sarah, he still had a cop's wits. He knew every way into and out of the building from the human trafficking case that took place on the same property. How, or why, did a veteran cop who chose the location and knew the layout let a murderer armed with a knife get so close to him? He should have dropped him as soon as his head became visible. The entire case hinged on this, and Dodge couldn't put the pieces together. And what about the booby-trapped container? That's a whole new ballgame. Murdering hookers to Ted Kaczynski? And who fired the shots at him and Beth? The Killer had never used a gun before, as far as Dodge knew. What changed? His head pounded and ears rang from the explosion.

After putting on a pair of athletic shorts and t-shirt, he slipped a low-ball glass from underneath the globe bar in his dining room and poured a double shot of Blantons. It was late and the brown liquid burned his throat. Like a shot of warm water. It took two swallows to empty the glass. When finished, he poured another drink. Only this time, he splashed in enough for a triple. He sipped from his glass as he walked over to the couch and gazed out the window. The red car parked in front of his house when he got home was now gone. The owner must have left or moved the car while he was in the shower. Dodge thought for a second about going and getting his truck and taking the vacant spot, but exhaustion won out in the end. He collapsed onto the sofa.

His mind wandered from the case to thoughts about Beth. He had hoped to see her sitting on the same couch he now laid on when he got home. She was not. Did she go to the airport and catch a flight back to Phoenix? Was she sleeping in a motel somewhere, avoiding him because of the danger he had placed her in? Or did she rent a car and make the twenty-five plus hour drive back home to Arizona? The thought of not seeing her again crept into his head and he became awash with sadness. He cared about her. More than he had cared about anyone in the past couple of years. He knew the feelings had always been there, suppressed by his inability to commit to or trust other people. But Beth was different. It was harder to convince himself it would never work. Even though thousands of miles and no less than six states separated them. Both loved their jobs. He would certainly never quit his and would never ask her to pack up and move across the country for him. Hell, he couldn't make a relationship work when the girl lived in the same town. He knew in his heart she could be the one, but the idea of another relationship ending in heartbreak and regret made him overthink the entire relationship. He let out a sigh and swallowed another mouthful of bourbon.

His eyes grew heavy. Unable to keep them open, he embraced

the exhaustion and drifted off to sleep. Dreams of Blanchard and Sarah filled the void. The pair were together. Trying to tell him something. But as hard as he concentrated, he couldn't hear them. He tried to get closer, but only found himself further away with every step. He ran, reaching out, trying to grab onto anything, but the pair faded into the distance.

Then a bright flash of white light jerked him from his slumber.

——~~~——

The room was square. A cold metal worktable sat in the middle. Each edge of the table measured the same distance to the opposing wall. The only light came from the lamp that hung above his work area, casting shadows on the walls as it gently swayed from right to left. Right to left. The walls were cement block painted white. Everything was white, even the ceiling. Everything that was, except the glimmering metal worktable. And the girl strapped to its top.

He watched her from a corner of the room. One of the two closest to her head. The light from the swaying lamp never quite reaching his sanctum, he stood silent in the shadows, waiting for her to wake up. The blow to her head was harder than he had intended. She had even thanked him for coming to her rescue before he swung the piece of wood he found outside the container, hitting her on the temple. He wanted to say how stupid she was. He was going to save her. Not her physical body as she had asked for, but her mortal soul.

His eyes held their gaze on her naked body as she woke. Leather straps across her chest, feet, and hands. Her arms and legs struggling against the bindings. He watched her eyes dart around the room, searching for something, anything, that might look familiar. Any hint of where she might be. After a few minutes, he saw the despair set in. A realization she wouldn't be able to escape. Her legs stopped flailing. Followed by her arms and then the muscles in her face. Leaving an expression not of fear but of exasperation. It was a look he knew well. He saw it in all his victims, eventually. Most times, as his hands tightened around their necks. Unable to stop him in their weakened state. Gasping for air. It lasted for only a few minutes before they succumbed to the inevitable results of his powerful hands crushing their airway. Broken capillaries in the eyes. Purple lips. Oh, how he loved the deep purple hue of the lips after he saved them. It was like a timer used to tell when a cake finished baking. When the lips turn purple, the soul is free.

The woman's head turned. Her eyes squinting, trying to focus on his form as he appeared from the corner. A piece of white linen protruded from her mouth, preventing anything above a whimper from escaping her lips. A smile stretched across his face as he approached the table.

"I realize this may be a bit of a shock to you," he said as he circled the steel table. "Sarah, is it? Some people say we are twins, my brother and I, but I think we are more than that."

Sarah said nothing. Her body shook. Her eyes following her captor's every move.

"I rarely reveal myself in such a way, but the end is drawing near. I must finish my work before I'm not able to continue." He ran the back of his hand along the side of her face, following the jawline to her neck and then across her chest. "In the past, I incapacitated my vict—chosen ones. Having them calm made it easier for me to complete my work and free their soul."

He gazed at her face as he told her what her fate would be. The expression in the eyes always gave it away. Pupils dilated, and the color drained from the iris. The eyes turned gray, a color of no hope and despair. This is the part he relished the most. When they realized their sins, agreeing to let him free them from their torture filled lives.

"That's it. Just relax. I will soon save you from the eternal hell you have experienced." His hand ran across her breasts and down her inner thigh. "But first, I need to do something."

Tears ran down the Sarah's cheeks. He watched as she tried to stretch the gag in her mouth by using her tongue to force it out. But the rag and her body's reaction to the shock of being kidnapped, not once, but twice, must have left the inside of her mouth as parched as desert sand. He leaned over. His lips brushing her ear.

"I'll remove the gag if you promise not to scream. It won't do you any good. I built this room myself. Lots of insulation to keep nosey neighbors from hearing me while I work. And if you do scream, I will gut you right here and eat your soul, devouring it so you can never move on from this existence. Do we understand each other?"

Sarah nodded.

He reached out and dragged the rag out of her mouth, placing it on her neck. Then he straightened up and placed his hands in his pockets.

"What's—," she stuttered. "What's your name?"

He stared at her body. She shivered, so he reached under the foot end of the table and pulled a sheet up until it reached her neck, folding it back on itself as if he was making a bed. He tucked the edges of the sheet along the length of her body. First one side, then the other. Once finished, his hands slipped back into his pockets.

"I'm sorry. I forgot what your question was."

"Thank you for covering me up," she said. Her voice trembling. "I asked what your name was."

"That's right," he said. "Don't you read the papers? I'm The Savior."

She stared at him for a moment before speaking again.

"No. I mean, what is your real name? What did your parents name you when you were born?"

Every ounce of experience, every bit of information attained over the years from his work, screamed she was stalling. *But there was no harm in playing along for a moment*, he thought. It might be fun. Besides, there was always time to take pleasure from this part of the game.

His eyes focused intently on his project. Hers stared back. Full of dread and fear. In fact, the whole room stunk of fear. It hung in the air like a fog. He again decided to play along.

"The people that raised me used to call me Evan. I never cared much for that name. It lacks any sense of exploration or devotion. I prefer a good biblical name. Jacob or Isaac would have been better, I feel. But anymore, I don't even know what name someone would call me. It really doesn't matter, I suppose. I won't be alive long enough for any of it to matter."

"I'm going to call you Evan. If that's alright with you?"

He smiled. He thought it might make her feel better. A brief gesture showing maybe she was reaching him. Of course, he knew that would never happen. No one could extricate him from his task. He was too dedicated to let anyone, or anything, distract him from his work. She smiled back at him. It had worked. It always worked.

He pulled an old dirty rag from his front pocket. Its pungent odor was familiar to him. Before his project knew what was happening, the rag smothered her face. His hand created a seal around her mouth and nose. Her eyes rolled back in her head as the chloroform did its job, leaving only the whites showing. His hand slipped from her face only when he knew she was unconscious.

"Can't have you wriggling out of those restraints," he said, tossing the rag on the table next to her still body, before turning to leave. He had faith in the parole agent and knew it wouldn't take long to find him, so he needed to move fast.

CHAPTER 25

THE WATER WAS HOT. It felt good to him as it ran down his body, washing away the grime of the past couple of days. Now he just needed to clean his mind. He dried off and got dressed, then put a cup of coffee in his system in three swallows. He drank it so quickly after pouring, the hot liquid burned the roof of his mouth. He refilled his travel cup, locked the door behind him and made his way to the task force office where Renquest waited with copies of the medical examiner's reports. One for Blanchard and one for Boynton. Dodge pretended he didn't see the bright yellow folders resting in front of his chair at the conference table. Choosing instead to sit on the opposite side. Placing as much distance between himself and the reality of what loomed inside those reports.

Renquest glanced at the folders, then at Dodge, pulled out a chair beside his partner and fell into the leather covered seat.

"We're gonna get the son-of-a-bitch."

Dodge said nothing. The words echoed in his ears. He was listening but couldn't hear.

Renquest reached across the table, pulling the yellow folders in front of him. But he didn't open the reports.

"We don't have to do this right now. We both know what it says."

Dodge took in a deep breath and sighed.

"How? How are we going to get him? We've got nothing."

"That's not completely true, and you know it. We know the neighborhood he steals his license plates from, which means he likely stays close to the area." Renquest leaned back in his chair. His stomach pushing out from his shirt. "We also know the victim he has this time."

The words bounced around in his Dodge's head. The thought of losing another victim was a hard pill to swallow. Knowing the person and having had interactions with her only exacerbated the situation. He had lost soldiers in battle. He had lost friends on the job. All good people. Co-workers and soldiers with integrity. But it never got easier. Every time was like a wound that refused to heal. Festering and burning under the skin, eating at the fabric of his soul. He couldn't let it go. The losses attached to him like the end of a piece of tape stuck to the roll. Once you found the edge—you must keep digging your nails under it to get it to release. Even then, the tape usually tore, forcing you to start the entire process over. Again, and again. Never able to get the tape loose with a clean edge, without leaving a little behind. There was always something left behind. A constant reminder of his failures.

He wondered about the other officers working the case. Would they have the stomach to do whatever it took? Did they have the guts to ride the dragon? The one person whose loyalty and drive to get to the truth he never questioned was his partner. Doubting Renquest never crossed his mind. Partners were good like that. Throw in a dead cop. That's like pouring jet fuel on a smoldering fire. Instantly, turning it into a flash fire, burning as hot as the sun. A fire only justice for the victim could put out.

Dodge pushed his chair back from the table. "I need to think." His hands digging into his pockets, searching for the magic cure. Grasping for that friend that never let him down, only to come up empty. Any hope he had was fleeting.

"Here." A small cardboard box slid across the table, landing in Dodge's lap. "I hate those things, but I need you to come up with a plan here, and we are running out of time."

Dodge cupped the rectangular box in his hand and smiled as he stood and walked toward the elevator. He had forgotten about his rules since trying to quit smoking, which coincidently broke the rule of never quit. It was time to get back to the rules. *Do what works*, he thought, tossing the wrapper and the little piece of aluminum foil that sealed the pack into a trash can by elevator doors. He pressed the UP button. He needed an overview. To see the complete city. And he couldn't do that from the streets. The building the task force worked in was only ten stories, but easily made it one of the tallest buildings in town. A bird's-eye view would give him sightlines. From North to South and East to West. He felt a rush of energy as he stepped out onto the roof.

Covering the roof was a layer of small stones and pebbles about two inches deep. As he walked across the surface, his feet sank, creating a grinding noise with each step. The stones had been the brainchild of a city planner a few years earlier. The city received funding from the federal government as part of a green initiative. The goal was to get towns and cities across the country to provide more green space to help reduce the rise in temperatures caused by increased hard surfaces, like cement and asphalt, and heat absorbing rubber rooftops. The town council created a green spot on the roof of the city's tallest building to try and convince other commercial property owners to take part. Lead by example, they thought. They decorated the roof with benches and small potted trees to provide some relief from the summer sun. Native tall grasses lined stone pathways, which were also bordered with native flowers and other plants. It was quite beautiful. The city forgot one thing. Summer in Virginia is as hot as Hades and as humid as Miami. The last place people wanted to visit in July was a rooftop closer to the fiery apex in the sky. Eventually, the city stopped maintaining the space and removed everything but the gravel. City planning at its finest.

As he approached the north side of the rooftop, he stopped about three feet from the edge. His body naturally recoiled as he peered over at the street below. The Air force veteran was afraid of heights. He never understood why he had this irrational phobia. It had always troubled him and he considered it one of his biggest flaws. He had jumped out of airplanes hundreds of times, and while he didn't find it particularly fun, scared wasn't an emotion he felt while dangling from under a silk canopy at five-thousand feet. But standing on a rooftop or looking out the window of a tall building tied his stomach in knots. Maybe it was because he didn't have a parachute anymore to slow his rapid descent if he fell. Or maybe while in the employment of the Air Force, not having a choice in whether you take the leap factored into his psychological reaction. Exit the plane on your own, or someone will assist you. The guy helping you out the door wasn't jumping, and it mattered little if you went on your own or it took a little shove to get you out of the plane. In fact, it became another rule for him, jumped or pushed, sometimes you must take the leap.

After taking a deep breath to calm his nerves—he took one step back, then stared out towards the north side of the city. In his mind, he pictured the farmland and open fields past the city limits and suburbs. Closing his eyes, he imagined driving back into the city—through the fields and past the row of houses making up the boundary between country and suburbs. The houses were all brick and wood sided. Small front yards with detached garages. The distance between the homes shrinking as he neared the city center and the edge of downtown. Nothing stood out to him or pricked a hidden memory, causing him pause.

His right foot behind his left, toes touching the ground, he made a military turn to his right and walked to the east ledge of the roof. A little closer to the edge than before. A breeze blew. He noticed a tingle on the back of his neck. He stared out toward the city limits, to where sheriff's deputies found the body of the first victim. Why did The Savior take the body so far out of town, transporting her miles from the area where he left the other victims? After his visit to the crime scene days earlier, there had been an itch he couldn't seem to scratch. Something was off. It was like trying to pound a square peg into a round hole. You could just keep hitting it until it crammed its way into the space, but the peg would fit better in the hole cut specifically for it. Cases didn't get solved by trying to make a theory fit a scenario. The facts formed the theory and the theory molded into a scenario.

Dodge stood silent a few minutes before turning right and again walking the perimeter of the rooftop until he was staring over the south side of the roof. This time, his eyes focused on the areas where he found Blanchard's body. The rusty metal rooftops of the warehouses shone in the distance. From where he stood, he couldn't make out which building they had found Blanchard. But he didn't need to physically see it. The entire complex now carried a burden of what had happened there. He could feel the blood pumping through his veins. His head pounded with every heartbeat and his cheeks flushed. Anger pervaded his stomach and pushed out the queasiness cause by the height. Instinctively, the fingers of his right hand drummed the holster strapped to his hip. Tap-tap-tap. Tap-tap-tap. At first, Dodge didn't notice the nervous twitch, but soon his primal brain picked up on it and he shoved his hand in his pocket. Twitches are a sign of weakness. He didn't have time for weakness. Not now. Not until he had Sarah back.

The parole agent counted his steps as he turned and made the walk to the adjacent edge of the rooftop. Twenty-five. That put him at center, facing west. The sun was directly overhead, and he felt the warmth of its rays as they hit the back of his neck. A bead of sweat formed on his brow. He studied the far-off streets and houses in the residential neighborhoods that lay beyond the brick and glass buildings of the downtown area. West is the direction the city had really grown over the last twenty years. While he was a transplant from the Midwest, even he could see expansion had favored the west side of town. Newer streets and sidewalks. More chain restaurants and strip malls. Businesses go where the people are.

His gaze focused to the left. An inch, maybe. But a mile away, that inch expanded to ten blocks. The same neighborhood where he and Renquest stumbled upon the corpse decomposing in the bathtub a few days earlier. It was also the same area where all the license plates The Savior used were taken. That area was important. Though the reason eluded him, every bone in his body told him those streets, and those houses, had some significance to the killer and his plans for Sarah.

As he stared into the distance, dread replaced the anger in his gut. Dodge knew he needed to find Sarah. And fast. Her captor had grown bold and as he stood near the ledge peering out over the city, he couldn't help but feel the end was near. Only he had no sway over how it was going to go down. Like a driver losing control and skidding on a wet roadway, first, sliding towards the ditch, then over-correcting. The rear of the car getting ahead of the front, no way to bring it back. Eventually, winding up a crumpled heap of twisted metal wrapped around a tree or telephone pole. Time was running out.

He lit the cigarette dangling from his lips. The rush of warm air into his lungs felt comforting. A calmness overcame him.

Another long drag and his mind cleared. Thoughts started lining up. Not the order in which they happened, but spatially. The front part of his brain took over. A map built in his head. The bodies. The crime scenes. The warehouse and the neighborhood where The Savior stole the plates he used to disguise his van. Then it hit him. They... he had been looking at this all wrong. The killings were never about the girls. This was about revenge. It was all about Blanchard. The killings started in Vegas with Blanchard, which followed him here. Blanchard was now dead, likely at the hands of The Savior. He pulled the phone out of his pocket and made a call to the state police.

After speaking with the station commander, Dodge's suspicions were confirmed. He flipped the still lit cigarette over the edge of the roof, watching it float to the street below, before turning toward the roof access door. The pebbles ground under his feet until entering the cool darkness of the stairwell. By the time he navigated the three flights of stairs to the task force's floor, a renewed sense of purpose consumed him. It was the first time he felt like there had been headway made in the case. It also pissed him off. He couldn't believe he had ignored what was right in front of him this whole time. The farther he descended into the stairwell, the clearer the picture became.

As he rounded the corner and stepped into Renquest's office, he stopped. For sitting in a chair, talking to his partner, was Beth. She looked up at him and smiled.

The high-back chair squeaked as Renquest adjusted his weight and leaned into the worn leather padding. "That's a pretty smart girl you got here."

Dodge looked at Beth, then back at Renquest.

"What's going on?" His attention now turned to his friend. "I thought you had gone."

Beth looked down at the table, shifting her weight from right to left. "I was on my way to the airport. I didn't know if I wanted to be part of this anymore, I mean two dead cops and a serial killer. It was all a little too real. Dodge, I knew Blanchard."

Dodge stepped into the office and propped his butt on the corner of the table.

"You could've gone home. We wouldn't have thought any less of you. This isn't your fight and frankly, I shouldn't have brought you into this shit show. For that, I am sorry."

The old chair squawked again as Renquest leaned forward, placing his hands on the desk and pushing himself to his feet. "I for one, am glad you did. For once, Paul Dodge did something that might help us solve a crime." He smiled. Beth smiled back at him. "Go ahead, tell him. I don't want to steal your thunder."

Beth turned to Dodge. "I was on my way to the airport to see about catching a plane back home, after I left the—the place where we found Blanchard. Like I said earlier, I wasn't sure if I wanted to be part of this or not."

Dodge nodded.

"Anyway, in the taxi on the way to the airport, something just wasn't sitting right with me. The way the killer followed Blanchard out here. How Blanchard left Vegas after the first round of killings has always left a foul taste in my mouth." She stopped to take in a deep breath, then exhaled. "No self-respecting cop would leave in the middle of a serial killer case. Not one that became personal, anyway. I mean, maybe if he planned to retire, but then to up and move and get right back into the business again? It's strange."

"Those are the very things that have been bouncing around in my head for days," Dodge said.

"I imagined that would be bothering you," Beth said. Her voice cracked as her excitement became more visible. "Being the most stubborn person I have ever met, I figured that would be an itch you couldn't help but scratch."

Dodge and Renquest both nodded in unison.

"I see why you two are partners," Beth said, her head shaking. "As I was saying, I just didn't get it. Blanchard was a lot of things, but he wasn't a coward, and he wasn't a quitter. So, I had the cab driver drop me off at the library downtown. It took a little coaxing with the head librarian and a flash of my badge, but she let me use the research area reserved for news media. It was just a hunch, but I knew there had to be more of a connection between The Savior and Blanchard."

"And you found something?" Dodge asked.

"I did. First, I looked into the coverage of the murders back in Vegas. It was pretty bland. Nothing popped up over the last twelve months. But when I searched for our friend Captain Blanchard, that's when things got interesting."

"What did you find?" Dodge asked, his body leaning into the conversation.

"I found an old article in the Las Vegas Sun about a family coming home from a trip to the Grand Canyon. It seems their car blew a tire and veered into oncoming traffic. The parents, Jon and Racheal Blanchard, died at the scene along with the driver of the other vehicle."

Dodge scratched his head. "Let me guess. There was a kid in the car."

A smile crept across Beth's face. Her white teeth shone through her red lips. "There were two survivors. Both boys."

"Son-of-a-bitch." Dodge leaned back onto the desk. "Blanchard has a brother."

"Oh, it gets better," Renquest pointed to Beth. His finger wagging between her and Dodge. "Finish telling him what you told me."

Beth took a drink of coffee, then cleared her throat. "During the investigation into the accident, the police interviewed the two boys, just to make sure they covered all their bases. It seems one boy got sick while at the Grand Canyon and the family had to pack it up and head home early. The other son was upset with his brother for ruining the family's one summer trip. He had wanted to go on a tour of the Hoover Dam and knew he would have to wait a few years before the family could afford to take another vacation. It took some digging, but I was able to uncover the boy's names. The angry boy's name was, Evan Blanchard."

"And the sick boy's name was Don Blanchard," Dodge said.

Beth nodded.

"Brothers?" Renquest asked.

"Not just brothers," Beth said. "Twins. Do you have any siblings, detective?"

"No. I am an only child."

"You see, all siblings share a bond. A sort of spiritual

connection if you will. But twins—they share things on a much deeper level. University studies have shown some twins can even read each other's minds. They have been known to form their own languages and are even cases of twins dying hours after their siblings."

The room went momentarily silent before Dodge spoke up.

"What happened after the accident? I mean to the two boys."

"I made a call to the Clark County Child Services office and was able to get some records, what hadn't been lost or destroyed, faxed to me."

"They released information involving juveniles to you?" Dodge asked.

"This happened over twenty years ago, and all parties involved are now adults or dead, so the social worker gave me what they had. I had to fill in the rest with newspaper articles and old police blotters. From what I read, there was no immediate family willing to take them. Or at least not Evan. But Child Protective Services would only release the boys to family if the parties agreed to take both. It's common practice to keep siblings together when placing them in a foster home."

"And let me guess. Evan was a disturbed child, and everyone knew it?"

"I couldn't access any reports because juvenile court records are confidential to help protect the child's identity, but it would explain the lack of family willing to take him in," Beth said.

"I'm gonna go out on a limb here," Renquest said. "Solitary, cruel to animals?"

"You guessed it. But it didn't stop there. There were police reports of a boy at the facility abusing other children. One victim even had cut marks on his abdomen and chest. I found a small article in the local paper, but of course everyone involved were minors, so no names. But from the reports the social worker gave me, it wasn't long after that they found a home for Don. Without Evan. That's where the paper trail stops."

Renquest turned to his partner. "What do you think?"

"We always knew there was a connection between Don Blanchard and the murders. Both here and in Vegas. I hadn't put it together in my mind yet. But it all makes sense. The way the case was personal to both men and why the killings stopped in Vegas and started up here again."

"But the one thing I don't understand is why did Blanchard ask for you? Why get someone else involved in the case?" Beth asked.

"He needed someone not connected, not invested in the case."

"But why?" Renquest asked.

"Because he knew he couldn't stop him. He needed help, and someone probably mentioned my name. Or he came across an old article on one of our cases."

Renquest and Beth nodded.

"Where were you at earlier?" Beth asked.

Without looking at her, Dodge thew his thumb up toward the ceiling.

Confused, Beth glanced at Renquest, who had sat back in his chair.

"The roof," he responded.

"Why were you on the roof?" she asked, turning back to Dodge.

"Because I can't smoke in here."

"Wait, I thought you were trying to quit smoking?"

"I am."

"But you started again?"

"No."

Beth shook her head. "But you just said you went to the roof to smoke. And why wouldn't you just go out to the street? Why the rooftop?"

"Because you can't see the city from the street. Not as a whole, anyway."

Throwing her hands up, Beth shook her head in defeat.

Renquest used the pause in conversation to ask Dodge what he learned while staring at the city from the rooftop.

"A lot," he answered. "Now that we know the why of the murders, we need to focus on the where. We must find Sarah, and I think I might have an idea where she is." Pointing at Renquest, he said, "Do you have a map of the city?"

"I'm sure I can dig one up. Why?"

"I need to test something out. Can you get the map for me?"

Renquest left the office and returned less than a minute later with rolled up grid map of the city. He spread the map out on the table and the three used items to secure the edges from curling up and rolling back into its tubular shape. Beth took a stapler from Renquest's desk to hold down one corner. Renquest used the corner of the speakerphone on the table and placed it in the middle of a short side of the map. Two birds, one stone, so to speak. Dodge pulled the extra magazine from his belt and placed it on the last corner. The three stared at the map of the city laid out first in six larger squares or quadrants. Each main quadrants was then divided into four smaller areas and those into four smaller and so on until the city was broken down to manageable half block radiuses.

Reaching into his pocket, Dodge pulled out a handful of coins and tossed them on the map. "Where was the first body found?" he asked, as he reached for a penny.

"Right here," Renquest said, pointing to a spot on the map just outside of town.

"And the second victim?"

Again, Dodge picked up a coin and placed it at the spot his partner pointed to on the map, showing where they found the second body.

"Now the third."

The three investigators stood straight and looked at the map. Three points, but no discernable pattern.

Beth spoke up. "It was a good idea, Dodge. Sorry."

"It's not enough to go on," Renquest said.

Dodge leaned in. His frame casting a shadow over the map, while he studied every inch. Every street and intersection, until he eventually reached across the table and took several coins. He began placing them, one at a time. Studying the map for a moment before placing each on a different location of the city. The last coin in his hand was a quarter, which he placed at the edge of the map. The western edge. Then he stood and stepped back as the other two gazed at his creation.

CHAPTER 26

IN THE PARKING LOT outside police headquarters, Dodge and Beth sat in his truck, the map from the task force office spread out across her lap. Its sides overhanging her legs, curling up on the seat next to her. All the spots Dodge marked with coins in the office were replaced with black circles made from a magic marker he found in a desk drawer in the conference room. Each mark joined by a thin black line. Points from east to west and north to south. All connected. Linked. Converging at one spot on the map.

"Are you ok?" Beth asked.

Dodge nodded, belching to himself, trying not to let the smell of bile and stomach acid escape. A swig of coffee from a cup that had been sitting in the console, still warm, but only from the heat of the day washed the taste out of his mouth.

"This must be deliberate. Right?" she asked.

A long silence went by as Dodge studied the map one more time. His eyes traced every line marked on its surface. His brain replaying every detail at each crime scene, trying to disprove what he knew to be true. That's how one avoids bias. A researcher's job is to create a hypothesis and after gathering all the available information on the topic, find the weakness and tear apart the hypothesis little by little until there is nothing left but a weak, malnourished argument. Then you start all over again. Investigations worked much the same way.

But not this time. The lines he had drawn crossed and intersected at different spots on the map. At first glance, the spiderweb of black lines and street grids appeared to be random. A bunch of indiscernible marks with distinct beginning and ending points. He had placed everything he could think of on the map, including Captain Blanchard's murder and tomato soup guy. The stolen license plate locations. And for good measure, he marked Sarah's abduction scene and the street corner she worked. But after staring at the map, Dodge noticed two points where all the lines came together. One was near where he and Renquest found the dead body in the tub. The other was more frightening. More personal. He didn't want to believe what his eyes were seeing.

That damn red sports car parked on the street in front of his house. Something about that car ate at him all night. He just couldn't put it together. Now he knew.

"We are going to have to split up," he said.

Beth looked up from the map and parsed her eyebrows. "I don't think that's a good idea."

"Neither do I, but it's how we are going to have to play it."

"Jesus Dodge, getting stabbed and almost blown up didn't teach you anything? We can't play his game. The smart play is to wait for Renquest and the entry team. We can hit the house in the burbs first. Then we can check the other address."

"If we hit one house before the other, someone is going to die. Sarah or an old lady and possibly her dog. I'm not willing to take that risk. Are you?"

Beth looked at him and heaved her shoulders. "What if he has the place wired to blow, like he did the container in the warehouse?"

"I've thought about that a lot. I don't believe he wired that box."

"Who else would've?"

Dodge shrugged. "Could've been a hundred people. It's not a secret dealers use that place to store their drugs. The whole thing felt like amateur hour to me."

"Amateur hour? It killed a cop and damn near us! And if there were drugs stashed, why didn't the dogs sniff them out?"

"The dogs were explosive dogs. I never had the drug canine crew go back in. Once the coroner removed Blanchard and Boynton, I assumed our work was done. But I'll bet all the money in my bank account if we have a narcotics dog do a sweep of the warehouse, we will find drugs. Probably hidden behind a faux wall at one end of a container."

Beth had a puzzled look on her face. "But why was that container rigged to explode? There was nothing in it. And where was Sarah?"

"True. There was nothing in that container. Blanchard had to have stashed her in one of the other crates. There are still some details I don't have figured out yet, but it doesn't change what's in front of us now."

"I still don't know why anyone would choose that specific container to open."

"The lock," Dodge said.

"What about it?"

"All the other containers had rusty old padlocks hanging off them. I think I even saw a combination lock dangling off one. But the one that Boynton opened. It had a nice, new shiny lock. That's what first drew my attention to it over the other containers. It looked like someone was trying to keep something valuable inside safe."

Beth's eyes widened, and he knew she understood.

"Once someone got blown up from breaking into that container—others would hesitate before trying it again."

Dodge nodded.

"So, you don't think Evan will rig the houses to blow once we are all inside?"

Dodge paused before answering. It was an enormous risk to take. His adversary was certifiably insane. No one could dispute that, and Dodge was moving forward on gut instinct alone. The sheer volume of things that could go wrong was so large, he couldn't afford to think about it. He was breaking about ten of his own rules, not to mention a half a dozen department ones. He looked over at Beth, who was clearly waiting on an answer.

"I don't. That's not his style. He wants a one on one with me. That said, make sure Renquest has the bomb squad on standby. No need to take any more chances than we must."

"What about you?"

Beth's tone dropped an entire octave. He could see the concern in her eyes. He understood that, and he felt the same about her. Though he would never outwardly show it.

His hand moved to her left thigh, attempting reassurance.

"I still say this is the worst idea you've had, but if we're going to do it, we best get going," she said.

Dodge turned the key, forcing the engine to life. He checked the mirrors before easing into traffic and heading toward the west side of town. The black truck maneuvered through the rush hour traffic, its emergency lights flashing and a whelp of the siren as they approached busy intersections. Beth used his phone to call Renquest and bring him up to date in the changes in the plan the three had hatched in the office while studying the map. He could tell by her reaction, his partner was about as excited as she had been to split up and take the two houses at the same time. His partners were correct in their assessment of the situation and the hesitancy they both felt, but there seemed to be no other way. There had to be two teams hitting the houses simultaneously. Renquest and Beth at the house in the burbs and he at the house on Scott Street. His neighbor's home. The old lady with the dog. He quickly quashed any arguments from Beth about who went to which house. Renquest and the entry team would ensure her safety. He alone would deal with Evan Blanchard. Evan wanted it personal and that was what he was going to get.

Dodge stopped the truck two blocks from the house on McQuery Street near the six hundred block of Jackson Avenue.

"Program Renquest's number into your phone." He told her to put the number in as her emergency contact so all she had to do was press and hold the number one key if she got into trouble.

"I'm going to call and have a uniform come by and pick you up. Wait here and do not go to the house without Renquest and the entry team."

"What about you?"

"I'm going to go home and make sure my place is secure. Then I will call dispatch and request backup to my location."

"You won't go in until they arrive?"

"I'll wait."

Beth grabbed his arm. "I mean it, Dodge. Wait for the backup. Don't go into that house alone. You said it yourself. That is exactly what Evan is hoping for. A showdown between you and him."

Dodge smiled, leaned out the window and kissed Beth. She held the moment longer than he expected, making him pull away so he could leave.

"I gotta go. Remember, wait here for Renquest and the entry team. Do not go to that house by yourself."

"I won't. I promise. Call me as soon as you get to your house. We can be there in minutes if you need us."

"Just get the girl. She will be in there, hopefully alive."

With that, Dodge pressed the accelerator and drove away, knowing he lied to Beth. He would not call for backup. He knew this was going to end with blood. No Hollywood blockbuster movie ending. Two men standing in the street. Their eyes locked. Waiting, watching for the slightest tell. Then a draw. Two shots, but only one bullet makes its mark. He would put Evan down as soon as he saw him. A cop killers' death.

He made a right-hand turn on to Scott Street and slowed as he neared his townhome. The element of surprise was gone, and it didn't matter. The tires came to a screeching halt in the middle of the street and the truck rocked to a stop. He reached under the dash, flipping the switch to disengage the emergency lights. His Glock slid out of its holster with a hiss as the metal frame slipped from the plastic holster's grip. Using his index finger on his right hand, he felt for the bump along the frame, confirming a round was chambered. The magazine fell into his left hand with a push of the release on the left side of the frame, below the trigger guard. His fingers pressed down on the last round. It was a full magazine. Fifteen plus one in the chamber. Sixteen chances. He liked his odds.

The truck door swung open, and he piled out—weapon in hand. His eyes darted at the front door to his house, then back across the street. There it was. The little red sports car, sitting in front of the house where he saw the old lady with the little dog enter the other day. It wasn't a coincidence. Two days in a row, the same car, new to the neighborhood, parked on the street near his house. The odds were against it. If he was a betting man, and he was, Evan Blanchard was sitting in the house across the road, watching his every move. The old lady and her dog, most likely dead. The rage bubbled to the surface as he crossed the street, toward the red door adorning the townhouse. His steps calculated. Each one taken with purpose. Three strides and he reached the sidewalk, slowing, making sure not to trip over the curb.

His finger twitched. Sweat rolled down his forehead and into his eyes. He used his left arm to wipe the moisture from his brow, which his body seemed to produce ever greater quantities of as he approached the front door. His eyes focused on the front window, but the blinds had been pulled shut. As he approached, he slid to the hinge side of the door. His left hand reached out, grasping the doorknob. It turned. He paused. A deep breath in. The door eased open as he pushed inward. He stood in the doorway—the muzzle of his weapon pointed straight ahead. His eyes slowly adjusted to the change in brightness. He was in a small entryway that opened up into a larger room. The hinges of the front door squeaked as he closed it behind him. It was a tactical move, preventing him from being silhouetted against the light from outside.

His heart raced as he advanced into the next room. The room was dark, except for dim light trickling in from a space between a door and the floor across the room and to his left. It was eerily silent in the house. The hairs on the back of his neck jumped to attention. *The old lady that lived here had a dog*, he thought. Yet, there had been no barking. Not a good sign as that damn dog yapped every time it crossed paths with anything having two legs on its daily walks around the neighborhood.

Policy in these situations was to call for backup and hold the perimeter. He knew it because he was the author. There had even been a promise to Beth he would call and wait for patrol officers to arrive before going in. It was a stupid promise. He lied when he told her that, knowing he would never call for help and wait for some beat cop to show up, increasing the number of people whose safety he needed to worry about. This would end today. It would be him or Evan Blanchard, but one of them would leave the house on a gurney.

He concentrated on the little strip of light coming from under the door. If someone was moving in the room, they would break the light and a shadow would form giving him an idea of where Evan was in the room. A shadows thickness can even tell you how close the person was when they moved. It wasn't exact science, but if the person was standing right next to the door, the shadow would be almost black because of the lack of light able to pollute the area between the person and the door. The further the individual stood from the door, the more the light from the surrounding area saturated the floor in front of them, producing a lighter shadow. It was one of those experience lessons learned over a long career. But it didn't matter right now. Nothing was moving on the other side.

As his hand extended to test the doorknob, his mind turned back to the warehouse. During the chaos of finding Captain Blanchard stabbed and discovering the dead officer's twin brother, Evan, was a serial killer, Dodge had lost track of the fact he had been shot at. He pulled his hand back. Who had been firing from the window? Initially, he hadn't believed it was Evan Blanchard, but if it was, there was a good chance he was armed. Was he on the other side of the door, muzzle pointed at eye level and ready to fire as soon as a careless parole agent or cop stepped into the room? The fingers on his left hand twitched as they came to rest around the grip of his Glock.

"Shit. How could I make such a rookie mistake?" he whispered.

It was too late now. The error caused a paradigm shift. Forcing him to play defense and not offense as he had planned. A change in plans now could have serious implications. Sure, things always went heels up during an operation. Bad guys had a way of making you feel like being upside down on the back of nowhere. But whether it was kicking in a door, and finding you were now outnumbered, or finding a semi-auto assault rifle shoved into a couch cushion after you had had somebody sit and wait while searching a house—the strategic component remained the same. Offense was the dynamic that kept the mission moving forward and provided the edge. Defense killed momentum. Defense left men vulnerable and gave them time to think. Think about gunshot wounds and funerals. Little sons and daughters weeping beside flag-draped coffins. Defense was for bad guys.

The clock in his head was ticking. The longer he waited, the louder the sounds became. Tick-tock. TICK-tock. TICK-TOCK. He needed to make a decision. Go in or wait for backup. Every second put him further behind his adversary, increasing the chances of becoming a statistic. What he needed was more time. More time to run scenarios. To figure out the best way of switching the momentum back in his favor.

He heard a loose floorboard creak. A small amount of light slipped through a gap at the bottom of the door. He strained to make out the slightest variation in the escaping light's brightness. At first, he thought he saw a shadow cross away from him. It was fast. He stared at the spot. A long moment passed, and nothing. He couldn't wait any longer. The situation wouldn't change. He needed to adapt. To overcome.

Again, his hand reached out, this time securing the door handle, turning slowly. The mechanism clicked as the bolt slid out from the plate that held the door closed. His back still tight against the wall as light flooded into the dark room as the door opened. Shadows bounced across the floor and walls. His mind raced as objects in the room became visible. A table. Standing lamp. A chair in the corner. Evan Blanchard.

CHAPTER 27

HEART RACING, DODGE MOVED HIS WEAPON to the ready position. His eyes fixated on a new target. Evan Blanchard stood in front of a bookcase between two high-back reading chairs. There was no way Dodge could have seen him lurking in the shadows before he opened the door. The small amount of light escaping through the space between the floor and the bottom of the door barely made it five feet before the darkness consumed it. That half of the room was black as a moonless night. Had he been facing the door instead of opening it with his back to the wall, it would have been lights out. A flag-draped coffin paraded through the downtown streets. Shots echoing across town from the twenty-one-gun salute, followed by a full military burial. But he hadn't turned his back. He still had a chance.

Evan stood motionless. A smirk on his face. Dodge knew the darkness had afforded his opponent an advantage. One for which he hoped he was wildly overconfident. As the situation progressed, the corners of his lips turned down. The veteran agent and former soldier had seen the look many times on the faces of his adversaries, realizing they now had to make a choice. Live or die. They could only choose one. The large knife dangling from Evan's right hand revealed the choice that had been made.

The two stood in silence for a moment. Dodge spoke first.

"Evan Blanchard?"

"You figured out who l am. That's very good, Detective."

"Parole Agent," Dodge replied.

"What?"

"You called me, Detective. Technically, l am a parole agent. I work for the Department of Corrections and am assigned to the police as part of a sex crimes task force."

Evan said nothing.

"I thought we should get the titles right, since you went through all this trouble just to get my attention. And you have it. So, what do you want?"

His head tilting to one side, Evan stared at Dodge. His body remained motionless.

"Is my brother dead?"

"He is." Dodge's eyes broke contact with Evans' to glance at the knife suspended from the end of his hand. "Is that the knife you used to stab him?"

"Oh, Agent..."

Dodge interrupted. "You can just call me Dodge."

The smile on Evan's face returned for a brief second. "Oh, Agent Dodge. I thought you were smarter than that. I didn't kill my brother. In fact, it was just the opposite. Watching him suffer brought me great joy. I *never* wanted it to end. You see, death was too good for him. What he deserved was to live with what he did to me. Live every day, longing, wondering where he went wrong. Knowing he was always one step behind me—unable to save the trash he swore to protect."

Dodge watched Evan closely. Specifically, the hand brandishing the knife. The light coming from the room behind Dodge illuminated the stainless-steel blade. If Evan's hand twitched, the reflection from the blade would give his intentions away. He needed to keep him talking. Stalling long enough to give Beth and Renquest time to get Sarah to safety and send the calvary his way.

"If you didn't kill your brother, then who did?"

"Why don't you turn around and see for yourself?" Evan asked.

"There is no fucking way I turn my back on you as long as that shiv is dangling from the end of your arm."

Evan let out a laugh. "See, that's what's wrong with the world today. There's no trust."

Dodge raised his weapon to eye level. "I could put a bullet through the bridge of your nose then go into the room with no worries. How about I do that?"

Evan's eyebrows raised. "But then you wouldn't know why I did it all. Think about all the questions everyone is going ask you, and you would have no answers to give."

Dodge fought the urge to just shoot and be done with it, but something inside of him knew Evan Blanchard was right. The investigator in him needed to know why.

"Place the knife on the ground and I'll look in the room. But if you move too fast, if I even see a glean in your eyes—I will put you down where you stand. Is that clear?"

"Crystal," Evan said, as he placed the knife on a seat cushion of the high-back chair to his right.

Dodge watched. The muzzle of his Glock pointed at Evan's chest. "Now take one step back."

Evan complied. A smile still stretched across his face.

"Now, interlock your fingers behind your head."

Again, Evan complied.

Every hair on his body tingled. His ears burned. Something wasn't right. Why the hell was Evan still grinning? But he needed to see what was in that room. He slid his left foot one step to the left. Keeping his weapon firmly pointed at Evan's chest, he slid his right foot. He repeated the motion. First his left foot, then his right. The front sight of his Glock never moving more than an inch from center mass. His body was now in front of the open door. His neck made a popping sound as his head turned and he peered over his right shoulder.

Bile filled Dodge's stomach, twisting it into knots. For there, tied to a chair in a corner of the room, was the old lady that lived in the house. Her feet bound with rope. A rag shoved into her mouth and held into place with duct tape. The tape wrapped around her entire head several times. In her lap was her little white dog. Its stomach had been slit from neck to tail. Its contents splayed out across the old woman's lap. Dodge looked into her eyes. She was alive, but the eyes staring back at him were dead. A dark charcoal grey, almost black. A doll's eyes.

He watched as her eyes moved from him toward the bed across the room. A quick glance back at Evan, who's smile stretched so far across his face, Dodge thought the corners of his mouth might tear. His eyes shifted back to the old lady, still focusing on the other side of the room. Dodge spun one hundred and eighty degrees to his left, keeping Evan in his sights as he turned.

He quickly saw what the old lady had been looking at. There was a large canopy bed directly across the room from her. A post shot up from each corner, holding an upper frame from which a thin decorative sash ran the perimeter. It would have been a beautiful piece of furniture except for a man lying on it. His arms and legs bound to the four corner posts. His stomach split open, same as the dog. Only the man in the bed was still breathing. Dodge could see his chest heaving up, then down. The breaths appeared labored, as one would expect with most of the man's innards now spread across his chest and groin. His eyes were closed, and Dodge knew he would be dead soon. There was nothing he could do to save him.

"That's the man that killed my brother. You can arrest him if you like, but I don't think he is going to make it to trial."

The sight of the man dying on the bed and Evan's statement caught Dodge off guard. He had been sure that Evan was the one responsible for stabbing Don Blanchard and shooting at him and Beth outside the warehouse. As far as he knew, there was no one else there. So, who was this poor bastard butchered on the bed?

Dodge's focus returned to Evan. His weapon still raised. "I don't understand. Who is that, and why would he kill your brother? And who was taking pot shots at me from the roof?"

"Well, I never got his name. But I guessed he was the manager for the storage building. I think he didn't like Don snooping around in his little operation. That was always one of my brother's biggest flaws. He could never leave well enough alone. Always having to dig and pry into things that were none of his business. This time it cost him his life." A brief silence passed. "After he stuck that knife in Don's gut, he must have panicked when he realized he killed a pig. You should have seen him. All panicky and running around like a, how do you say, decapitated chicken."

"Like a chicken with its head cut off."

"That's it! So quaint. But it was clearly his first time. You know, I envied him at that moment. The first time is the best. As hard as we try, we never can replicate the first time of anything. The first kiss. The first intimate experience with a woman. Your first kill. Every time after the first is like chasing the dragon. It's an addiction."

Dodge remained silent.

"Have you ever killed anyone, Agent Dodge?"

Still Dodge said nothing. His eyes locked on Evan.

"You have," he said, a slight upturn in his voice. "I can see it in your eyes. Killing does something to a man. It changes you. Makes you more aware. The experience also makes it easier to spot one of our own. And you are one of us, Agent Dodge. You reek of death."

Dodge decided to try and get the conversation back on track. "You never answered my second question. Who shot at me?"

Evan nodded toward the man on the bed whose chest had now stopped moving. "I guess you won't get to put him on trial. That's a shame. Justice is important. It's why... well, why I do this."

"If he killed a cop and tried to kill me, I don't give a rat's ass if he's dead. He got what he deserved. Sometimes justice is vengeful, and she will get to you what's owed," Dodge said, beginning to show the strain of the moment. His voice had picked up an octave and sweat ran down his brow and into his eyes.

"Oh, have I not been clear? I fully expect to suffer the wrath of lady justice, Agent Dodge. My time will come, and I will be judged on my sins."

Now Dodge smiled. "You mean, God? *Have I not been clear?* God can have you when I'm finished."

A deep roar of laughter burst from Evan Blanchard's mouth, echoing off the high ceilings of the old townhouse, reverberating through the room.

"You haven't even seen the best part," Evan shouted, in between his howling laughter. His hand outstretched and index finger pointed past Dodge into the bedroom. "Don't you want to see what's in the bathroom?"

His eyes focused on Evan. He felt his finger sliding from the frame of his Glock and on to the trigger guard. One shot. That's all it would take. One shot to the head and this would all be over. It was becoming more difficult with every passing second to fight the urge to give in and squeeze the trigger. It would be messy, but Dodge was sure the old lady wouldn't mind. Nothing a little paint couldn't cover up. His finger transferred to the trigger. His front sight raised slightly and was now pointing at the bridge of Evan Blanchard's nose. Flip the switch and lights out.

But he couldn't do it. Not like this. He needed to know that Sarah was safe before dispatching Evan Blanchard. He took in a deep breath, easing his finger from the trigger.

"If you so much as blink, I will split your head like a canoe. Do you understand me?"

"I wouldn't miss this for the world, Agent Dodge. I'll be right here when you are ready. Would you like me to slide to the right, just a little? When all is disclosed, you'll have a better view of me. Besides, I want to see your eyes at that moment. The moment it all becomes clear to you."

This was all wrong. The game had shifted. He was playing defense again. Dodge couldn't seem to keep the lead. Every time he gained leverage, Evan Blanchard took it back. Dodge wondered what Evan wanted him to see in the bathroom. It was probably the old lady's husband or cat strung up like Jesus Christ. The thought of tomato soup guy flashed in his head. He shuddered.

Dodge nudged the muzzle of his Glock to the left and Evan took two steps and was now directly across from him. The light from the room lit up his face and, for the first time, Dodge saw Don Blanchard staring back at him. The hair was different. Evan's skin was more weathered. A sign of a hard life on the streets in a desert town like Las Vegas. But anyone could tell the two were twins. Seeing a dead man's face staring back made him uneasy. Something about it wasn't natural. He shook it off and turned his attention to the door behind him.

With one eye on Evan Blanchard, he began moving toward the door, with a quick glance at the old lady. Her head was hanging, and tears ran down her cheeks. She had given up all hope. Maybe she knew something he didn't. His heart raced. He felt the bile from his stomach making its way up his esophagus and into his throat. He swallowed hard, hoping it would quell the burn. It remained. As he passed the foot of the bed, he peered at the dead man. His skin color had already faded, as gravity did its job once the heart stopped beating and blood pooled in his backside. He had turned greyer as the pink hue had drained from his skin. The entire room smelled of a jar of old pennies. The metallic scent was thick in the air. So thick he could taste it, which made the burning in his throat even worse. His gag reflex was trying to engage, as he fought back the urge to vomit.

He approached the bathroom door and looked back at Evan Blanchard, the light shining on his face. A broad smile stretched from ear to ear. His eyes reflected red in the light. Like how eyes appear in a Polaroid picture. Every bone in Dodge's body told him to get the hell out of there. It was a trap. His subconscious screamed at him to shoot, grab the old lady, and head for the street where he could wait in safety for back-up. But he couldn't stop. Something stronger than his rules, pulled him toward whatever awaited in that bathroom.

The bath was small. A double vanity with a marble countertop on the right as he entered. A toilet with help bars mounted to the wall for people with disabilities and trouble standing on their own was tucked between the end of the vanity and the far wall. A small linen closet faced the toilet, and the bathtub to his left, partially obscured by the door which opened inward. The only light was coming from the bedroom. Dodge reached in and found a light switch to the right on the inside wall. His fingers gently brushed the toggle and flipped it up. Three wall lights mounted above an overly large built-in mirror came to life. He squinted and turned his face away for a few seconds, then peered back into the room.

As he looked in the mirror, he noticed the shower curtains pulled aside, fastened to hooks secured into the wall on each side. A white liner shielded him from seeing inside. All he could make out was a shadow the size of a person. *Shit*, he thought. *Sarah.* One more glance back at Evan, whose smile had somehow grown larger and eyes that were open wide as a kid on Christmas morning, stared back at him.

He pointed the muzzle of his weapon through the doorway and at Evan. Using his other hand, grasped the edge of the white liner between his fingers. The burning in his throat was more like a fire now, like he had drunk from a bottle of hot sauce. His stomach ached from the excess acid, and it felt like a rubber band was clasped around it, drawing it into a tight bunch. He took a deep breath in and blew it out. His hand slid the white liner back. Evan Blanchard cackled in the other room. The sound of his laughter pounded in Dodge's head like a bass drum.

He couldn't stop the vomit this time.

CHAPTER 28

HE USED HIS SHIRTSLEEVE to wipe the vomit from his chin and mouth. The effort to hold his reaction back was noble, but what he saw in that bathtub untied the knot binding his stomach like pulling on one strand of a shoelace. In seconds, what remained of the lunch he had eaten earlier found its way to the surface. His head jerked, turning away from the body hanging in the shower. He didn't want to see her like that. But the mirror. The mirror kept Cortez in his view. It was as if she was staring at him from the other side of the looking glass. She didn't seem real, like a mannequin in a store window. Dodge turned back and looked over his shoulder at the woman he had shared his bed with two days ago. A red line stretched from one ear to the other across her throat. Blood soaked her white blouse. The same one she had been wearing the last time she had left his house.

Dodge had wondered why he hadn't heard from her. He had been so wrapped up in trying to run background on Captain Blanchard and find Evan, he chalked her lack of action up to not having enough information to take to her editors for an on-air story. He had been wrong. And this time, Cortez had paid for his sins.

"I'm sorry," he said as he pulled the white liner closed.

Evan's laughter had stopped. Dodge pushed the door against the side of the tub and stepped out of the bathroom, staring at the old lady as he passed. Her head hung low. Nothing but low whimpers coming from behind the rag shoved in her mouth. He continued past and into the room where Evan Blanchard still stood. The smile on his face was gone. The spark in his eye had disappeared. He just stood there. Not moving. Not talking. A statue.

He stopped, leaving about six feet between the two men. His eyes glanced at the chair. The knife was still resting where Evan had placed it. Why hadn't he grabbed the knife while Dodge was busy finding Cortez in the bathroom? It would have been so easy. He could have made it to the bathroom before Dodge would've even known what was happening. It's what he would have done. *Take advantage of every opportunity in a fight, because you may not get a second chance,* was a rule.

It was at that moment that he realized his mistake. The damn gun. He had forgotten about the gun. The storage warehouse manager splayed out on the bed, had had a gun. He was the one that took the shots at Dodge and Beth at the warehouse. Evan had abducted him after he killed Don Blanchard. The gun would have still been on him. Dodge had underestimated his adversary. All the victims, up to this point, died from strangulation or knife wounds. Not a single firearm used. Until now.

Dodge didn't even see the gun in his left hand until it was too late. His focus had been on Evan's right hand. The hand that had held the knife. The explosion from the end of the barrel blinded him. His ear drums cracked from the sound of the round leaving the muzzle. He felt the round penetrate his left shoulder, spinning him around until he faced back into the room with the old lady and the dead guy on the bed. His eyes met the old lady's. Her pupils wide as dimes, watching him fall to his knees. A tear ran down her cheek. She must have known she would be next.

Dodge tried to swing his body around, but before he made a quarter turn, he felt a burning in his back. He looked at the old lady again. She had closed her eyes. Her head turned away from him. His hand raised to his chest. He pressed it tight, but the blood seeped out. The wound was a through-and-through. But he was sure the round had pierced one of his lungs. He was having trouble taking in air. It was like he was drowning and there wasn't a drop of water in sight. Unable to take a full breath, he struggled to stay upright. His core weakened and he collapsed to the floor.

Blood ran out from under him. The light in the room faded. His hearing became distant. Like echoes in a canyon. Each breath was more laborious than the last. He closed his eyes. *Just make it quick,* he thought.

Flashes of light. It must have been the shots. Evan had finished him. Was he dead? The pain was gone, but he couldn't move. It was as if it had lifted him to a higher plane, looking down at the world below. But it wasn't clear. Everything was fuzzy, like an Eighties console television. He could make out shapes, but not objects. Muffled voices. He strained to hear what was being said. But one stood out. A woman's voice. It was Beth. She had come. Dodge concentrated on the sound of her voice. Things became clearer. He could see her.

He tried to speak, but the blood in his mouth muffled the sound.

She knelt over him; her hands gripped his shirt, and she was shaking him. Yelling his name.

"DODGE! Damn you. You promised you would wait. Why didn't you wait?"

He saw Renquest standing behind her. His hand on her shoulder, pulling her back as the paramedics crowded around him, cutting his shirt off, placing electrodes on his chest.

"CLEAR!" one paramedic yelled.

Everything went fuzzy.

"Charging two hundred! CLEAR!"

The lights flickered. Dodge felt himself falling. He had never been in zero gravity before but imagined this is how it must feel.

"Charging three hundred. CLEAR!" the paramedic screamed again.

It felt like someone hit him in the chest with a sledgehammer. A massive thud. Then everything went black.

CHAPTER 29

HE SQUINTED AS THE SUN SHONE brightly over the bow of the sailboat. The water was calm—small waves lapped against the side of the boat, gently rocking it. The temperature was perfect. A slight breeze danced across the deck, billowing the sail, pushing the craft, and splitting the water—he held one hand on the helm, guiding it toward the setting sun. A drink in the other. This was his happy place. Why had he ever left *Kelly's Dream?* He purchased the boat with money willed to him by a lover whose past had caught up with her. Murdered. It was the same story heard all over the country on local news channels. A couple of small-time crooks hear someone talking about money they have and decide it's easier to take from that person than it is to earn their own. In the end, all Kelly's killers got was a few hundred bucks. A beautiful life snuffed out over the price of a fancy meal.

"Dodge."

He looked around. He was alone. There was no one on his boat and nothing but open water surrounding him. *Must have been a gull*, he thought.

Then he heard it again. A woman's voice calling his name. It was distant at first but grew louder each time.

"Dodge. You need to wake up."

His body shook. He couldn't control it. He stood. Something pulled at his arm. His hand let go of the helm and he stumbled backward. The sun, bright in the sky a minute ago, had now faded. The voice continued to call to him. He turned and walked toward the sound. A light appeared in the distance. *Kelly's Dream* was gone. He was now in a tunnel. His pace increased as he ran towards the light. His hand reaching out. Then something took a hold of his right hand and pulled him through to the other side.

His head pounded. His eyes felt glued shut as the light tried to pierce the veil of darkness.

"Let me wipe some of the sleep from your eyes," he heard a soft voice say.

Dodge tried to move his arms.

"You have little strength right now," the voice said. "It'll take a few hours before you can move freely, so just relax."

He felt the warmth of the wet washcloth as she gently wiped the crust from his eyes.

"There you go. You can open your eyes now."

The initial burst of light burned his retinas, forcing his eyes shut again. A moment passed, and he eased his right eye open. Then the left. Giving each one a moment to adjust to the brightness. A young woman's face looked down at him.

"Welcome back, Agent Dodge." It was a woman. She was dressed in nurse's garb. She smiled and turned to an older lady behind her. "Find Dr. Chu and tell him his patient is awake."

Patient? What was she talking about? Had something happened? The last thing he remembered was... Then it all came flooding back. The house. The old lady. Cortez. Evan Blanchard. He looked down at his body. A bundle of tubes and wires snaked around the bed. Ends plugged into machines that beeped and clicked. The other end connected to his hands and arms. His lips moved as he tried to speak, but no sound came out.

"Your mouth is dry. Let me get you some ice chips," the soft voiced nurse said.

She left the room and returned a few minutes later with a small spoon and a plastic cup filled with ice. Using the spoon, she placed a few of the ice pieces into his mouth. He didn't chew them. Instead, letting the crystals dissolve and melt, the water slowly wetting his tongue and throat.

"Would you like some more?"

Dodge nodded.

The nurse shoveled a slightly larger pile of ice onto the spoon and placed it in his mouth. He chewed the ice this time. Swallowing the smaller chunks as they melted.

"There, that's better," she said.

Dodge cleared his throat. It was scratchy, but he could speak. "Where am I?" he asked.

"You're at County General. The doctor will explain everything when he gets here. Just try to relax until then." The nurse stood and turned toward the door. Then she stopped. "Oh, I made a call to Detective Renquest. He wanted to know as soon as you were awake. He has been here almost every night." She pointed to a chair sitting in the room's corner, under the television. "Dinner time. Just like clockwork. Technically, your insurance is paying for the meals, so we bring him yours. Some nurses like to flirt with him, but he just sits there. Reading out loud to you."

At that moment, an older man walked into the room. His long white lab coat and stethoscope dangling from around his neck gave him away as the doctor the nurse had been referring to.

"Good afternoon, Agent Dodge. How do you feel?" The doctor said, moving to the bed's side, looking at the monitors perched above Dodge's head.

"Like I get hit by a Mack truck."

The doctor nodded. "What do you remember?"

Dodge closed his eyes and drew in a deep breath. Pain shot through his chest. He winced.

"Yeah, I would advise against breathing in too deep for a few more days. It's going to take some time for your lungs to adjust."

"How long was I out?" Dodge asked.

"Two weeks."

"Two weeks?" Instinctively, he looked at his wrist, but there was no watch strapped to it. "What happened to me?"

The doctor stepped closer and grabbed the chart hanging off the side rail.

"They brought you into the ER with two gunshot wounds. One to the upper left chest which collapsed your lung. The second entered your back and pierced a major artery going into your heart. The paramedics stabilized you and once in the operating room, I repaired the artery and stopped the bleeding. There is a patch on your lung and a valve installed to drain any excess fluid. It was touch and go for a few days, but we took you off the respirator after seventy-two hours. We removed the drain a few days ago, which is causing the pain when you breathe. It should subside over the next couple of days. You have a medication button there on the side of the bed. Use it when you need to."

Dodge looked around the room and then back at the doctor. "When can I get out of here?"

"It'll likely be another week, but things are going well. We can re-evaluate in a few days. Do you have any more questions for me?"

Dodge leaned his head back into the pillow. "Was anyone else brought in with me?"

The Doctor half-turned and gestured toward the door. "Detective Renquest requested that we not talk to you about anything concerning what happened before you arrived. He should be here any minute."

With that, the doctor and the young nurse, who gave Dodge a smile, left the room. He wondered what had happened at the house. Details were coming back to him. The old lady tied to the chair. The guy on the bed. His guts tossed across his body like a dead deer laying along the side of the road. And Cortez. That was the worst. Her throat cut from ear to ear. Her face still bearing the look of terror that must have been going through her mind in the last seconds of her life. She would haunt him the most.

Renquest showed up, as the nurse said, right around dinner, but not planned this time. He came as soon as the hospital had notified him Dodge was awake. He stood in the doorway. Staring. A look of relief on his face.

"Well, don't just stand there all gap mouthed. Come in," Dodge said. He was glad to see his friend.

"I see you're still playing up the getting shot thing. How many nurses' numbers you got so far?" Renquest said.

"Oh, they're being overcautious. I should be out of here in a day or two."

Renquest reached across the metal railing and touched his partner's arm. "Glad to have ya back."

Dodge smiled.

"So, tell me what happened. I remember nothing after the first shot."

Renquest walked to the other side of the room and pulled the chair the nurse said he spent so many hours in over the past week. He took off his jacket and draped it across the foot of the bed, then sat down, melting into the green cushions.

"When we, Beth and I, got to the house, it must have been five or six minutes after the last shot. You were lying in the doorway to the bedroom. There was a lot of blood, and you didn't seem to be breathing. The Paramedics..."

Dodge interrupted. "Skip the part about me. We all know how that turned out."

Renquest looked down at the bed.

"It's ok. I remember seeing Cortez in the shower," Dodge said.

Renquest shook his head.

"She was dead long before we got there. Probably long before you did as well."

"What about the old lady?"

"She was still alive. Tied to that chair. Her dead dog laying across her lap. I don't know why Evan let her live. I mean, she will never be the same. No one sees what she did and stays right in the head for long. After we interviewed her, one of her kids came and picked her up. Took her to Texas to stay with them. Houston, I think. Anyway, last I talked to her, they were putting the place up for sale. Probably have to be an out of towner that buys it. Everyone here knows what happened in that place. A local wouldn't touch it with a ten-foot pole."

"The gutted guy on the bed?" Dodge asked.

"The manager of the warehouse where Don Blanchard was killed. We think he is the one that stabbed him, took shots at you, and had the container rigged to explode. I would have liked to see him fry after a nice quick trial, but he got what was coming to him."

Dodge tested his legs by pushing his feet against the weight of the blankets. They moved. He then pushed his body back and sat upright. He flinched at the pain in his chest as he took a breath.

"You sure you should move like that?"

"I'm fine. Just needed to get off my back for a minute." Dodge stared at his partner, who was staring back at him. "What about Sarah? Did you find her?"

"Yeah. She was in the house directly across from the place where we found the floater in the tub. She is alive and even came by to see you a few times. Those flowers over there," he said, pointing to a small bunch of red and yellow roses sitting on the windowsill. "She brought them Saturday. I thanked her for you."

Dodge glanced at the roses sitting in front of the window but said nothing.

"As for Evan Blanchard, he is in the wind. Gone before we got to you. The crime scene guys think he strolled right out the front door. The deadbolt on the back door was engaged. Couldn't have done that after leaving without a key. And why the hell would've he? No sense in locking a door to a house after leaving a couple of dead bodies and a wounded old washed-up parole agent leaking on the floor. Ain't got a clue where he went after he left."

"Was there a little red sports car parked along the street when you and Beth arrived?"

Renquest scratched his chin. "Not that I remember. Why?"

Dodge stared at the tubes and wires dangling from his wrists and arms. "I don't know. I noticed it twice outside my house but hadn't given it much thought. Suppose I should've paid closer attention."

Renquest stood and turned toward the window. His hand combed through his thinning hair. "You know what I don't get? Why not kill the old lady? And after taking the time to snatch Sarah, why leave her alive? None of this makes sense."

Dodge crossed his arms over his stomach. His eyes again fell on the mess of wires and tubes connected to his body that made him look like a medical experiment. A Frankenstein's Monster. He turned and peered out the window.

"Evan Blanchard is a psychopath. There is no reasoning behind anything those types of people do. We have been studying serial killers for over fifty years now. Other than being able to create a general profile, we have learned shit else. A reasonable explanation for an unreasonable event is a logical fallacy. It's considered unreasonable, for a reason."

"I suppose you are right. Do you think we will see Evan Blanchard again?"

"I don't know if he will ever show up here. It kinda seems like he accomplished all he wanted to in our town. His brother is dead. We have nine bodies in the morgue. And he gets to move on. A new patch of victims. New causes."

"We may have lost this one, partner."

Hearing the words come out of Renquest's mouth didn't sit well with the veteran agent. He never was one to let the past be the past. At least not professionally. And he knew his partner felt the same way. In his bones, deep down in the depth of his soul, he knew he would meet Evan Blanchard again. He wasn't sure when or how, but their paths would cross once more. It was like that with the first man he had shot, Grayson Heller. Grayson just kept popping up into his life. He had no reason to believe The Savior wouldn't do the same.

Renquest stood and grabbed his coat off the foot of the bed. "You might want to give your girl a call."

"She was pretty pissed, huh?"

"I thought I was going to have to keep her from killing you herself once the paramedics revived you."

"Maybe I'll just leave that one be for a while," Dodge said.

"Your choice. Sure, seemed like a good one, though. Not sure I could miss out on that. But hey, if there is one thing, I have learned over all the years we've been partners. You're gonna do you. Nothing anybody can do to change that."

With that said, his partner turned and walked toward the door and into the hall.

"Shit," Dodge said. "I'm gonna need a ride home when I get out of here."

CHAPTER 30

DODGE WAS READY TO BE HOME after nearly a month in the hospital. The food alone was enough to force a person to heal up as soon as possible, to escape the inevitable toilet trips an hour after choking down the last bite. He was sure the doctors put something in the food, a mild laxative, just to get the patients that could move up and walking. Whatever it was, he would be glad to be back in his own house. Eating his own food and sleeping in his own bed. He wasn't supposed to have any alcohol for a month or two, but ever since the nurse wheeled him out of the hospital's front doors, he thought about little else. He now could add having been shot to the list of wounds he suffered and lived through. One drink wouldn't kill him.

The taxi pulled up to the curb and stopped in front of his townhouse. He took a twenty out of his wallet and slid the bill through the open passenger window, telling the Middle Eastern man behind the wheel to keep the change. Five bucks. It was a good tip. He watched as the cab pulled out into the street, turning at the next intersection, and disappearing out of sight.

After a moment, he turned to the house across the street, leaning on the metal cane the hospital forced him to take for support. The doctors had told him he would need the cane for three to six months. He felt two to four was a better goal. It would take work, but he would soon have his strength back and be back at work.

The one thing he knew was he needed to ditch the aluminum pole the hospital called a cane. It looked like something an elderly person on television would use in a Medicare commercial. He would go shopping for a new one. Maybe oak or teakwood. Something more suited to his style. He could call the Veterans Administration to see if they would pay for it. He had never used a single service from the VA before, but maybe it was time. Pride is partially to blame for being where he was. Shot twice. Multiple dead bodies. A cane. Pride, she was a fickle bitch.

There was a For Sale sign in the front yard of the old lady's house. She must have decided not to own a home where two people died, her dog tortured and killed and an over the hill parole agent laid bleeding out on the bedroom floor. He couldn't help but wonder if deep down, she feared the killer might return for her and that is why she didn't want to stay. He didn't blame her. Looking at the house gave him the chills, and he wondered the same thing. Would Evan Blanchard come back to finish what he had started? Would Dodge, the old lady, and Sarah ever really be safe? Time would tell.

He took one more glance up, then down the street. The curbs absent of red sports cars and white panel vans. He shrugged his shoulders and walked to the stoop, taking each step gingerly. The pain was still there. He felt it with each step up. On the last stair, he pulled his keys from his pocket and unlocked the door. The blast of air hit him, assaulting his nose. He had left something out on the counter. Probably cheese or some kind of perishable food. It still smelled better than the hospital he had been in. He would clean it up, but first he needed to see about that drink.

ABOUT THE AUTHOR

CHRISTOPHER (CHRIS) FLORY spent ten years with various correctional departments as a probation and parole officer, specializing in the supervision of sexually based offenders and criminal street gang members. He is currently employed as a contractor for the federal government as an intelligence analyst.

The Savior: A Paul Dodge Novel is the author's third novel in the *Paul Dodge* series. He has also been featured in academic journals and professional conference papers while attending undergraduate (BA Indiana-Purdue University Fort Wayne '00) and graduate school (MA Purdue University '15). He is currently working on the next book in the *Paul Dodge* series.

Chris now lives in Northern Virginia with his wife and dog Shadow. He enjoys spending time with his family, baking and outdoor activities.

Connect with Chris online at:
christopherflorybooks.com
Twitter: @AuthorFlory
Instagram: @authorflory.

TRUST MISPLACED

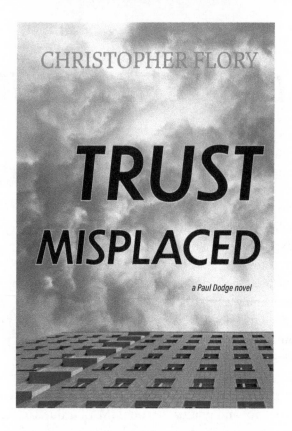

PAUL DODGE IS NO STRANGER to the dark side of crime. As a parole agent and a member of the local Sex Crimes Task Force, he knows what depravity lies in the shadows. But when an investigation into a local sexual predator leads him to a photo of a judge's daughter and another young girl ends up dead, Dodge quickly realizes he doesn't know whom to trust.

In the most dangerous case of his career, Dodge races to detangle a growing web of lies and corruption. His life and career are both on the line in this high-stakes case, and a single misstep could end them both.

LAST RAYS OF DAYLIGHT

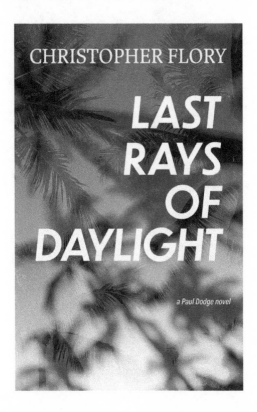

A HURRICANE, DRUGS, AND A RUTHLESS KINGPIN land Dodge in a deadly tropical mix.

In the wake of a hurricane, a young girl is found dead in a shipping container in St. Thomas. Short-handed with agents and residents picking up the pieces after the storm, the FBI calls in Paul Dodge, who was taking an all-too-rare vacation in the sun and sand.

The case quickly escalates and lands the agent in a world of gangs, drugs, and human trafficking. Dodge will need to rely on his years of training and military skills if he is to survive the coming showdown and find justice for the victim.